She'd been betrayed by someone she trusted.

It felt awful.

She snatched a pillow from the head of her bed and clutched it, muffling her mouth in its softness. Was she going to cry?

No, she decided. She wasn't. She'd hold out for more information. There was so much that she didn't know. More she *didn't* know than she *did* know. And knowledge was the key out of her prison, she felt more and more sure.

I'll go find out. I'll hunt *down my answers.*

She paused before the mirror of her dressing table.

Did she *look* like a girl who deserved to be betrayed?

Thick dark hair pulled back in a simple braid. Gray eyes, slightly reddened, even though she had not cried. Pointed chin, a little wobbly.

No, she didn't look like a girl who deserved betrayal. But she did look like a girl who wasn't getting enough to eat. Did she? Really? Chin a little pointier, cheeks a little thinner, eyes and temples a little stretched?

Maybe. Or maybe not. She felt hollow inside, and scared. Which made her face look scared too.

I'll figure something out. She'd figured out a lot already. *I'm not giving up.*

Also by J.M. Ney-Grimm

CAUGHT in AMBER

A MYTHIC TALE

by J.M. Ney-Grimm

Wild
Unicorn

ISBN-13: 978-0692531587
ISBN-10: 0692531580

Designed by JMNG

Cover art:
"Gentle Young Woman" by Ipb / Dreamstime.com
"Bellver Castle" by Jyothi / Dreamstime.com

Interior illustration:
"Antique Clock" by Vtorous / Dreamstime.com

To all those who wander and are lost,
may you find your way and your safe harbor

With praise for
Miles,
who enjoyed
all the clever bits
and couldn't turn the pages
fast enough

And with endless gratitude to
Laura and Amy –
if I said thank you
from now until tomorrow,
it would not be enough

TABLE OF CONTENTS

Caught in Amber

FIRST

Glad Sun, Secret Shadow

BENEATH HER HAPPINESS lay something darker, something fear-stricken, something cruel and cold.

It skulked and lurked.

It coiled beneath the threshold of awareness, seeking a vulnerability, seeking entrance.

It was evil, and it threatened her.

But she awoke happy.

The glad sun streamed in through four point-arched windows, filling her bedchamber with light.

She stretched and blinked and rejoiced. Then fell back against her banked pillows, grinning and studying the rollicking cornice molding that stretched around her room where the walls met the ceiling. Small carved suns with curling rays and merry faces somersaulted along the frieze as though they couldn't keep still. That was the way they should be: energy-filled, laughing, and replete.

She threw her covers off. The soft, oh-so-soft white sheet with lace edging it. The light wool blanket, white with a satin band. The sky blue silk quilt, tied with crimson knots and embroidered with silver swans and golden stars. Lovely and cozy and comfy.

Phlumph! The covers landed at the foot of the bed.

She laughed and turned her own somersault, flopping atop the tumbled bedding in a tangle of white nightgown and untied ribbons, her braided hair unraveling in dusky curls around her shoulders.

She lay there a moment staring up at the ceiling, painted to depict a gloriously blue sky and a towering cloud castle from behind which burst the jolly sun, cousin to the ones in the cornice.

The darker something that hid behind her content loomed a moment, then fell back.

Quiescent for an interval, but ready to strike.

She considered attending to it, pursuing it, finding its dread lair, confronting its terror. But her happiness called her. Why be scared (or terrified), when you could be happy? She *could* be happy, so she *would* be happy. *Hah!*

Embracing happiness, she scooted down to the end of her bed and sat up, legs dangling over. The head of the bed was tall: two gilded gryphons with wings upraised, ready for the downbeat that would lift them into the air, red cherries clutched in their beaks. The bed's foot was much lower, a simple curve of wood, gilded to match the gryphons, which barely cleared the thick mattress. It pressed into the backs of her thighs, mundane and comforting. She *would* be comforted. Clinging to comfort, she scooted forward a bit more to rest her bare feet on the floor, satin-smooth red oak boards, cool and unadorned.

She studied her surroundings. They felt familiar. They should. This was her room.

It *felt* familiar. And yet it wasn't. She didn't know this place.

Which was scary.

The looming shadow underneath the sunshine reared up within her.

She blinked in bewilderment. How could this cheerful room harbor monsters?

Blue-and-white striped wallpaper covered the walls from the cornice to the chair rail. Paneled wood painted soft blue filled the space between chair rail and floor. That cheerful shade of blue seemed the very color of pure happiness.

Three tall, tall windows with their pointed arches at the top and deep sills at the bottom pierced one long wall. And the sunlight flooding through them belonged to the summer morning of a day filled with treats and surprises.

And yet . . . a shadow, a doubt, a devouring hunger poised . . . somewhere. Where?

She could feel it, cruel and biting.

She felt as though she were two persons. One sitting in the sun and anticipating loveliness. The other crouching in darkness, fearing the advent of . . . what? Something dreadful. Something ravenous. Something hostile. To her.

It scared her. And this strange split within her scared her more.

She glanced at the sunlit striped walls of her room, the merry suns in its cornice, wanting to keep their promise of delight.

I can choose, she told herself. Choose the light. Or choose the darkness.

Her hands clenched the silk of the quilt beneath her, crumpling the smooth softness with her fingers.

I choose the light.

And the darkness fell back before her determination.

A fourth window occupied the wall to the right of her bed's head board. It gave onto a view of rolling hills, grassy with stands of trees green in summer leaf. She was high up and could see a long way to the distant horizon.

Where was this beautiful countryside?

She didn't know it, even though it too felt familiar.

There was that peculiar split again. Something that felt familiar, but had no place – none at all – in her memory.

She shivered despite the warmth of the air.

Within her room – it was generously sized and high-ceilinged, but not so spacious as to make her feel small – two wardrobes and two blanket chests of red oak, a gilded dressing table, and a writing desk stood against the walls. Fine, heavy stuff. Two armchairs upholstered in crimson were placed before an elegant marble hearth. No fire or wood there, just the polished brass andirons. The air was pleasantly warm from the sunlight.

She paused, there on the end of the bed, fighting to retain her confidence.

What came next? In this room that was hers and yet . . . wasn't?

Why could she remember so little?

Why did this room seem both familiar and utterly strange?

Where was she?

And what should she do next?

A memory of waffles assailed her, crisp on the outside and soft on the inside, their pockets dripping with melted butter and strawberry preserves. She could smell the savory strips of bacon beside them and the citrusy orange segments in a small dish next to the plate.

Breakfast! Breakfast was what came next.

She stood abruptly and hurried to the paneled oak door, turned the brass knob, and slipped out.

The door opened onto a small vestibule, more a passage through a very thick wall than a real antechamber. Its walls were coffered wood painted white, blending into the white marble of the hallway just beyond.

She pattered out to the hall, bare feet on cool marble floor, nightgown swirling around her ankles, as she gazed wonderingly around.

The hall was so grand, carved with marble pilasters and marble alcoves and rounded marble vault overhead. Frosted glass globes held by white brackets in the shape of wings adorned the walls.

So . . . she was in a palace or a castle.

She looked to her left.

The hallway dimmed in that direction, with no windows to light it, only the subdued glow of the glass globes on the walls. She felt an intuition that she should go that way, but it didn't look very promising.

Did the dark terror that nibbled at the edges of her cheerful curiosity lie that way?

Maybe.

She wanted to find people – friends? – someone she could ask questions of. Someone who might help. She did need help, didn't she?

Her mood wobbled again, from blithe to scared and . . . alone?

Uncertain, she touched a finger to her lips. They were very dry, so dry that flakes of rough skin tickled her fingertip.

How long had she been without water? Her lips shouldn't be this dry after merely a night of sleep.

But she wasn't thirsty. Not even a little bit.

She looked to her right.

That was a more inviting prospect.

The glass globes remained unlit, for their glow was unneeded. Large bay windows along the left wall – overlooking a diminutive enclosed court – flooded the hall with cool light.

Numerous doors lined the right wall, and the hall's end offered a choice of ways: several branching passages, stairs up, and stairs down.

She would go in that direction. There had to be someone else waking up behind one of those many doors.

Please gods!

She fought her fear yet again and turned right.

The first door yielded a parlor that looked like a wedding cake. Silver gilt, white satin and lace, crystal and mirrors. The pretty clutter of it repulsed her. As did the faint scent of roses lingering on the air. Someone she knew – an enemy? – did she have enemies? Someone she didn't like, at least, would have loved it.

She didn't go in.

The next door down revealed a child's playroom, with bright murals and vivid red, green, and blue furnishings.

But no children. No nurse. No one at all.

The tall rocking horse seemed to mock her. She could remember rocking on just such a plaything in the past – back and forth, back and forth – feeling comforted by the motion.

The snippet of happy memory – contrasted against this empty, lonely room – chilled her.

The formless dark that waited under the veneer of the castle swelled and overpowered her.

She huddled against the door frame in terror of something she couldn't see or understand. A formless animosity.

What was this place?

Why did it seem both wonderfully splendid and ominously haunted? And where *was* everyone?

With effort, she pried herself away from the playroom doorway and set off down the hallway.

The next room was a water closet. Oh, piffle. That was the last place she'd find help.

She wouldn't bother checking the rest of these closed doors. This wing of the castle felt deserted. A slew of parlors and nurseries and bedchambers would do her no good, if they were all untenanted. She trotted to the end of the hall and turned left. There had to be someone somewhere.

The castle was *huge*.

Corridors and more corridors, with chambers along all of them. Vast galleries with views of interior courtyards. Spiral stairs to more towers than she could count. Formal staircases down to grand receiving rooms. Ballrooms, stillrooms, dining halls.

And all of them unpopulated. All of them subtly tainted by a wrongness beneath the splendor. A hostility that roused itself at intervals before receding again.

Where *was* everyone? What had happened? Why was she here?

Who was she?

That question shocked her.

She hadn't realized – not really, not truly – that she didn't know who she was. How could that be? She felt dizzy.

Only blankness greeted her when she tried to cast her thoughts back to before she awoke in that sunny bedchamber – *her* bedchamber. Nothing and more nothing.

Abrupt terror shot through her.

How could she not remember anything? Not even her own name! She desperately wanted answers. But how could she find answers when there was no one to ask?

She sagged beside a square pilaster in a barren reception hall, fighting tears.

Her lips were even drier than before, the skin flaking off when she ran her equally dry tongue over them. She should be thirsty. She'd been trotting through this pile of a castle for . . . who knew how long? It felt like a *long* time. Her legs were tired, and her bare feet ached from pounding against the hard marble floors.

How could she not feel thirst? But she didn't.

She pressed the heels of her hands against her forehead and swallowed hard, gathering determination. She would hunt through the castle as she might hunt game in the woods.

She would dig up some answers. Somehow.

Straightening her shoulders, she set off again, twisting and turning through the sprawl of corridors, choosing her way almost at random.

When she stumbled upon a small, square, white door – unpretentious – hidden behind a fluted white column, she felt her first whisper of hope.

Every other space she'd visited had been obvious, open to anyone. Open to her.

This door was secret, meant only for those in the know. Which was definitely not her. She knew nothing at all, even the things she *should* know. Perhaps there were answers beyond this portal.

She'd almost given up on people. Surely she would have seen some sign of them, if anyone were present. But answers . . . she *could* not give up on finding answers.

She turned the unadorned brass doorknob, pushed the door open, and looked through.

Her heart leaped within her.

This had to be it!

The door was hidden behind a column on the other side also, a column of polished green marble in a whole line of them, like cypresses along an avenue. Across the hall – more magnificent even than any of the hundreds of spaces she'd passed through – another line of green marble columns flanked the wall.

She stepped through the door.

And almost fell.

Like the blow of a giant's sledgehammer, or a mountain falling on her, the animosity lurking behind the castle's grand veneer slammed down on her more terribly than any of the other times it had roused.

Her knees shook, as though she bore a heavy weight on her shoulders. The hatred oppressing her was that palpable.

She could hear her breath whistling in and out as though she drew near the end of a grueling race. Could she stand?

No, that wasn't the question. She was standing. Standing and trembling.

Could she take a step? Could she walk?

She wanted desperately to step *back*, step out of this pounding animosity. Return to the empty desolation she'd been ranging through, where the malice slept uneasily, but slept nonetheless.

She took a step forward.

Oh, gods! Not forward. She wanted to go back.

And yet . . . back held no answers, no people, nothing. She had to go forward. If she could.

She took another step forward, and another, passing around the towering green column into the open space of the hall and along it.

She found she *could* walk. Walking was no more difficult than standing. It was just being here that was hard, withstanding the malevolence that powered down so unceasingly.

She went on, steadily. Clinging to some trace of stubbornness inside her that quivered under the onslaught, and yet did not succumb.

All the spaces beyond the concealed door were very grand: vast in size with tall coffered ceilings and impressive colonnades, connected by broad halls and impressive stairways. These rooms were for show, not use. Receptions for heads of state, audiences for ambassadors, award ceremonies to honor heroes.

Still she went on, determined to learn something from the differences in this wing of the castle. Wrest some advantage from them.

The enmity increased. She could feel pieces of herself – not her body, which trembled, but her *self* – shredding away. If she kept going, would even her stubbornness be pounded into oblivion? Taken the way her memory had been taken?

The malevolent presence was worst in the resplendent entrance hall.

The capitals of the columns, far overhead, dripped with crystal and gold ornament. Enormous fresco murals depicted warfare between colossal heroes and equally colossal monsters. Black marble flooring, polished to reflectivity, gave the illusion that leviathans swam its dense shadow as kraken hunting the sea.

Most daunting, the great double bronze doors to the esplanade outside – formed of eight panels each, depicting yet more battle scenes – were barred shut.

She sank to her knees. Which hurt, more hostility slamming up from the dark marble.

There was nothing for her here. Not even exit.

She'd not let herself think of escape until now, when the sight of those doors – the heavy bars above her head – proved it impossible.

She was trapped in this awful castle.

Her mouth stretched in a silent scream.

The skin of her dry lower lip split, its pain sharp within the bludgeoning hatred.

She felt warm wetness well from her split lip, saw the shining scarlet drop of her blood fall through the air, and splatter on the polished floor, wherein the bright reflections and dark shadows moved, signs of the leviathans hunting below the surface.

Oh, gods!

Were they the source of the malice pounding her? Would one immense behemoth surface to the taste of her blood, open its cavernous maw, and swallow her down?

She cringed, there on her knees, bent and expecting her destruction.

Stolen Thirst

THE MALEVOLENCE emanating from the ceiling bent her head yet further.

The menace rippling beneath the floor bruised her knees.

Another drop of blood fell from her lip.

She pressed the dry underside of her tongue against the split skin to cover the cut. She had to move. Now. Leviathans or no leviathans.

Reluctantly, she placed her palms on the floor – resisting the ache that leapt into her hands – and pushed up. She gained her feet and fled, stumbling, lurching, back to the small door behind the column and through it.

The lifting of the demonic enmity was so sudden, she felt light as a hot air balloon. Had she left the floor to float above it?

She burst into tears. Tears of relief. Tears of belated terror. Tears for the memories she did not have.

And then she was running again.

The heavy demon menace of the state rooms was absent, but she could no longer ignore the sleeping darkness that roused and turned and slept again in these friendlier spaces.

She wanted her bedchamber and its safe warmth, longed for it, was desperate for it.

More by instinct than knowledge, she dashed onward.

She'd found the staterooms by accident. She'd have to find her way back by accident too.

And yet some intuition guided her when a choice must be made. Left and right, and left and right again. On and on. She was almost surprised when she discovered herself running down the hallway with the bay windows on her right and the rank of closed doors on her left, a dimmer stretch ahead.

And there was the open door to her room. Her room! It hadn't disappeared altogether!

She'd been afraid it wouldn't be there. Like in dreams where you were perpetually lost. That nothing she knew would be there, even the things she knew only from this morning. That she would be condemned to wander unknown spaces with a hauntingly familiar feel until she perished.

But her room was here. Sunny and safe and warm.

She threw herself onto the bed, burrowing her head in the pillows, yanking the covers up over her shoulders. *I'm home! I'm safe! I'm alright!*

And she was. But she wasn't. Still she could feel the sleeping malice in this part of the castle.

She huddled there a long while, feeling the soft firmness of the mattress under her, so unlike the hard and dangerous floor of that demonic entrance hall. Feeling the light softness of the sheet and blanket wrapping her shoulders, enfolding her in care and . . . love?

Her shaking calmed. *She* felt calm, there in the bright warmth of her bed.

Gingerly, she probed for memory, hoping this safe space might help her discover something. But there was nothing. Which was terrifying all over again. But she refused to give in to it. She couldn't give in. Giving in – as she had in the dreadful moment when her lip split and bled – had gotten her nothing.

She fought her fear down.

But nothing else changed, here under the covers and the pillows.

Eventually she realized *she* would have to do something. Nothing would happen here of its own accord. There were no maids in the parlors, no footmen awaiting her call, no one at all. She was alone in this vast pile of elegance.

Cautiously, she poked her head out from under the pillows and pushed the covers back.

Her room was the same. Same rollicking suns, same sunny windows, same silent furniture.

She swung her legs over the side of the bed and to the floor. She went over to the dressing table and sat down on the delicate stool drawn up to it. Silver brushes – two of them – a tortoiseshell comb, and a hand mirror lay on its agate surface. A large framed wall mirror hung above it.

She wondered all over again: *who am I?* What would she see in the mirror? If she looked? She *had* to look.

Pushing the accessories aside to rest her elbows there, she leaned her chin on her hands and studied herself.

Grey eyes, with dark circles under them. Straight short dark brows. She'd always wanted delicate arching brows. Small, blunt nose. Why couldn't it have been a charming retroussé? Or aristocratically aquiline? Her – mother? sister? friend? – someone had admired hers. Said it was cute. *I don't admire it.* She hadn't then. She didn't now.

Full lips, pale and very, very dry, fringed in flakes of dead skin. Why wasn't she thirsty? Something was very wrong with that.

Pointed chin. No cheek bones yet. *I'm young.* How young?

Fourteen? Fifteen? Sixteen? Again she didn't know. But one of those seemed about right.

Dark, curly hair, just below her shoulders, tangled from her night's sleep and now wholly escaping its braid. Had it been a night? Or longer? She suppressed the terror that question brought. She was getting better at suppressing terror.

Looking at her reflection didn't trigger any memories.

How could she know so little of herself? Of her history? Only her core sense of *I am, I exist, I live* remained.

What is my name?

Oh, gods! She didn't even know that.

Not Desirée. Not Aimée. But it was a name like that that meant something. Something nice. Beloved?

I wish!

She couldn't bring it to mind.

I hate this!

And she did. How could she be . . . happy? Even after the loneliness of searching the deserted castle, her confusion when she first realized that she remembered nothing before her awakening here, and her terror in the demonic wing, she could feel herself reviving. Was she a naturally cheerful person?

Maybe.

I'll choose a name. I won't be nameless. I'll be Fiona. Or Freya.

No. I'll be Fae.

The name Fae felt good. Felt *right*.

She scrutinized her reflection again, not seeking identity this time, but assessing what was plain to see. The dark circles under her eyes could mean nothing good. Was she ill? She didn't feel ill. Just . . . a little empty?

But her lips? So pale and dry, flaking with their dryness. When had she last had water? Not since she awoke, that much was sure.

Thirst or no thirst – and she still had none – she had to find water.

She was still in her nightgown. She supposed she *could* go seeking water in her night clothes. But she'd rather not. She'd already sought people and answers so clad and found . . . great enmity. She needed the armor of daytime garb to face . . . whatever she found this time.

I'll find water, she told herself fiercely. She *had* to find water.

She picked up the larger hair brush and began brushing her hair, working the tangles out.

A diamond tiara lay in the top left drawer of the dressing table. *No.*

Hair clips, combs, barrettes, and ties were in the top right drawer. *That's better.*

She rebraided her hair and pinned it up around her head in a coronet. She'd never worn it that way before. Somehow she knew that. But why now?

This was a room for a princess.

How else, when it was beautiful and spacious and located in a castle. But *she* was not a princess. Nor a serving maid. Nor lady-in-waiting. Nor a knight's daughter. All those stations in life felt irrelevant. She wouldn't wear the tiara, but she could try to live up to her surroundings. Or try to fit in.

She checked the wardrobe to her left.

Oh, heavens! Ball gowns in silk and floating georgette and velvet. *No!*

The right wardrobe held day wear: muslin gowns with fitted bodices and long skirts. Not quite like what she normally wore – whatever that was – but they would do. She chose a pretty yellow one with elbow sleeves and knotted buttons down the front. There were undergarments in a few small drawers inside the wardrobe: chemises, camisoles, petticoats, drawers. Fussy stuff. She chose the bare minimum – camisole and drawers – and forewent the hose and shoes altogether.

She was ready. And still she wasn't hungry or thirsty. She pinched her upper arm. Hard. Yes, it did hurt. This wasn't a dream.

She fought shy of the door. The hall outside – the *castle* outside her room – harbored that dozing evil. What would happen when it roused completely?

She turned left. Toward the dimness that she had rejected the first time she made this decision. Intuition – the same intuition that had returned her to her bedchamber from the demonic entrance hall – told her that left was the correct direction.

Perhaps the kitchens lay that way.

She squared her shoulders, reaching for the optimistic person she sensed she might be.

I will be hopeful. I'll even be cheerful. The statements had gritted teeth behind them, but she would make them true. She gave a little skip, even though she didn't feel like it, and then felt her heart grow lighter in the wake of her pretense.

Hah! Pretending helped.

Some. A little.

She would keep pretending then.

The hall went on and on, then turned into a stairway that was almost a ramp, so broad and shallow were the steps, curving gradually around a wide spiral, down and down from one generous landing to the next.

She descended for longer than she'd walked the hall above. At the bottom, a wide and low-ceilinged corridor led through an open doorway into the kitchens. She felt her eyes widening. Castle kitchens were . . . big!

She hadn't known. How could she *not* know? The not knowing still made no sense.

And didn't feel good. Not good at all. She should know *something*. There was too much of *nothing* in her thoughts, more nothing than anything else.

She pushed down her fears yet one more time to focus on her surroundings.

Castle basements were . . . fancy!

Low shallow vaulted ceilings extended away from her, supported by thick whitewashed piers at intervals, until they reached the walls with a scattering of dark, unpainted wooden doors with iron rings as handles.

Closer to her were marble counters on stone pedestals, wheeled tea carts, ice chests, jelly cabinets, plate hutches, a vast hearth laden with a bouquet of pot hooks, a rotisserie, and a toast rack, plus copper pans and iron stew cauldrons. Every kitchen tool she could imagine and many more she couldn't.

But no cooks.

The place was silent, empty of people – like all the other spaces in the castle – a cool white expanse lit by low-arched windows placed high in the outer walls.

No cooks and no food.

But what about water? Every kitchen had water. Had to have water. For cooking. For washing up. It was water she needed. Water that she was seeking.

Her lips felt *crusty*, they were so dry.

Her eye fell on a deep, square porcelain sink set into a wooden cabinet against the wall, with porcelain drainboards on either side. Two copper faucets protruded from the backsplash, each sporting a porcelain cross-handle.

Water!

Oh, gods, *yes!*

She rushed over to the sink and turned the handle on the right with the letter "c" in the center where the four porcelain lobes met. The knob was stiff, and its metal shaft groaned. She gave it another twist.

It loosened abruptly, and then –

Nothing.

No gush of water. No trickle of water. Not even a single drip.

No water at all.

The First Godmother Door

THE LEFT HANDLE – the one marked "h" – also yielded nothing.

The sink was as dry and useless as all the rest of this shadowy vault.

Her disappointment was so bitter, she could almost taste it in her dry, dry mouth. She bent to rest her forehead on the rounded lip of the sink. It was very cool and hard.

The crusted flakes of skin on her upper lip caught on those of her lower one. In longing, she dredged up mental pictures of water. A stream babbling through woods. A spraying fountain in a grand marble plaza. A river flowing beneath the many-arched stone bridges of a city. A cascade rushing down natural stone stairs.

And then memory engulfed her. Real memory, not just random bits of knowledge surfacing willy nilly.

At some point in her past, she had stood before an outdoor pump, its pipe rising from a bare damp spot of earth amidst moss. She must have been very young, because the top of the pump handle reached her shoulders. Someone else's hand – a large, capable hand – worked the handle up and down, while clear water burst from the spigot.

A male voice with a hint of laughter in it instructed her, "Hold your paws under the stream and you'll do. That's right."

She'd looked down at her hands. They were very, very muddy. She'd been making mudpies, and when she finished with the fun she hadn't known what to do.

The water was cool and smooth compared to the warm gritty mud. She turned her hands over and over in its flow, rubbing them and watching the dirt sluice away.

"Did you know that water is more important than food, little minikin?" the man working the pump asked her.

She liked his voice. It was kind and tender. Unlike the other voice. The cool woman's voice that had scolded her for the mud. But she didn't know the answer to the man's question and shook her head.

His finger pointed to her wrist. "There's a bit there to wash off," he urged her.

Her arms were bare – was it summer? – so she thrust her forearms under the stream. Oh! That was a little too cool!

"There you go, mignonette. All clean!"

The memory ended there. She wished there were more of it. She'd rather be there than here, back with the gentle man and the water. Instead she was leaning against a cold, dry sink in a deserted basement kitchen.

She pressed her forehead harder against the smooth porcelain, not wanting to confront her solitude.

The kind man's words echoed in her thoughts.

"Did you know that water is more important than food, little minikin?"

Dear gods, he was right. She might last weeks, nearly a month, without food. Working to solve her predicament – even though she didn't understand it, any of it – the whole while. Or most of it.

But without water . . .

By tomorrow, she would be weak.

The next day she would grow nauseated, and her thinking, unclear, foolish even.

And the next day . . .

The next day would be her last day. She would drift into delirium and die.

Dear. Gods.

She thrust herself upright and fled the kitchens, fled her bleak realization, running back up those long, shallow stairs and back along the upper hallway.

The light in the miniature courtyard visible through the bay windows had changed. No longer the clear, cool light of morning casting long shadows, nor the strong and hard-edged light of noon shining straight down, but the softer golden light of afternoon. Late afternoon.

The courtyard itself was in shadow. And the turquoise sky above held the luminous depth that came with evening.

Gods! Was the day nearly done? It felt both interminable and too short. As though she'd been searching – first for people, then for answers, and now for water – for either forever or just an hour or two. Her legs wobbled with fatigue, and her feet ached even more than before. The palace floors were hard, and she'd been walking with little rest since she awoke.

She had a feeling that such walking wasn't unusual for her, but that she was accustomed to softer footing. Mosses, grasses, pine needles, bare earth. Natural, outdoorsy surfaces. Not smooth marble or polished oak. Though the wood was better than the stone.

But she needed this day to last a little longer. Long enough for her to find water. She needed it not to be evening. Not yet.

She stopped briefly in her room. The cheerful suns frolicking around its cornice lifted her discouragement a little. Looking at the golden gryphons on the headboard of her bed, she felt stronger. Strong enough to go on, at least. And going on was what she had to do. Even if it meant she continued her search in the darkness of night.

Lifting her chin, she set out again.

Eventually, she fetched up in a conservatory. That is, she thought it must be a conservatory, because of its glass-paned roof.

But there weren't any plants. Just a bare white floor of tiny hexagonal tiles traced by a pattern of black arabesques. A birdbath stood in the middle.

The birdbath held water.

Water!

She approached it almost cautiously. Would this prove to be just another promise with disappointment in its wake?

The water was clean. No dusty film on its surface. No green mold discoloring the basin's stone.

She should be thirsty. Desperately thirsty. *Should* be, and wasn't. But the water drew her as a candle flame drew a moth.

She touched her forefinger to her lips. They were beyond dry and cracked. They must have split again, because she could feel more than one thread-like scab. Her tongue clung briefly to the roof of her mouth, it was so dry.

Why *didn't* she thirst? So much about this made no sense.

If she were dreaming, she wouldn't be thirsty. But if she were dreaming, it wouldn't hurt when she pinched herself. It hurt.

The sun must be very low. The tint of the sky had deepened, even in the short time that had elapsed during this latest search. She thought it was a short time. Time was so hard to judge in this place, with all the clocks stopped at one minute to twelve. The conservatory stood wholly in shadow, lit only by the luminous sky.

She bent and kissed the water, opened her lips, and sucked the liquid in: wet, cool, and quenching – everything water should be. She drank a long draught, paused, and drank again. It felt very, very good as she swallowed.

Her dry lips and tongue grew slick and scummy, as though covered in sticky mucous. Which was nasty, but better than the dangerous dryness that had preceded it.

She rubbed her lips, and the mucous came away on her fingers. Oh! It was the dry, dead skin now mixed with water that had created that slimy film. She'd never been so parched before. Never had that happen before.

She drank until her stomach felt overfull and stretched with it.

How would she know when she'd drunk enough? She could remember the sensation of thirst, even though she could not feel it. She could remember that when she was very, very thirsty – as thirsty as she'd ever gotten, which didn't seem very much, compared to this – a few modest goblets of water weren't enough. She'd needed three or even four.

This water couldn't quench a thirst she didn't possess, but her body felt like a flower showered by rain, reviving in the moisture.

She lingered beside the birdbath, sitting down on the floor, tailor fashion, and watching the blue of the sky deepen. Each time the fullness in her stomach abated, she sipped again from the birdbath.

The conservatory grew dimmer, still light only because its glass roof admitted all the remaining radiance of the translucent sky, and the white marble walls and white tile floor reflected it.

Her mouth and throat and tongue felt moist again, and her lips.

The birdbath remained full. Had she drawn the water line down at all?

Maybe.

Abruptly it all seemed too much. She sank to the floor, huddled against the pillar of the birdbath, her cheek pressing its stone.

Who had done this to her?

With that question – feeling angry, terrified, and lonely – fresh remembrance swept her under.

In memory, she stood in one of the castle hallways outside a door unlike any she had seen this morning. It was small, not grand at all, with a point-arched top. Many of the castle windows had that pointy arch, but none of the doors. Not even the small, square door into that dreadful demonic wing.

This door was carved in bas relief and painted to depict a beautiful young woman. She wore a flowing garment fashioned from cloth of silver and begemmed with stars. Masses and masses of curling blond hair floated around her as though she lay on water. Her face was very sweet.

A tall woman stood beside this door, her hand on its knob. She wore a long, severe, fitted gown of black velvet and a black satin cloak. Her dark hair was confined in a snood at her neck. Opals shone from it. Her face was as severe as her gown.

She turned to speak to – *who am I?*

Gods! Who am I? Surrounded by old memory, she remembered more recent memory. Remembered that she had named herself. *I'm Fae! I decided that.*

The woman turned to speak to Fae. Her voice was low and gentle, wholly unlike her face and her garb. "I am going away for a year. I leave you responsible for my home. Will you shoulder this task?"

Fae nodded. She wished to please this formidable woman. "Yes, milady, I will."

Milady issued further instruction. "You must command my servants."

"Yes, milady."

"You must stay within doors."

Oh, but that was a hard promise. "Yes, milady."

"And you must never open this door, nor allow any other to do so."

"Oh, no, milady."

"Good." She looked so different when she smiled: warm and loving and giving. "I love you, child." She turned away and departed.

The memory ended there.

Fae stretched out her hand as though she could grasp this snippet from her past and hold it. As though she could say, "Wait, please wait," and the stern, but loving woman – Milady – might stay and comfort her. As though she could catch hold of the departing memory and be pulled by it into the rest of her history.

"Please," she whispered, which did no good at all.

She was alone and severed from her past entirely. She felt empty and very, very lost.

Who *was* Milady? Did she have a name? A real name? She must, but Fae could not recall what it might be.

What was her relation to Fae? Not mother. Definitely not. An older sister? A family friend? An aunt? That felt right. Aunt. But with more of a connection to Fae than kinship, something personal. A governess? No, she'd taught Fae, but not on subjects like arithmetic or the use of globes. More intimate things; how to be a good friend, when to apologize after you'd wronged someone.

Apologizing. That meant something.

Had Fae wronged someone? Had Milady wronged someone?

Fae straightened, still sitting there on the conservatory floor, and pulled away from the pedestal of the birdbath. Her cheek felt sore where she'd leaned against the pedestal. She rubbed the skin, feeling the indents made by the fluted stone.

Abruptly she knew who Milady was: *my godmother!*

But nothing more than that.

I'm not going to unearth anymore about her now, she decided. *What about that door?*

She was sure it was somewhere in the castle. But where?

The first star shone in the deep and radiant sky above. The conservatory had grown very dim, its pale surfaces still gleaming faintly through the shadow.

A second star appeared and Fae felt the sleeping malice of the castle shift and wake. A sensation of sharp nips traveled down one arm to her wrist, as though she pinched herself.

No sign of the pinches showed on her skin. No bunching or wrinkling of her flesh. No redness. But they hurt!

She leapt to her feet in panic.

This was what she'd feared from the moment that she'd escaped the demon of the staterooms. That its twin – drowsing in the living spaces – would rouse and assail her.

She plunged through the nearest doorway, running toward her room and safety, carried along the darker hallway by her momentum.

Tearing scratches raked her legs, while needle-like stings jabbed her ankles.

The hall was worse than the conservatory – much worse – but it was too late to go back.

She stumbled down a stairway buffeted about the head by slaps. By some miracle she didn't fall, and the next stretch of corridor was better. Tall windows lined one wall, tall mirrors the other. The reflected light meant she could see where she ran. And the pain – clustered nipping, scratching, and stabbing – diminished.

She came to a corridor where the glass globes glowed, shedding a warm light on the white marble floor and walls. She could sense the malicious attention of the castle's evil – more goblin than demon – but the pain ebbed completely.

Fae slowed, then stopped.

Beyond this lighted area, the hallway was dark. Did the dark harbor the goblin torture?

Could she stay here in the light? Safe?

She cast a quick glance over her limbs. No bleeding cuts or purpling bruises. No remnants from the pain at all.

The light globes flickered, then went out.

Oh! Gods!

And a feather of scorching heat sizzled across her shoulders.

Fae ran.

Her race through the shadows became a blur of torment, stinging hurts that might have seemed minor if delivered solo, but were unbearable in an overlapping sequence. The goblin presence behind the pain strengthened, until its caustic glee hurt her awareness as much as its pinches hurt her body.

She was sobbing when she reached the hallway outside her room.

Sobbing and gasping.

Her legs felt like limp cloth beneath her, as though she might collapse before she achieved her door. The doorway to safety.

"Please, please, please," she whispered, straining to take those last, necessary steps.

"Oh, please."

And then she was stumbling into her bedchamber.

The moon had risen and shone through the windows, illuminating the furnishings, the walls, and the ceiling.

Fae stared up, then moaned.

Black and silver in the moonlight, goblin faces leered down at her from the cornice, seeming almost to cackle in evil glee.

Fae's legs gave one last wobble and folded.

She fell back, landing hard on her rear, and then bumping her head. She hardly noticed the pain from the fall amidst the goblin pinches and pokes.

Through the tears pooling in her eyes, she gaped at her room's transformed ceiling mural.

The moonlight illuminated a fortress built of smoke, coalescing from sullen coals. The hint of a demonic face – eyes agleam with malice, lips curved in the enjoyment of pain – gloated over its terrible victory.

Fae shrieked and rolled, somehow regaining her feet.

A gleam of pearlescent black caught the corner of her gaze as she whirled, aimed she knew not where.

Oh, gods! Were the gryphons – *her* gryphons – as changed as her merry suns and her fairytale cloud castle? To bats or winged snakes?

Please, please, please. Someone come. Someone help. Someone make the monsters go away.

Weren't monsters supposed to crouch *under* the bed?

She squeezed her eyes shut.

A streak of agony sliced up her arm, from wrist to elbow to shoulder, deeper than any of the scratches that had preceded it.

Surely her flesh was split to the bone with blood gushing from the wound.

Her eyes flew open, and she saw her gryphons. *Her* gryphons. Magnificently changed, to be sure, but still *hers*. Black and sleek with opalescence shining on their feathers. Beautiful and fierce in her defense.

Desperate, she leaped for her bed.

As the mattress received her and the softness of the linens enfolded her, all pain ceased. The goblin rancor muted. The demon hatred abated.

By day, the golden strength of the gryphons protected her happiness.

By night, their dark intensity protected her from harm.

She cuddled down in the nest of her bed. A tide of relief flowing across her exhaustion swept her into slumber.

She lay dreamlessly for a while, vaguely conscious of being protected, savoring it.

Then her dreaming began, and her sense of safety popped like a soap bubble.

She stood on a hilltop in the night, before her the flames of a bonfire leaping into the starless sky. Black-robed men and women capered around her, screeching and gibbering, their faces mad with evil glee.

She glanced down to see that her hands were chained behind her to a stone pillar. The uneven light flickered over runes deep-carved into the rock.

The crowd of witches parted.

A woman in a voluminous, hooded cloak approached. She put back her hood to reveal a pale, stern face – Milady's face, but with red eyes, not gray. Black horns sprouted from her brow, wrapping around the sides of her head like a crown before their tips turned up just past her ears.

Dreaming, Fae's heart felt as though it would pound right out of her chest.

The demonic woman parted her cloak, raising a stone dagger in both hands as though she made offering to some dark god.

Fae struggled to be free, but the chains at her wrists held fast. Indeed, chains bound her ankles as well.

The demon gripped the dagger's hilt in her left hand and licked its blade with an impossibly long tongue. The blade's edge split her tongue in two. She smiled and bent toward Fae's neck.

Fae lunged away from her as though it were possible to sink her body into the stone pillar behind her.

It wasn't.

The two halves of the tongue slid around her neck, slimy, hot, and strangling. An instant later, the knife pierced her. She tumbled into darkness, falling and falling and falling, a scream streaming from her dreaming throat.

SECOND

No Provision Made

⁂

As SHE FELL, the darkness scourged her, malicious like the goblin watchers taunting her as she dreamed.

Then the darkness changed. From a caustic, hostile flatness to a velvety, living depth of night.

Stars pricked out in the night, a moon rose, and she realized that she did not fall, but floated in cool water, its ripples spreading out from her face, catching glimmers of silver light.

The burning tension and pain in her breast ebbed away.

A ribbon of gold and lilac grew on the horizon, and a sliver of the blinding sun appeared.

⁂

She awoke to daylight and her bedchamber in its daylight guise: merry suns gamboling around the cornice, fairytale castle beckoning in the sky mural on the ceiling, robin's egg blue wainscoting.

The breath huffed out of her at the relief of it.

The castle's dark malice slept. Her room was safe. *She* was safe. For now.

But she didn't linger in bed. Her bursting bladder shot her out into the hall, seeking the water closet she thought she remembered from yesterday.

Where, where . . . there!

She dove through the narrow door, swung it shut, and pounced on the commode.

The closet held all the necessities: a generous stack of loo tissue on a narrow shelf, hand towels on a rail beside the washbasin, a cake of soap in a dish. Windowless, the yellow-paneled walls glowed under one lamp, which was lit. The globe's bracket resembled a moth's wings.

Fae studied it a moment. This was the first rendition of insect wings she'd spotted. Were there others? Did insect wings denote one sort of space, avian wings another, and the wings of legendary creatures yet another? That could be useful information.

The loo tissue was soft and thick, but she scarcely noticed this luxury, distracted – and dismayed – by the color of the urine in the commode bowl: a deep ochre, too dark, unhealthy.

Water. She had to devise a system for water. One that would work. That didn't rely on bodily sensations, since she had no thirst reminding her to drink. And something that would permit her to carry water with her.

Casually, she pulled the chain to the cistern mounted high on the wall above the commode. No water flowed to flush the bowl. Of course; the kitchen taps had been dry also. She tested the spigot over the wash basin. Nothing. The soap and towels would be of little use for handwashing without water.

Discouraged, she levered herself to her feet.

She checked her reflection in the mirror over the wash basin.

Her lips were pale and dry again, with little flakes of peeling skin. The circles under her eyes were lighter than the day before, but still present.

I could die of thirst without ever feeling thirsty.

She started to touch her finger to her face, then stayed her hand. Wash first.

She lifted her chin, grabbed the soap, and marched herself back out the closet door, down the hall, and into her room.

She dragged an old-fashioned ewer and basin out of the daywear wardrobe – it had been tucked behind the skirts of the dresses – and trotted upstairs to the conservatory.

The sky through the glass panes of the roof was a very light, bright blue – fit for the robe of a goddess who brought happiness cupped in her hands.

Fae dipped water from the birdbath with her ewer and filled the basin, which she'd set on the tile floor. She crouched to wet her hands, lather them with the soap, and then rinse them.

A line of drain tiles encircled the conservatory near its walls. She poured the dirty wash water out above them.

There. Hands clean.

Then she drank and drank from the birdbath. Only when it felt like her stomach would burst with another mouthful did she stop. Just like yesterday, the water level of the birdbath did not dip. So very odd. Was the birdbath fixed in time, always existing at the moment of its fullness? Like the clocks that showed the time as always one minute to twelve? Was she the only element here that moved from the present into the future?

Leaving the ewer and basin in the conservatory, she scampered back to her room to change her dress. The yellow gown from yesterday was wrinkled, since she'd slept in it. And she didn't want to face this castle rumpled and disheveled.

Its sleeping evil might lie quiescent now, but its goblin nipping – or worse, its demon sledgehammer – might wake at any minute. Fae shuddered. She needed to be her strongest self today.

The coronet of her braid was falling out of its pins. She took it down, unplaited it, brushed the tangles out, and rebraided it in two quick pigtails.

She bundled the wrinkled yellow dress into the hamper in the corner and chose an aqua dress from the wardrobe of daywear. Its bodice featured a placket of tiny pintucks and pearl buttons. She found a matching ribbon in a dressing table drawer and tied it around her wrist. *Every time I catch sight of the ribbon, I'll take a sip of water. After I find something to carry water with me.*

But first she had to *find* that something for carrying water.

She headed for the kitchens, counting her steps, hoping that knowing the distances between places in this castle might help her understand it better. Somehow she doubted that it would. This castle wasn't understandable, wasn't reasonable. But she had to try. There wasn't anyone else.

Loneliness congealed around her.

She squared her shoulders.

I can do this. She had to.

Seventy-five steps to the curving ramp of the stairway. One-hundred-eighty-six stairs. Although the treads were so deep that she took two steps on the flat for each step down. Then seventeen steps through the vestibule to the kitchen archway.

She performed some rough arithmetic. More than six-hundred footsteps.

That gave her pause. Was there some significance to the number? Should she see what lay six-hundred steps away from her chamber along all the different routes possible? Maybe.

But water organizing first.

The kitchens were brighter than before, with the morning light shining in through the windows set high in their underground walls. Unlike the upstairs, there were no glass globes to illuminate the vast space. Instead, plain iron brackets held oil lanterns. But the lanterns were empty of oil. By evening, it would be very dark here.

Fae shivered, remembering what the dark held.

She surveyed the many counters dotting the expanse, some supported by metal legs at their corners with a broad shelf underneath, others featuring enclosed cabinets with doors. Taller pantry cupboards flanked the massive pier-like pillars that upheld the shallow vaulted ceiling. There were a lot of nooks to search.

She sighed.

The sooner she started, the sooner she'd find what she needed. At least she could rule out the cluster devoted to baking, the one accoutered for grilling and roasting, another devoted to drinks.

That still left a lot.

She searched.

Eventually, next to a closet filled with brooms, dustpans, mops, and buckets, she discovered a repository of camping gear: portable cooking pans and utensils, a tiny spider-like stove with a bottle of fuel, nesting tin dishes, and a water canteen. It was an odd shape, round and flat, made of metal, and nested in an olive green canvas sling with a shoulder strap.

She slung the strap over her head, to rest it on her left shoulder, while the water vessel hung at her right hip. Yes, that would work. Except there was no water here.

She touched her lips. Dry again, in spite of her drink from the birdbath after she'd washed her hands. How long ago was that? It was so *annoying* that she couldn't judge the passage of time. That her body gave her no sensation of thirst. That she was here at all.

What had *happened* to her?

Not now, Fae, she told herself. *Just get on with it. Fussing won't help.*

But she wanted to fuss. To whine. To have someone who cared. Someone *else* who would tell her to stop whining.

Back to the conservatory she went. First up the ramp of spiral stairs that seemed to climb forever, then through the hallways. She tried skipping, just because she could. It seemed to help press her fear down far enough that she could ignore it.

Fine. She would skip. Feeling scared only made everything harder.

She scampered up a straight flight of stairs. And turned a rebellious pirouette in the upper hall.

Better and better.

She was reclaiming some courage. She *needed* courage.

The slumbering evil of the castle roused and turned and returned to sleep.

Fae's shoulders hunched. She unhunched them and turned another pirouette, more defiant than anything else.

Through the glass-paned conservatory roof, the sky had deepened from the pale, clear purity of early morning to the stronger hue of full morning. The shadow of the eastern wall had shrunk toward its base, a modest crescent on the tiled floor. The day was passing, the sun rising, despite the timelessness of this place.

She took the metal canteen out of its sling.

A piece of paper fluttered to the floor.

What?

She snatched it up.

Script writing in black ink adorned one side.

Fae, you must *stay alive. See to your physical sustenance first of all. No provision has been made for you.*

✐

Her fingers clenched on the scrap of paper.

A cold feeling – fear and relief co-mingled – stabbed her belly.

Someone knew she was here. Someone who cared about her. Someone who wanted to help her. She felt both less lonely – someone's awareness held her – and more lonely: that someone wasn't here.

But, Olympus above! No provision made for her food and drink. The birdbath must be an overlooked remnant from when the castle was inhabited. From when someone opened the two casement frames on one side of the glass roof to let doves fly in. She could see the long chains, looped on a stanchion, that connected to gears at the window latches.

Where would she find a similarly overlooked detail that could feed her?

Bird seed, assuming there was any, wouldn't do it. Hay for the horses, assuming she found the stables? Same. Dried banana chips for a pet monkey? Well, she could certainly *eat* them. Assuming there had been a pet monkey. But banana would not sustain her . . . however long she was stuck here.

I need to search for food.

Except that water must come before even food. She *had* water, here in the conservatory. But it was too far away from . . . safety. She never again wanted to run the gauntlet of goblin pinches and goblin spite as darkness gathered in the maze of hallways between the conservatory and her bedchamber. Her bed. It was only her bed that was safe, protected by her gryphon guardians.

She checked the flip side of the paper scrap she held in her hand. Nothing.

No, wait a moment.

She held it closer. There was a watermark, pure white against the softer white of the paper. Shaped like a gryphon, like the gryphons on the headboard of her bed.

Huh.

She turned the scrap to study the writing again. What was it about those fine, elongated loops on the up-strokes and down-strokes of the letters?

The chill in her belly deepened.

Sweet Marionya! The handwriting was her own.

The returning sense of being entirely alone, entirely dependent on her own limited resources in this castle, appalled her. While the puzzle of how the note had come to be tucked in the canteen pouch bewildered her.

Had she been here all along, her memory of the previous day stolen in the night?

Surely not. She could remember yesterday – all too vividly – even though she remembered nothing *before* yesterday. Besides, she'd have perished within a few weeks, if she had to learn the rules of the castle anew each morning, find water and food enough before the sun set. This was already her second day – she *hoped* it was only the second day – and she still had no food.

Like her thirst, hunger was absent.

Had she known she would be here and left herself helpful clues, like this note, in advance?

If that were the case, why had she not avoided this imprisonment altogether? It was imprisonment. She was pretty sure of that. But why? And by whom? And why had she consented to it? She was equally certain that her consent lay in the paradox somewhere.

Or had some impostor learned to form her f's and l's and y's just as Fae did?

The note was addressed to her. Did that mean she'd guessed correctly when she named herself Fae?

She bit her lip. The sharpness of her teeth on the soft flesh felt good. At least she felt pain properly, even if she didn't experience hunger or thirst.

Intuition told her that Fae was not really her name, but maybe someone had called her that once.

She unscrewed the cap of the canteen and submerged it in the birdbath. The water gurgled in through the opening, large air bubbles burbling out. When it was full, she lifted it, dripping. Was it leaking? No, that was just water from being immersed.

She screwed the cap back on and wiped the sides with her palm, flicking the rest of the wetness off the surface. Then she bent and drank from the birdbath, feeling her lips grow moist again.

The water in the basin remained the same level.

Did nothing change in this palace? Save herself, becoming dry without water? Would she grow emaciated, if she could not find food?

Water first, Fae, she reminded herself. *Water,* then *food.*

She needed large containers, really large and more than one, that she could fill with water and set in the hall just outside her room.

She returned to the kitchens and ransacked them for what she needed.

The serving carafes didn't really hold that much. She'd have to make too many trips every day to the conservatory.

The huge soup kettles were better – maybe two gallons? – but hugely heavy.

Eventually she fetched up at a nook in the wall she'd missed before.

Three shallow steps descended to what looked like a sidedoor to the gardens. But within the doorframe was no door, only an expanse of plastered wall. As though the opening had been bricked in, the way nobles had bricked in their windows when the crown declared a fenestration tax.

Or the way guardians of the public health during plague ordered stricken households bricked in to die.

Who had ordered Fae bricked in?

Did they intend *her* to die?

Too Heavy a Burden

THE SLEEPING EVIL of the castle stirred, muttered, and turned over to slumber on.

Fae shivered and stared at the blocked doorway. Who had bricked her in? And why?

No answers came to her, but she felt a renewed longing to get out, to leave, to escape. Were all the doors barred – like those colossal bronze doors guarded by the demon – or blocked, like this one? If she searched hard enough, would she find a door that was not locked?

Did the arched door she'd seen yesterday in memory stand somewhere in this immense pile?

If she found it, could she escape through it? Was that why she'd remembered it?

She felt an impulse to run until she found that godmother door. Never mind the water. Never mind food. Just get out! Now!

She'd roamed through so much of the castle yesterday, and not even begun to see all that it might show her. The godmother door might be just around the corner. Waiting for her to find it. Waiting to offer her freedom.

But she'd not seen any sign of it yesterday. Why would she find it now? And, if she did find it, why would it provide escape? She was just wishing – wishing oh-so-strongly – and wishes were just wants. And wanting alone wouldn't get her anywhere.

Water, Fae, she reminded herself yet again, and looked at the walls flanking the nook with the plague door.

On the right wall hung shoulder yokes that milkmaids used to carry their burden. On the opposite wall, a shelf held six milk cannisters: tall, tin vessels with broad necks, lids, and curving handles that swung out of the way of the top openings.

Perfect! Absolutely perfect for her purpose.

She tried the yokes on her shoulders.

The first that came to hand was for someone broader than she, but the second fit well. At each end of the yoke dangled a rope ending in a sturdy hook. She placed the curving handles of the cannisters in the hooks, one to each side. The whole contraption felt pretty light, fairly comfortable. She suspected the full cannisters would be a different matter. *Cross that bridge when you come to it,* she told herself.

About to start for the conservatory, she paused.

She wanted more than two cannisters. Two would do, but if she had more, she might be able to stockpile enough water for several days, not just one or two. She could always come back for the extras, but why make unnecessary trips?

With a little fiddling, she found she could thread the wood of the yoke through two of the cannister handles, and then put one cannister in each hook as well. That wouldn't work when they were full, but empty cannisters were fine.

The upper cannisters bumped her arms as she walked. At the top of the long ramp of stairs, one cannister slid down the wood of the yoke and fell down the rope to clang against the cannister secured by the hook, both containers swinging wildly into her knee.

She got everything repositioned and took the steeper flight of straight stairs more slowly.

As she entered the conservatory, the aqua ribbon on her wrist caught her eye. Blast! Sipping from her canteen wouldn't have been possible while she toted milk cannisters, but she hadn't even remembered.

She put her burden down, took five quick swallows of water, and then set about filling the cannisters.

They were too big to fit in the birdbath. Even if they'd been shorter, the water was too shallow to allow her to immerse them the way she could her pancake-shaped canteen.

She'd need a soup ladle. Or something like that.

The basin and ewer she'd used to wash her hands caught her eye. Of course! The ewer was exactly right.

Even using the ewer, filling two of the milk cannisters took a while. She counted ewerfuls while filling the second one: sixteen. What had she been thinking when she envisioned using a soup ladle? Great and little gods, she'd have been ladling until dusk at that rate!

Recalling the dark halls from the conservatory to her bedchamber, she shuddered. *Tonight* she would be in bed well before dark.

But it was still morning as yet, and she wanted the other two milk cannisters that still sat on the shelf next to the plague door. She took the yoke back with her to the kitchens. But she forgot again about drinking from her canteen.

In addition to the milk cannisters, she snagged a drinking ladle – that held a lot more than the soup ladle and might come in handy – as well as a tray and eight water goblets. Modest ones, not the generous tumblers that a racemaster might give to competing sprinters after they crossed the finish line.

Carrying the loaded tray while balancing the shoulder yoke and cannisters was tricky.

This time she *remembered* that she should sip from her canteen, but both her hands were otherwise occupied.

On her way to the conservatory, she stopped at the bay window across from the water closet. Bare plant stands resting on a white-tiled floor filled the alcove. Some were small and circular, others rectangular and shelf-like, and one was shaped as stacked tiers.

This would be the perfect watering spot. Near to the safety of her bedchamber.

No, her *chamber* was dangerous. But her *bed* was safe. And she could pour washing water into the sink in the water closet.

She left the tray and glasses on a shelf-like stand, but ferried the cannisters and ladle on to the conservatory.

She decided to move the two full cannisters before filling the other four. She fastened their handles to the yoke's hooks, crouched a little to fit herself under the yoke, and pushed to straighten her legs.

She could not. The yoke held her bent.

She wasn't strong enough to lift thirty-two ewerfuls of water.

Even lifting just one cannister with her arms in order to pour some of its contents into an empty cannister proved beyond her.

She glanced at the glass roof above her.

The sun had cleared the eastern wall during her last trip to the kitchens. Not high noon just yet, she guessed, but getting there. She scrubbed the back of a hand across her brow. Sweaty.

She glugged a bunch of long swallows from her canteen – draining it – and then refilled it.

She looked at the two full milk cannisters, the yoke with its loops of rope on the mosaic floor, and the four empty cannisters. Sighing, she dragged an empty cannister next to each of the yoked cannisters, removed the lids, and started ladling. The necks of the cannisters were wide, but not wide enough to admit the ewer.

She'd known that drinking ladle would be useful. Thank goodness she'd known.

When the full cannisters were down to nearly half their previous volume, she could lift them and walk. She didn't waste her burdened test steps, but carried on toward the archway out.

She had to stop and rest twice while traversing the upper hallways. Getting down the stairs was plain scary. She couldn't hold onto the bannister, and her balance felt precarious with so much weight on her shoulders. But she made it.

At the bay window, she set the cannisters down on its tile floor. She dipped each of the goblets she'd left there into a cannister, filling them. How many glasses would fill her canteen? She eyed it. Maybe four? Say four. She'd measure the next time it was empty.

Meanwhile, she had a plan. If she drained her canteen only once during the day, she'd drink from all eight goblets in the evening. If she swallowed down the contents of her canteen twice, she'd drink four goblets. Three canteenfuls, and no goblets needed. Unless her lips were dry.

Cumbersome, but it was a system that didn't rely on thirst. It would keep her alive.

What next? More water carrying?

Or look for food?

She rubbed her sore shoulders. Food, she decided. Godlings, yes! She had enough water for now. She could carry more later.

Six flights of straight stairs down (plus five landings) she arrived at the castle stables.

The stables were fit for a king's horses: parades of prancing stallions carved on the limestone cornices, bas relief flowers garlanding the stone pillars, and fine oak panelling forming the stall partitions.

When she passed through the broad, squarish doorway into the space, the scent of clean straw on the cobblestone floor and hay in the manger racks swirled around her, grassy and warm, like afternoon in a meadow.

With the aroma came memory.

In memory, she stood under the sloping roof of a half-walled smithy, holding a horse by the bridle strap, crooning wordlessly to calm it. Her tuneless song blended with the soft humming of the smith. He stood with his back to her, bent over with the horse's left foreleg drawn up between his legs, rasping smooth the surface of the hoof.

The dimness of the space, lit by the flickering of the coals in the forge, contrasted with the golden evening in the pasture beyond the timber half-walls. The tang of woodsmoke mingled with the metallic smell of hot iron and the comforting one of living horseflesh.

The smith broke off his humming to address a question to her.

"Theophane's an independent sort. Don't you think her freedom would be enough for you?" He carried on rasping – scrape, scrape – while he awaited her answer.

Theophane.

The name brought a face before her mind's eye; a purposeful woman with direct gray eyes, high cheekbones, thin nose, and pale blond hair braided close to her head.

My cousin, realized Fae. *My cousin who studies fencing and the arts of war. Who knows how to drive a chariot and plan a battle.*

Did Fae want to learn how to fight with a sword?

No, but she did envy Theophane her license to do as she chose.

Fae's voice, as she answered the smith, held a touch of scorn. "Backed by the patriarch, her father. Where would all 'Phane's freedom be without his support? What if he'd insisted she learn the arts of hospitality and domesticity? Would she be practicing fencing passes, exercising in the gymnasium, and reading *The Book of Five Rings* without Hadrien's support? I think not!"

The smith shifted his left hand more firmly under the horse's toe, thrust the rasp into a holster on his thigh, and plucked the horseshoe dangling by one heel from his back pocket. He held the shoe against the sole of the hoof. "Hmm, hmm. Almost, but not quite."

He removed the hoof from between his legs and let the horse place it back down on the ground. Rather than walking directly over to his forge, he turned to face Fae. His hazel eyes looked at her kindly, but his mouth, framed by neat brown mustache and beard, was firm-lipped. His hair, straight and close-clipped like his whiskers, conveyed the same "meant-for-business" approach that seemed to be his character.

My uncle, she realized. *Leander*.

He ran his fingers through his hair from brow to crown. "I take it you've no admiration for your aunt."

Fae snorted. "Sariah? She organizes her entire day – and every day – around Hadrien. She gets up early merely to pour him tea during his breakfast, schedules her marketing for when he is busy, and invites friends according to whether he wants entertaining company or peaceful solitude. And they're not even her friends. They're his!" She consciously relaxed her hands on the bridle strap. The horse whickered his approval. "No. Aunt Sariah is all wife and nothing but wife. I can't understand how she's so happy. I'd be bored to tears."

Leander smiled and then turned toward his forge, gripping the horseshoe with tongs and thrusting it in amongst the glowing coals. He pumped the bellows twice, and then stood watching the shoe take on heat. "And Pallas?" he suggested over his shoulder.

Fae didn't bother to get riled this time. He was baiting her. In a teasing, friendly way, but still . . .

"Pallas is worse than Sariah." She could just see this other aunt of hers, crooning over her infant daughter and sewing baby clothes.

Leander turned further around toward her, his left eyebrow arched. "Really! How so? Pallas rules her own demesne without interference."

"And that's exactly why it's worse," retorted Fae.

Leander retrieved the shoe from the forge and placed it on the anvil, holding it steady with the tongs, while he shaped the red-hot metal with ringing blows from his hammer.

Fae raised her voice so as to be heard. "Sariah makes Hadrien's comfort and happiness her life work, but it's her choice to do so. Hadrien doesn't make her. And if he ever told her how she should manage the housemaids or the cook, she'd either laugh or hand him his head. She doesn't brook interference."

Leander shifted the horseshoe from its flat-lying position to looping over the horn and carried on hammering.

Fae knew he was listening, despite his focus on his task.

The horse nudged her free arm, and Fae scratched his poll. Phlegon liked a little attention when being shod.

"Aunt Pallas would wean her baby from breastmilk to goat's milk, if Hadrien ordered her to. Or dress the wee thing in wool instead of thrice-washed linen. Or dose herself with fennel tea."

"Your uncle would never do anything of the kind. He respects your aunt's wisdom and expertise." Leander held the horseshoe up to eye level, studying it. The metal had cooled from cherry-red to black, but the heat still quivered off it. He tilted the shoe, then plunged it into the bucket of water beside the anvil.

"That's not the point. Hadrien respects Pallas, but Pallas doesn't respect Pallas. And Hadrien's only her brother. Not her father or her husband."

Leander was attaching holding clamps to the still-hot horseshoe. He brought it over to the horse, positioned himself to grip the lower leg, and ran his hand down over the fetlock. Phlegon lifted his hoof, and Leander neatly pulled it between his thighs. Holding the shoe by the clamps, he pressed it against the hoof bottom.

A cloud of smoke plumed up, accompanied by the smell of burning hair.

Phlegon tossed his head, but made no other fuss. He was an old hand at this.

"Hadrien *is* the patriarch. I'd obey his orders." Leander lifted the shoe, let Phlegon take his leg, and walked back to the anvil. He set the shoe down, then returned to examine Phlegon's sole.

Evidently it wasn't satisfactory, because he gripped the hoof between his legs again and embarked on some dainty pruning with the hoof knife. Leander was a perfectionist about fitting shoe to sole. It had to match exactly.

"But you obey because you took an oath to do so, not because you doubt yourself."

Leander pruned Phlegon's sole a bit more, then grabbed his rasp to smooth the new parings.

Fae continued her argument. "I just don't think it's fair that Hadrien's the patriarch. Back before the dark aeon, even before the golden age, in the time of innocence, Gaia was matriarch. Why shouldn't we have a matriarch again?"

Leander let Phlegon's leg go once more, and tested the heat of the shoe resting on the anvil. Cool enough, evidently, because he removed the holding clamps and carried it over to check it against Phlegon's hoof. He grunted, secured Phlegon's hoof between his thighs, and pulled his driving hammer from its loop. He snagged a nail from the pouch on his belt, lined up the shoe with the hoof, and started pounding the nail in. *Ting, ting, ting.*

"So you'd prefer obeying a matriarch – the way you obey Hadrien – to obeying a patriarch?"

Leander bent the nail where it emerged through the hoof wall, clipped and bent the nail tip, then started on the next nail.

Fae pondered obeying a matriarch. No, it didn't appeal. She didn't really want to obey anyone. But obedience wasn't really the heart of her problem. It was its own issue, separate from this. What she *wanted* was for women to possess the same degree of authority as men. It wasn't fair to compare any of her aunts to Hadrien, precisely because he *was* the patriarch. The proper comparison was aunts to uncles. But even there, the women came up short.

Leander pulled the clinching block from its holster beside his rasp and placed it below the first nail end on the hoof wall. One precise rap on the nail head, and the nail was clinched. He moved on to the next one. And the next. *Rap, rap, rap.*

When he finished, he pulled forward the hoof stand and set Phlegon's hoof on it. He brushed his thumb over the hoof wall, nodded, and then rasped the clinched nail ends smooth. Another moment and he was done, the hoof stand tucked back against the wall, and Phlegon with his hoof on the ground.

Leander stroked one hand down Phlegon's neck. "There you go, boy. That's better."

"Uncle, do you believe me wrong?" Fae pleaded.

He turned from patting the horse to touch a hand to her shoulder.

"No, sweetheart, but you'd be better working on your own freedoms rather than those of others," he told her.

That advice went right down to the ground through her body, through her heels. She could feel its rightness and its challenge, both then in memory, and now as she looked around the stables of this time-frozen castle.

Were there any freedoms to be had here?

Bearing It

⁂

FAE PONDERED THE FRAGMENT of memory she'd just relived. It felt *good* to remember. No, it felt *great* to remember. But she wanted more, much more. Who were all those people? Aunts and uncles and cousins, yes. She got that. But what had happened to them? Where were they now? Where was she herself?

What has happened to me?

Her family seemed important, perhaps governing the fate of populations. And large; with an extended kinship. But she couldn't call up any details to match those vague intuitions. She'd better keep on with the tasks at hand. She still needed to find food. And each of the memory spurts she'd experienced had been triggered by places here in the deserted castle.

I'll put the puzzle pieces together when I have more of them.

But she needed more pieces. Many more than she had now.

The stables were huge. Aisle after aisle of stalls and generous loose boxes. More grooming alcoves than she could count. Dozens of tack rooms with filled saddle trees and wall brackets festooned with halters, leads, and more. All of it fashioned from warm red oak.

Dozens of record rooms held leather books full of breeding records as well as ranks of pigeonholes organizing papers about specific steeds.

She pulled out one parchment at random. The paper crackled as she unfolded it. Neat script detailed the peculiarities of a steed named Pyrois, who pulled a phaeton and was harnessed using either the traditional four-in-hand or the more challenging random hitch.

Pyrois.

Glorious godlings! Pyrois was Phlegon's brother.

Pyrois had been stabled here. Undoubtedly Phlegon as well. Had her entire family of aunts and uncles and cousins once dwelt in this castle? Along with their horses and dogs and falcons in the associated mews?

She stared at the record room in which she stood. Two walls of glass-doored bookcases. Two walls of pigeonholes.

Had she ever been here before?

It did not seem familiar. Nothing in the castle did. Except her bedroom. And even that felt familiar and unfamiliar at the same time.

Many, many doors studded the outer wall of the stables – big wide affairs with mesh-protected windows set into their upper halves. That is, they looked like doors, but lacked hinges and latches.

Fae was not surprised. Not after the great barred portal in the staterooms and the plague door in the kitchens. There would be no easy way out of this place.

Her big find was in one of the many feed storage rooms.

The fancy bins – red oak adorned with carved horse scenes and lined with tin – were all empty of the sweet feed that prudent stable masters locked away from their charges. But six bags of unopened oats were stacked on the platform of a small, four-wheeled hand cart. She flung herself on the top bag, embracing it.

Tears started in her eyes. *No, Fae. No crying now. There's work to do,* she admonished herself. But the relief of it . . . !

Food. She had food! So long as she prepared it properly – soaking it overnight in acidulated water to make it nourishing – and cooked it, she could eat oats.

Acidulated water. That could be a problem.

No it wouldn't. There had been a big bottle of vinegar in amongst the brooms and dustpans in that kitchen cabinet. Milk whey would have been better, but vinegar would do.

She tugged on the handle of the cart.

It didn't budge. The bags were *big*. And heavy.

She tried hefting the top bag in her arms.

She could do it. Just barely. But lugging it all the way to . . . where would she lug it to?

C'mon, Fae. Plan this properly. Where will you do your cooking? The bay window where she had her water. She could move some of the plant stands out to give her more floor space and rearrange others to serve as work surfaces and storage shelves.

I can do this. I can survive. For the first time she felt confident.

Arranging it all was hard work. She sweated. But she remembered to drink often enough that her canteen was empty before she got back upstairs.

First she dragged all but two of the feed bags off of the cart. She pulled the remaining two to the bottom of the stairs, then went back for the next two, and back again for the last two. One by one, she carried the bags up all the stairs.

Ugh! Her arms felt like jelly when she set the last bag down.

She reached for her canteen, remembered it was empty, and grimaced.

Then she shrugged and walked the hallways back to her bay window. The necks of the milk cannisters were wide, but not wide enough to admit her canteen, so she held it over the opening while pouring water from a water goblet. The canteen took three-and-a half gobletfuls. She drank the remaining half goblet plus two full ones.

She felt better for the water.

Her body never signaled thirst, no, but there were subtler sensations that she was beginning to learn. Subtler discomforts that vanished when she drank. That was probably a good thing. Maybe she wouldn't accidentally die of a personal drought.

She smiled wryly.

Next came bumping the cart up the flights of stairs. It was too bulky and heavy to carry. And it kept trying to drag her back down as she wrestled it, tread by tread, upward. But she did it. After that, transporting the oat bags to her cooking bay was easy.

She fetched the vinegar, a big mixing bowl, a dish towel, and the camping stove and cooking gear from the kitchen.

No way to open the sturdy burlap of the oat bags.

Back to the kitchen for shears, a measuring cup, the nested camping dishes, the steel fuel bottle for the camp stove, *and* an extra fuel bottle hidden under a crumpled ground cloth.

Then she started the oats soaking: two cups of oats, add water to fill the bowl, uncork the vinegar and pour a dollop in, stir, cover the bowl with the dishcloth.

She wasn't yet done. Oh, the *oats* were done for now, but *she* was not.

She glanced up through the windows of her cooking bay. The courtyard it overlooked was so small and the castle walls so tall here, that she couldn't see much sky. Where was the sun? Not in view, as it would be around the noontide. Was it afternoon already? She'd done a lot: hauling water and hauling oats.

One token of the passing time – and her success in drinking – was reliable. Her bladder was bursting again.

She opened the door to the water closet.

It was just as she'd left it: charming lemon-painted wall panels, glowing lamp, mirror over the washbasin, and commode full of pee. It smelt strong and unpleasant.

She bit her lip and went about her necessities.

This time she had plenty of water for a thorough washing up. After her hands were clean, she poured all of the water in the least full milk cannister into the commode, using the strong stream of water to manually flush it.

There. That was a better way to leave her water closet, fresh for next time.

But she needed to complete her water-hauling chores, if she were going to have enough for washing, cooking, and drinking.

Up in the conservatory, the shadow of the west wall stretched partially across the mosaic floor, but not all the way. And it wasn't even near to climbing the east wall. The sky overhead shone very blue. Early afternoon then, she guessed. Which was good. She wanted to do more than sort out water and food today.

Now that she knew she could survive, the desert loneliness of the castle and the sinister feeling that underlay its grandeur grated on her. Doing something to break her prison felt more and more necessary.

She *had* to get out of here.

But she couldn't skip the basics, much as she wished someone else would do them.

She'd brought the cannister she'd emptied with her and filled it to the just-above-halfway mark first. Then she added enough water to the two partially filled cannisters to take them from just-below-halfway to just-above-halfway. And finally she filled the two remaining empty cannisters.

When she arrived at the top of the stairs with her loaded shoulder yoke, she paused and set the cannisters down. What had she been thinking this morning when she simply walked down the staircase?

I must not have been thinking! Because it had been a crazy thing to do. What if she'd fallen? Broken a leg? Or her neck? There was no one to help her if she were injured.

This time, she pulled one cannister down step by step.

Scrape.

Klung!

Scrape.

Klung!

The metal rang like a bell each time it lurched downward onto a stair tread.

When she reached the bottom, she went back for the second cannister.

Climbing the stairs one more time to get the shoulder yoke, she thought for a moment. It made more sense to get all the cannisters to the top of the stairs at once. Then she could drag each one down, and then carry them to her cooking bay.

The odd cannister was a pain.

She dragged it along the upper halls, and that proved so awkward that she fetched the oat cart to ferry it – and the other four cannisters, two by two – through the lower halls.

I have a new system, she decided. Yoke for the upper halls, and only fill cannisters in pairs. Cart for transport from the stairway to the cooking bay.

It all took more time than she wanted it to.

She remembered to drink, and had to fill her canteen twice more. As well as going through the water closet routine another time. This time she washed her face. The cool water on her flushed cheeks felt good. She wished she could bathe her whole self.

She checked the sky again through the bay windows – fruitlessly – no sun in sight in the small piece of sky, of course; and then entered her bedchamber. Its windows looked east, but she could see the shadows in the gardens below lengthening. Late afternoon?

I don't think it's evening yet.

Did she dare go exploring? Or should she start cooking dinner? She didn't know how to work the camp stove. It would be prudent to figure that out.

Yes, it would. But she wasn't going to do it.

I want to know . . .

What did she want to know?

More than I do right now. What is this place? Why am I here? How do I get out? Especially that. *How do I get out?* The loneliness of the castle made her feel empty inside. The lurking malice of it made her feel as though she walked always under a sword dangling by a thin spider-strand.

I'm going to explore downward. Not the stairs to the kitchen, but some of the others she'd passed in her peregrinations.

The small godmother door that she'd seen in memory – the one that Milady had told her must never be opened – that was an important piece of this puzzle. If she could find that door, she'd learn . . . what? She hadn't a clue, but it was necessary.

And she couldn't bear to wait any longer to seek more answers.

ℰℓℐ

The Second Godmother Door

⌘

As it chanced, she didn't descend any of the stairways she'd bypassed before. None of them felt right, and she hurried past them.

Hurrying because she was only too aware of the afternoon passing.

She *had* to be in her bed before darkness fell.

Somehow she ended up in one of the tallest towers of the castle, near its pinnacle. She climbed a tightly winding spiral stair, the triangular treads so small that she hugged the outer wall to have room to place her feet. Narrow arrowslits, closed off from the open air by more modern glass, lit the stairwell at long intervals, giving it an underground feeling, even though she was high in the air.

Fae emerged from the stairs into a small, round chamber with a low ceiling. Its walls were white plaster, and a bright splash of sunlight through the single arrowslit made a line of blazing gold across the rough flagstones of the floor. The rest of the space seemed dim in comparison. One side of the ceiling sloped downward, where the next flight of stairs continued. She could see the first few steps through the open archway. On the other side, just below the sloping ceiling, a small pointed door was inset into the wall. It was fashioned of splintery dark wood like its frame. No painted bas relief adorned it. Fae could see the silver-gowned maiden in her mind's eye, but this door was plain.

And, yet, this *was* the door. She was sure of it.

She tested the age-tarnished brass knob. It turned under her hand. She could hear the spring in the mechanism twanging faintly. The air felt warm. She could smell a hint of cinnamon on it.

She hesitated.

Milady had charged her with seeing that this door was *never* opened.

Had the opening of it caused her present imprisonment?

Would opening it again free her?

Or would it usher in something worse?

Fae bit her lip.

And found herself caught up in another memory.

In her memory, she stood with Milady again, this time in a large, shadowy space with clerestory windows near its tall, beam-supported flat ceiling. A gymnasium? Maybe.

Under a balcony along one wall was a small, pointed door. In the painted bas relief on it stood a huntress, bow in her hand, quiver of arrows on her back. Her golden blond hair rioted in tight curls around her face. She wore a sleeveless blue tunic and green leggings.

Milady walked to the door, standing in the shadows under the balcony.

Fae followed her.

"I trust you, child," said Milady.

"I shall not fail you," declared Fae. And she wouldn't. It felt good to be trusted. She would be trustworthy.

"I depart for a year," said Milady. "My task will take that long."

Fae nodded.

"Will you be lonely, child?"

The correct answer would have been "no," but Fae was honest. "Yes, milady."

"Then this will be hard for you, I fear."

"Oh, no, milady! I could not fail you!"

Milady smiled. "Good. You know that you must never open this door, nor allow another to do so."

Yes, Fae knew. She'd stood sentinel over a door like this one before. And she'd prevailed. No one – including herself – had opened it.

"This door shall remain closed," she'd promised.

And with those words, as she heard them in memory, a lot more grew abruptly clear.

She had, indeed, guarded the door with the archer sometime in her past. And the door with the silver-gowned maiden. The door she stood beside right now, even though it no longer featured a maiden on its boards.

There had been a third door. She could see it clearly in her mind's eye. Small and pointed, like the other two. Ornamented, like the other two, but with a red-haired young woman, her tresses plaited in a hundred small braids, each only six inches long. She wore a golden breastplate and golden greaves on her legs and forearms, and a skirt of red leather straps over her thighs.

Milady had ordered Fae to guard this door, to ensure it stayed closed. Fae had done so faithfully.

And *that* was the problem.

Why had she been so obedient?

Why hadn't she wondered more, challenged more, explored more?

Because the shutting of those three doors, their uninterrupted closure, had led inexorably to her present fate. She was sure of it.

She didn't know quite how. Not yet. But she *would* find out.

And when she knew more . . . she would open those doors. She would find the other two. She would learn all their history. And she would free herself.

She studied the one in front of her.

Dark, dry, splintery wood. Dull, tarnished brass knob. Equally tarnished escutcheon plate. With a keyhole.

A keyhole.

Abruptly Fae twisted the knob again and pushed.

Pushed harder.

The door didn't budge. It was locked.

Fae sagged against the splintery wood, fighting tears. She'd been so sure that this door was her answer, her salvation, her escape.

But it was just one more dead end, one more hope quenched, one more incomprehensible piece in the puzzle of this castle.

A spark of anger lit within her,

She didn't want to spend a second night here. Even protected by her gryphon guardians, she would feel the goblins mocking her, feel the demon hating her, feel the flat deadness of the dark. But she didn't have any choice.

She lifted her head and straightened her shoulders. This door might not be *the* answer, but it was part of an answer. And this door's escutcheon plate possessed a keyhole.

She would just have to find the key.

Fae turned away, crossed the small landing area, and sat down on the top step of the spiral stair.

The cinnamon scent on the air smelled stronger, the warmth felt warmer,

Unlike every other room and passage in the castle, including her own bedchamber, this spot felt fully safe and welcoming. Not just a veneer over awfulness, but safe right down to its bones. As though the goblins and the demon were absent from it, not merely sleeping.

Maybe she could retrieve more memories, more knowledge, if she stayed here. And even if she didn't, it was a relief to be free of resisting the castle's lurking evil.

The stone of the step pressed warmly on her thighs through the fabric of her gown, as though it had baked in the sun for a long time. She leaned against the rough plastered wall, warm also. If only she could stay here, right here, until she got free.

She fingered a wisp of her hair that had straggled out from one of her two pigtails. She pulled the right plait over her shoulder, studying the dark, curling strands below the ribbon and the tidier braided length above it.

None of the maidens depicted on the pointed doors were dark: silver blond, golden blond, and flame red.

Spirit of the stars.

Spirit of the moon.

Spirit of the sun.

How did she know that?

She didn't know these women. But her cousins had played their roles in an entertainment once. A theatrical production.

Fae sighed.

She'd already delayed dinner preparation to search. She'd better not delay it again. The castle's night was approaching inexorably. Besides, finding food would do her no good if she didn't eat it. She sighed. Being so responsible felt . . . necessary here, but confining.

I'm not normally so serious. At least, she hadn't been. But then something had changed. She wondered what, and swung to her feet.

The looming sense of desertion and malice that characterized the castle returned full force when she reached the third step down from the landing. It oppressed her. And it took many, many steps down to get out of the tower.

Oncoming Night

֍

BACK IN HER COOKING BAY, she discovered that the tote for carrying the camp stove also held a parchment of printed instructions. Not her own handwriting this time – or anyone's – but the regular type generated by a printing press.

Thank goodness! On several counts.

A relief not to be confronted by another mystery. And a relief to have instructions. She'd never have figured out how to use the camping gear else.

The stove was a tiny little spider of a contraption. It came with a thin short metal hose, a tinder wheel, and a cylindrical baffle to attach to the outside of one's cooking pot.

She perused the directions carefully, not wanting to make a mistake.

First, check that the stove burner knob and the fuel regulator knob on the connector hose are both set to off.

She checked; they were.

Second, attach the fuel cylinder to the regulator end of the hose, and the other end of the hose to the camp stove.

That was easy. They were threaded like screws and could be twisted together.

Third, check for leaks by rubbing soapy water along the hose and the joints at both ends.

She had water, and she had soap. She applied it as directed, then cracked the regulator valve open.

No bubbles. No leaks. That was good.

Fourth, turn the burner knob on slowly, one or two turns. Strike the tinder wheel above the stove burner and light the gas.

Eeek! This was the scary part. She practiced with the tinderwheel three times, pulling the string on the wheel and watching as a shower of sparks fell from where the flint abutted the spinning metal. Yes, she could do this.

She turned the burner knob, snatched up the tinder wheel, and pulled the string.

The shower of sparks fell.

And the burner blossomed into flame with a soft *foomph*.

She'd done it!

Fifth, place your pot on the lit burner and adjust the burner knob to the heat level required.

She'd already attached the baffle that would concentrate the heat around the camping pot. Now she spooned some of the soaking oatmeal – sludgy and soft – along with its cloudy, viscous liquid into the pot. She added an equal measure of fresh water, covered the pot, and placed it on the camp stove burner. The burner was making a soft purring sound.

Next came the wait while the oats cooked.

It shouldn't be long. The oats had soaked enough to be ready for eating with just a few minutes of simmering.

She replaced the cloth over the bowl where the remainder of the oats continued to soak, and checked her stores.

Five cannisters of water as full as she could manage. One cannister only a quarter full. Five bags of oats unopened. One bag with just two cups removed and held closed by a clothespin. Eight empty water goblets. She'd used them to fill her canteen throughout the day.

The aroma of cooking oats began to fill the cooking bay. Like baking bread, but heavier and more grasslike. Her stomach didn't growl. Nor did it ache with hunger. It couldn't. Not here. But she found herself longing for her meal, even though her body could not. She *needed* dinner.

Fae lifted the lid with a spoon handle. She could feel heat radiating off the metal of the pot and the baffles belted to it. The oatmeal was beginning to bubble. She let the lid fall closed and turned the burner knob down, watching the flame to lower it without letting it go out. She didn't want the oatmeal to burn.

Where would she eat?

Right here, she decided.

She dragged the straight-backed chair from the writing desk in her room to a spot in the hall beside her cooking bay. One of the circular plant stands would make a fine table. She filled a water goblet, to have something to drink with dinner. Which surely was done by now.

She used the spoon handle again to lift the pot lid.

A cloud of steam rolled upward, fragrant with that oatmeal smell. *Mmm.*

She lifted the pot lid all the way off and set it to rest on the surface of the stove's plant stand. Then she turned the fuel regulator valve off. When the burner flame went out, she turned the burner knob to off.

The camp dishes were tin – like the cookware – flat, with tall slanting rims. Concealed between the top two and the bottom two was a small napkin wrapped around a plain fork, knife, and eating spoon.

Fae spooned some of the oatmeal onto one dish and found it grew too hot to handle. She borrowed a hand towel from the water closet and used it to grip the plate rim, moving the plate to her "table."

She sat, placed the napkin on her lap, and spooned up a mouthful of oatmeal.

Ow! It scalded her tongue.

She grabbed her water goblet and swigged, then swigged again, cooling the oatmeal and soothing the burn. A little more waiting would be needed, evidently.

What time was it? And how many times had she asked herself that question?

The sky visible through the windows had the jewel-like tone of early evening. *I bet the western horizon is showing gold, if I could see it.*

She still had some time. The stars had been out last night when the goblins awoke. But she didn't want to cut it too close.

She repressed a shudder. The castle was a scary place, but she was tired of being scared. She'd managed bravery a few times, in spite of her fear. She was going to try for it more often. And longer.

I can do it. I can be braver. Being braver is . . . more who I am anyway. That felt right. Being herself felt like . . . an important piece of this puzzle she was putting together. An important piece of regaining her memories and her identity.

I'll get free when I know who I am.

That felt true.

She stirred the oatmeal on her plate, then tested a tiny dab of it. Warm, smooth, and satisfying with that substantial oat taste. Like home. Like mother's rocking chair. Like drowsing by the fireside. *Mmm.*

She finished the plateful and served up two more. She felt no hunger to satiate, but she did feel something. A hollowness that needed to be filled.

She finished all of the oatmeal she'd cooked.

Washing up the dishes in the water closet basin proved somewhat cumbersome, because the basin was on the small side, and she had to pour all her water from the cannisters, rather than turning on the taps. She dried everything with another hand towel and set the cookware, utensils, and plates on the tiered plant stand she was using for storage.

Outside the windows, the sky glowed a deeper cobalt and the first star shone, bright and hopeful.

If only she could leap right up into that living blue. Escape from her prison by flying.

I wish I were anywhere but here.

But . . .

Oh, gods! The first star! She had to hurry!

The globe lamps in the hall had lit, glowing softly. Sweet Marionya, but she was glad this hall possessed lamps. Quite a few did not. Night was coming on. She needed to ready herself for bed. Now, right now.

I've done well, she reminded herself. *I've found food and water. Tomorrow I'll accomplish even more.*

The lamp brackets in her room were gryphon wings, to match the bedstead, and the glass globes shed light enough to chase the shadows out of every corner.

She could not wish to turn them down. She knew what lurked in the dark. She could feel the goblins stirring. But it would have been nice to watch the darkening landscape outside the windows. Perhaps there was a village hidden by distance or the brow of a hill, and she might have spied its presence by firelight flickering in windows.

She removed her aqua dress and underclothes, sniffing them before letting them fall into the hamper atop yesterday's dress. They smelt as fresh as if they were freshly laundered. How odd.

She bit her lip and retrieved the dress from the hamper. It would only get wrinkled – like the yellow dress. May as well hang it back up.

She sniffed herself. *She* was not so fresh. How would she manage a bath? She sighed, the sound loud in the silence.

The bracelet of aqua ribbon, still on her wrist, caught her eye. She touched her tongue to her lips. They were dry again. She drank half her canteen and pulled on her nightgown. Its soft cotton felt good against her tired body.

She unbraided her hair and brushed it. Static crackled between the boar bristles of the brush and her dark curls. She rebraided them in two pigtails and left them hanging down her back.

She glanced anxiously at the ceiling. The cloud castle remained a cloud castle illuminated by sunlight. It hadn't transformed into the sinister smoke fortress inhabited by a demon. The merry suns on the cornice were yet merry and sunny, not malicious imps.

But they would change when the lights went out.

I'll be asleep by then. I won't look. I won't see.

But she would feel them staring, gleeful in their ridicule.

She needed to hurry more. Her bedtime routine had relaxed her. She couldn't afford to relax. Not yet. Not now.

Hurry up, *Fae!*

She rummaged in the dressing table, trying some of the lower drawers, and discovered tooth powder and a toothbrush. Hurray! She could have a fresh mouth!

She jumped to her feet, lifted her arms, and did a quick dance step.

Hastening through the lamplit hallway, she dove into the water closet to clean her teeth and wash her face. The need to move her bowels, for the first time since she'd awakened in this castle, arrived while she patted her cheeks dry with a hand towel.

Manually flushing the commode afterward took a bit more water, a whole cannister rather than just part.

But it was good. It meant her body was working properly, digesting her food, taking in nutrients and fluids, expelling wastes. *It means I am alive.*

Back in her bedroom, she studied her face in the mirror. Same dark hair in neat pigtails. Same straight-looking gray eyes and straight brows. Same small snub nose and full lips. Same pointy chin. But the circles under her eyes were gone, and her cheeks showed a slight flush. That was good. The result of enough water and some food. But . . . was her face thinner? Two days and only one meal. Would it really show so quickly?

No. That was her imagination. But the oatmeal wasn't going to be enough. Not if she were stuck here for a really long time.

I won't be, she reassured herself. *I'll get myself out of here sooner than anyone would believe.*

The real problem was . . . she didn't believe it herself. And she was the one who mattered. It wasn't like there was anyone else to convince.

Stop it, Fae. Just go to bed and do the next thing, whatever that is.

Her bed felt like heaven, soft and supportive and cozy.

Through the windows, shadow shrouded the land as the sky turned from luminous cobalt to velvety indigo to living black. She knew how it would feel if she were out of doors: mysterious, depthful, and breathing. Behind the glass of her window panes, it felt flat, as stale as the water in her canteen.

Her eyes drifted closed almost immediately, despite the lamplight and the darkening panes of the windows.

I won't look, if I wake in the night.

And then she slept.

Sleeping, she dreamed of herself wandering the magnificent, untenanted castle.

She watched herself from afar as she emerged from her bedchamber to turn wondering eyes on the splendor surrounding her. Dream Fae explored with enthusiasm at first, but her energy quieted as she discovered that she was wholly alone. Her skipping muted to walking. Her wide-open interest changed to disappointment. When she discovered the birdbath in the conservatory, she was dragging.

Dream Fae transitioned from open to closed.

Dreaming Fae felt grief tighten her chest. Her dream was superimposing an older history onto the recent one of wandering the castle, but she'd lost something, sometime. And it hurt.

Sorrowing, she awakened in the moonlit night – the light globes long doused – and dived under the covers without opening her eyes.

She could feel the caustic glee of the goblins, the bludgeoning hatred of the demon.

Oh gods, oh gods, oh gods.

It hurt. Even though she couldn't see the malicious faces of the goblins or the implacable eyes of the demon. Even though her body remained free of pain – safe, here in her bed – her heart ached as though bruised.

She cowered under her blanket, fighting back tears.

THIRD

Searching and Seeking

⸎

DREAMING, she'd not known what she'd lost.

Waking in the night, she knew.

Her memories, her history, her very self. All gone on the tide of some unfathomable force, with herself washed up on an unknown beach where the gulls dove and pecked at her.

Except it was not birds that rent her heart, but the ridicule of goblin spite and a demonic will to destroy.

Clutching her pillow and shuddering, Fae wished the blanket over her head delivered the sense of safety it once had when she was little and in the grip of a night terror.

But it didn't. It didn't at all.

She could feel the nipping jabs of the goblins as though their hostility were hat pins stabbing right through the soft wool and the linen sheet.

Remember your guardians, Fae.

The thought felt like it came from outside of her, but it didn't. Some well of strength within her disgorged it at her need.

She didn't open her eyes. The imps felt stronger, and she didn't dare. But she did call her avian guardians to her mind's eye, dwelling on the dark power of the gryphons mantling their mighty wings at the head of her bed.

I'm safe.

Within that momentary respite, she slept again, dreamed again.

At first she thought herself repeating the dream of her earlier sleep: watching herself wander her prison.

But this girl's dark hair was straight, not curly. And she cried a lot more, explored a lot less.

She is not me, dreaming Fae realized.

Nor was this castle Fae's castle.

Its conservatory was rectangular and featured a shallow reflecting pool, not a bird bath. Its tiled floor depicted jungle flora with huge leaves.

The straight-haired girl lay down on her back in the reflecting pool as though to drown herself, but discovered the water to be to shallow.

She's my cousin, thought dreaming Fae. *My cousin Eulalie; Aunt Pallas' eldest daughter.*

Eulalie cried in the reflecting pool for a while. But when she climbed out of it, she seemed stronger. She changed her wet clothes for dry ones: lilac trousers with a calf-length lilac tunic, intricate cut-work ornamenting the hems of the garments.

She sat at the writing desk in her room – a room wholly different than Fae's, with gauzy violet curtains around the bedstead – and wrote page after page of . . . who knew what.

Then she explored the castle anew, determination in the set of her shoulders, and method in her quartering of the vast pile. She seemed to grow stronger with each stride.

I like her journey better than mine, thought Fae drowsily.

And yet . . . Eulalie appeared to be imprisoned as well, in a castle similar to – but not the same as – the one trapping Fae.

When Eulalie reached the small, splintery door in the tallest tower – the godmother door, and the one spot in Eulalie's castle that matched Fae's castle – Fae woke up.

✍

It was morning, and the glad sunshine shone in across the oak floorboards of her daytime bedchamber.

She felt better. *Much* better.

She was naturally cheerful. Wasn't she?

Feeling happy felt like regaining a part of herself. Like the promise of regaining yet more.

Fae sat up and, still sitting, bounced on her mattress; once, twice. *Must be something jouncy under the mattress.* She tried it again, laughing. She glanced up at the cornice frieze. The carved and painted suns there were laughing, too, but in a nice laugh-with-you way.

Today I'll find the second godmother door.

Today I'll put more puzzle pieces of memory together.

Today I'll get closer to escaping this place.

But first things first: water closet, hand and face washing, dressing. She chose a white gown with simple lines, a large square collar, and a sash. She took her hair out of its pigtails, brushed the tangles out, and braided it into one, big, thick plait down her back, with a white bow securing it.

Today I'll have breakfast!

She paused after testing the camping stove set-up for leaks. No leaks, but she'd recollected one small appealing detail from yesterday: there were salt licks in the horse stalls.

She scampered through the hallways, bounded down the stairs, and skipped into the stables.

I'm myself again. The real me. The happy me.

It felt good. Who cared if the castle concealed furtive evil? Who cared if it displayed surface cheer? Her good mood was all her own.

She plucked a block of salt from the holding bracket in the nearest stall and trotted back upstairs. Her thighs were burning at the top of the stairs, because she'd hurried.

Cooked oatmeal with salt – scraped from the salt block with a knife – was so much better than oatmeal without it. She ate every bite.

She washed up, tidied up, and set another batch of oats soaking. She filled the eight water goblets and filled her canteen.

Whups! No wrist ribbon.

She went back into her room for the aqua one and tied it into a bracelet.

Time for more exploring. More hunting. More finding of answers.

She checked her water supplies: two empty cannisters, three full cannisters, and one just a quarter full. She would work on refilling the empties tomorrow. That was why she'd decided to use six in the first place – so she wouldn't have to carry water every day!

Now . . . where might a gymnasium be in this massive pile of stone? She wanted to find that second godmother door.

I'll stick to the middle levels. No towers or cellars for today. Just echoing galleries with room enough for hundreds of people.

But she would search portions of the castle she'd not visited before.

Her bedchamber lay on the east, and all her exploration so far had been along the hallways and stairwells just to the west of it. With a few excursions to the heart of the castle, and one into the wing just south of her bedchamber – the demonic wing.

She shuddered.

She'd be avoiding that wing.

Instead she'd aim for the westernmost periphery, where the windows looked onto the sunset in evening.

Adjusting the canteen strap over her shoulder, she set out.

The sheer size of the castle impressed her all over again.

Stepping briskly, she walked passage after passage, gallery after gallery, peering through open archways, throwing open closed doors. The muscles in her thighs began to flag when she climbed flights of stairs, and her knees to ache when she descended.

She remembered to drink from her canteen.

Even as the water grew warmer, the mere wetness of it felt good on her lips, in her mouth, and as she swallowed. But there was more to it than physical sensation.

Drinking regularly felt like another small victory against the castle.

Just like feeling cheerful and optimistic was also a point for her.

She arrived at the far western wall more by accident than design. Even though she did possess a good sense of direction. Which helped. A lot. But the corridors of the pile twisted and turned so much, and the odd courtyard blocked even straight hallways, that planning a route was impossible. Drawing a map . . . daunted her.

I'll learn the layout, she vowed. But that would take time.

The long morning shadow of the castle stretched away over the gardens. The sun hadn't yet cleared the castle roofs. It might be early, if this were summer. It looked summerish outside: the lawns green and smooth, well-scythed; the flower borders bright with a riot of blooms; the vegetable plots verdant and overflowing with growth; the forest beyond the tended grounds well leafed out.

She quartered this western wing of the castle.

But she found no gymnasium. And no second godmother door.

❧

Staring out a window overlooking a rose garden, she bit her lip.

The long shadows had shortened quite a bit. The morning was advancing.

She *had* to find that godmother door. She was convinced that finding it was . . . necessary? Why did she think that? It wasn't as though someone had told her the conditions she must meet to regain her memories, her self, and her freedom. Or like she was playing a game with known rules.

She didn't know what might work. If anything would work.

All she had to go on was her intuition.

So she was going on it. And intuition told her . . . that she needed to remember . . . everything. That she needed to *be* herself, and not what this place made her.

That she had to find that second godmother door.

So she kept hunting.

As she hiked through the indoor spaces, she began to long for the outdoors.

She just wanted to feel the breeze lifting her hair, to hear birds calling, to smell the sneezy scent of grass pollen or the loamy aroma of fresh-turned soil. She *had* to get out of doors. And maybe, once she found some such connection to the open air, she could find a ladder. Or rope. Or tie the sheets of her bed together.

If I can just get outside, I'll be free of this place.

That didn't feel right. Getting outside wouldn't bring the memories and the freedom she needed.

But there would be people and meals and singing. Wouldn't there? Shouldn't there?

She'd have won.

There was that game metaphor again. Was this a chess match to be won or lost?

No, this was deadly serious, with her life in jeopardy. With everything in jeopardy. She *had* to win.

I will win!

And she had to get outside. Just *had* to.

But she found no door to the outside.

In desperation, she attempted to turn the crank of one of the casement windows. It didn't budge. Even if it had, the sill was a good twenty feet above the ground. She'd need a ladder, if she were to get safely down.

Angry, she plunged into the nearest room, a study.

Glass-fronted shelves lined its walls, holding hundreds of fat, leather-covered books. A wingback chair and ottoman occupied one corner beside a floor lamp. On the vast desk – a heavy mahogany piece of furniture – lay a blotter and a stack of parchment. A fountain pen stood in a stand next to a bottle of black ink. Atop a carved walnut box rested a massive paperweight – a crystal sphere larger than her fist and with an inclusion of colored glass at its center.

Fae snatched the paperweight up, ran toward the bank of windows behind the desk, and threw the globe at the lowest glass pane, flinching as she did so in expectation of the shattering crash.

The paperweight bounced off the window with a click, leaving the glass unharmed. It landed with a thump on the thick carpeting.

Fae collapsed on the carpet beside it, her cheek pillowed on the orb, while a storm of furious tears swept through her.

Damn! Damn! Damn!

Huntress in the Woods

ONLY WHEN HER EYES acquired that weird, dry ache that came with too much crying, her nose felt swollen and stuffy, and the dense pile of the carpet had abraded one knee, did she stop.

She lay there a bit, the glass orb right in front of her nose. The colored inclusion shimmered: purple, crimson, metallic gold. Was it a dragon? A phoenix? A gryphon? Or an abstract that resembled whatever the beholder imagined?

She sat up to delve for a handkerchief. Not in the cuff of either sleeve. Nor tucked in her bosom. Bother! She'd forgotten to provide herself with one. She licked her lips, tasting the salt of her tears and feeling the roughness of the skin. She'd forgotten to drink. The water in her canteen was flat and lukewarm by now, but its moisture refreshed her mouth and her dry throat.

Her face felt sticky. She borrowed the doily from a small table on the far side of the wingback chair, moistened the lacy weave with her stale canteen water, and then wiped her eyes and cheeks. A clean, damp face definitely felt better than a scummy, tear-smeared one.

She looked at the rumpled doily, looked at the bare table, and tucked the doily into her left sleeve. She had a feeling there would be a next time.

Unfortunately.

So, she couldn't get out. At all.

I need to find somewhere that the outside becomes part of the inside. A balcony or a raised terrace or a rooftop garden.

Except that getting out wasn't the answer. Intuition was all she had for guidance here. And intuition said that achieving her victory would be much more complex than finding an unbarred and functioning door to the outside or an open window.

This place was a puzzle on more than one level.

The first was figuring out what sort of puzzle or puzzles she faced.

The second was solving those puzzles.

Intuition pointed to several of the puzzles. She needed to find the second godmother door. She needed to *be* herself – holding onto optimism and good cheer. She needed to care for her physical wellbeing. And she needed to remember everything that she'd forgotten.

She looked out the window that had refused to shatter.

The day was very bright, and the shadows cast by ornamental trees and bushes were shorter than before. Noontide would arrive soon, but the afternoon and the early evening remained to her. She would not waste them.

She would continue her search. Searching had delivered her water and food. Searching had given her returning memories. Searching had brought her to the first godmother door.

She straightened her shoulders and left the study, the fallen paperweight still on the carpet.

As she pushed her legs up yet more stairs and then back down others, the happy mood of the morning crept back into her heart. She peeked into exotic anterooms and skipped defiantly along galleries.

The sleeping evil of the castle shifted and roused, the way it had all the day before, but did not wake. She counted that good enough. So long as the goblins slept, she refused to be afraid.

She entered the southern reaches of the castle, walking along a comfortable, low-ceilinged corridor. Instead of the white stone typical of so many of the castle's passageways, this one featured walnut panelling and a parquet floor, combining in its geometric design the dark brown of walnut with red mahogany and blond beech.

Substantial walnut doors studded the walls at regular intervals. Light from the window at the far end of the hall didn't penetrate far, but the lamp globes – supported on walnut falcon wings – were lit.

Fae could feel the heft of the first door as she opened it. The hinges were solid and well-oiled; it swung easily. Within was a gun room. Locked, glass-fronted cabinets displayed muskets of various vintages, their long shapes gripped by ornate brackets. One piece, chased with so much silver and gold filigree that it looked more like jewelry than a weapon, must have been a prince's gun from centuries past. A table with flat display cases held several pistols.

None of the guns interested Fae much, and she would have left the room almost immediately had there not been something more to her taste.

The fourth wall boasted four absolutely gorgeous recurved bows.

They were stored properly, unstrung, each with two padded wooden pegs supporting the riser (with its grip and arrow rest) in a horizontal position.

Unaware that she was moving, Fae walked toward them, raising her hand to caress the topmost bow. The riser was shaped from tigerwood, with vivid stripes of red-brown and black. It felt satiny smooth under her fingertips. The limbs were fashioned of birdseye maple with a glorious blond ripple.

She lifted the bow down, placing one limb behind her heel and pressing the other with her hand, then slipping the tail of the bowstring on.

Racks along the baseboard held ranks of arrows, point down.

She plucked one up and sighted along it. Straight. Beautifully straight.

She nocked it and moved into the ready position, left arm out straight to her side at shoulder height steadying the bow, right arm pulling the bowstring back, elbow high.

It felt marvelous.

Where can I shoot this bow? I have to shoot this bow.

She would come home to herself, if only she could. Maybe all of her memories would come flooding back.

There had to be a shooting gallery somewhere. No one could possess such magnificent weapons and not possess a place to enjoy them.

The shooting gallery proved to be behind the last door on the left before the hallway reached the window and turned.

It was set up for target shooting with muskets or pistols.

The space extended away from the door: a long, long stretch of paneled walls and parquet floor, ending in the hanging linen squares with black-and-white gun targets painted on them. Behind the targets, metal plates angled from the floor and ceiling, narrowing gradually to a slot where spent bullets would pass through to a collection bin.

A foyer area just inside the door provided room for spectators and loaders. Beyond it, the shooting bays, three of them separated by walnut-paneled baffles, faced onto the long firing lanes.

Fae found an archery target in a storage room off the foyer. It was a nice one: a thick circle of braided straw covered by the traditional archery target of fabric – concentric circles of white, black, blue, and red around a yellow bullseye – and supported on tripod legs.

She used an empty gun cart to wheel her target down the center firing lane, where she set it in front of the hanging gun target.

She trundled the cart back to the foyer and did a few quick exercises to ready her muscles for shooting: shoulderblade squeezes and the like.

The aqua ribbon on her wrist caught her eye. She swallowed three big gulps from her canteen, and then set it aside to sling the quiver of arrows, brought from the gun room, over her shoulder. She took up the exquisite bow, and moved to the center shooting booth, between the two baffles.

Deep breath in. Slow breath out.

The rest position, sideways to her target, bow down.

The ready position, arrow nocked, bow up, and bowstring drawn, elbow lifted high.

She released.

And the arrow flew true, straight toward the inner circle of the yellow bullseye.

Like a stooping hawk.

Like a springing lynx.

Like a striking snake.

Twang. Swoosh. Thunk.

She nocked another arrow and released, then nocked a third and released, placing both right beside the first in a neat, tight cluster.

It felt like coming home, just as she'd hoped.

I'm an archer. A huntress. A child of the forest.

And then memory came piling in on her.

❦

In memory, she bounded down a forested hillside. The dappled light of mid-morning shone through spring-green leaves, spotting the corrugated bark of hickories and maples. She *loved* that dancing sprinkle of bright specks. The slope was more open than many around Milady's lodge – no thickets of azalea under the tree canopy, just a few delicate dogwoods, past their bloom, but fresh with new-sprouted greenery.

Hidden by mats of wintergreen and the lacy fronds of ferns, last winter's leaves crackled under the leap of Fae's moccasinned feet.

A gentle breeze caressed her cheeks and rustled the foliage overhead.

The twittering call of a scarlet tanager darted through the air.

The soft thumps of her controlled leaps sounded like a drum, beating out her joy in running through the outdoors.

She could hear her companions behind her: the crackle of leaves under their feet, the panting of their breaths, a soft murmur when one spoke to the other, a dulcet laugh on occasion. They were close to the lodge yet. No need to adopt a hunter's stealth until they neared the crest of the ridge on the other side of this valley.

Fae ran out in front. Unusual. Calanthe was far faster and always took the lead.

The whippy end of a dogwood branch swiped Fae's cheek.

She jumped to clear a boulder suddenly underfoot amidst a tangle of ferns. The bunch and flex of her leg muscles felt glorious.

She deepened her inhalation, savoring the fresh green scent of the forest in spring and the earthy aroma of loam, moistened by rain and warmed by the seasonal change. Mmm. *This* was where she belonged. Among the trees, out of doors, stretching her limbs.

She glanced down. Green leggings clad her legs, a blue tunic her torso. Her arms were bare.

She could feel her quiver of arrows and her bow – strung and ready – bouncing on her back.

I'm free. I'm here. All is right.

She wasn't sure what alerted her to a change.

The movement of shadow?

The faint hint of musk in the air?

A muted throbbing of sound?

Something was wrong.

She checked her headlong rush – slowing to a walk, slowing her walk to a creeping stalk – and gestured a hunter's hand sign to her friends: *beware!* She heard their speed diminish, their footfalls go quiet. They were good, these girls. Strong archers, fast runners, savvy trackers.

Fae stopped beside the large trunk of a mature hickory, lifted her bow off her shoulder, and nocked an arrow.

Ready to shoot, she surveyed her surroundings.

Left, the hickory bole and a cluster of maples beyond it.

Right, a bare spot on the mountain, an expanse of lichen-spotted granite fringed by ferns, with more hickories in the distance.

Some ways ahead and downslope, a thicket of mountain laurel, its bushes clumped dead center, with more straggling away to one side.

Did something lurk in that thicket?

The rustle of movement drifted to Fae's hearing.

Then a grinning redhead emerged from the looser line of bushes. Her short braids stuck out all over her head, and her yellow tunic gleamed in a stray beam of sunlight. The bronze of her leggings was more subdued.

Calanthe.

Of course.

Fae eased the tension on her bowstring.

Strolling up the slope, Calanthe moved her fingers in the sign for 'first.'

Indeed she was. Fae's lips curved to mirror Calanthe's grin. Of course Calanthe was first. She'd probably turned back when she found herself so far out in front that it was boring.

Fae started to lower her bow. Then the sudden crackle of trampled underbrush and snapping branches sounded from the mountain laurels. Something large, solid, and enraged moved in the thicket.

Fae raised her bow again, and Calanthe whirled.

A brown bear, small eyes glaring red, jaws open, shouldered out of the bushes.

This was no bluff charge. Fae knew the difference. This was real.

The bear's dark pelt flashed gold in a shaft of sunlight.

Calanthe changed from grabbing for her bow – she wouldn't be quick enough – to drawing her hunting knife – which wouldn't be any kind of enough.

Evil at the Heart of the Rose

✣

THE BEAR SHIFTED its weight, preparatory to swinging its heavy, clawed forepaw in the blow that would smash Calanthe's red-braided head.

Fae loosed her arrow.

Twang. Swoosh.

The arrowhead ticked against the bead at the end of one of Calanthe's braids and –

Thunk!

– buried itself in the bear's skull, right between the eyes. Eyes so fiery an instant ago, flattened in death.

The bear's body slumped to the ground with a muffled thud.

Calanthe stood over it, knife poised.

It didn't move.

Calanthe sheathed her knife and glanced up at Fae. "I'm an idiot!" She shook her head.

Fae's heart hammered in the aftermath. She'd almost lost her friend. Right there; so quick; so irrevocable. Now that it was all over, she felt fear. But she refused to admit it aloud. "Perhaps you should pursue a runner's berth in the Theosian Games, rather than a hunter's role in my band," Fae teased.

Philyra's husky voice – casual in its tones – came over Fae's shoulder. "You know, you really should compete in the Games. You'd win the laurel wreath for sure."

Philyra. Calanthe.

Fae's attention returned abruptly to the shooting gallery in which she stood, her gaze still fixed on the tight cluster of three arrows in her target.

More names teased her. Thalia, Zoe, Oranthe, and Lydia. The rest of her merry little troop.

Her thoughts slid and spun, then focused.

On her very first morning in this castle, she'd wondered who she was and what her station in life might be. She'd rejected princess, chamber maid, and knight's daughter. But *now* she knew.

I'm a goddess!

Not royalty. Not servant. Not nobility. Just as she'd speculated before.

She was divine. The goddess of the hunt. Diana and her nymphs.

Diana?

No, that didn't sound right at all.

I'm not Diana.

In fact, no one she knew was Diana. Diana was a creature of myth, invented by the ancients to embody the human experience of swiftness, fierceness, the freedom and the glory of the chase.

And how could she be a goddess? A goddess wouldn't be trapped in a frozen castle, would she? Or lose all memory of who she was?

I'm not a goddess.

But something about it felt right.

Fae shook her head and went to collect her arrows from the target. She dropped them in her quiver and surveyed the shooting gallery:

walnut paneled walls, parquet floor, her canteen resting on a bench in the foyer area.

She retrieved her canteen.

What about the bow she'd slung over her shoulder and the quiver of arrows still present on her back? What would she do with them?

The castle hadn't served up enraged bears or pouncing cougars so far. Did she need weapons?

Maybe not, but she wasn't parting with them. They made her feel more like herself. They kept a little space between herself and the malice underlying the castle's surface.

After a bit more poking around – hunting – she found her way back to her cooking bay.

She couldn't see the sun in the limited patch of deep blue sky visible above the tall, narrow court outside the window. She'd just missed it, just missed the moment at high noon when the sun would shine from straight overhead. But not by much.

She checked the soaking oats. They were getting nice and mushy, the liquid thick and cloudy. There'd be more nutrition in this batch than the earlier ones that hadn't soaked as long.

She should have lunch, but she didn't want it. She could feel the longing in her body for nourishment. Not hunger; not an ache in her stomach. The castle didn't allow that. Just like it didn't allow thirst.

Thirst.

She'd been getting complacent about water and not drinking it.

I'll have water for lunch, she decided. As delicious as the oatmeal had tasted for dinner last night and for breakfast this morning, she didn't think she could eat it three times every day. *I'll cook a huge amount for dinner*, she promised herself. But she wouldn't skimp on water.

She drained four of the eight water goblets and topped off her canteen.

There. Now it was time to go hunting again. She wouldn't stop until she found it: the door with the archer depicted on it.

Except . . .

Sweet Marionya! She paused in shock.

The door with the archer on it. That archer had been herself in the role of Diana in the play *The Race of Atalanta*. She'd worn a wig, since her hair was dusky, not golden. And Calanthe with her spiky red braids – playing Apollo's daughter – had been rendered on a *third* door. While Thalia, silver gowned with clouds of silvery blond hair – Selene of the moon in the play – graced the first door.

Was *that* why Fae thought for a moment that she was a goddess? Because of a play? It was ridiculous!

In that instant her optimism and determination fled.

She felt stupid and very foolish.

As shame washed over her, the drowsing evil of the castle roused and roiled.

She bit her lip.

I can't afford to think ill of myself. This place seizes on my slightest weakness.

She swallowed hard.

I liked how Eulalie in my dream got stronger as she continued exploring this dreadful castle. I'm going to grow stronger too. And my way of being strong is to be happy. She smiled, with effort, and turned two pirouettes.

The stirring goblins lay still again.

Besides, she really didn't remember enough to draw any firm conclusions about anything. All she had were fragments of her past.

But she was recalling more and more. Eventually she would have enough pieces to put it all together.

I will figure it out.

She settled her canteen strap on her shoulder, checked her bow and quiver, and set out: seeking that second door. In memory, it had featured herself as an archer on it, but she suspected it would be plain here in the castle. Just like the first one.

The details of the castle were beginning to blur in her mind. Her feet ached from padding across the rigid floors. There were so many rooms and spaces, ornamented in every possible fashion and color palette.

But, despite the confused details, she was beginning to understand how the passages connected and how the different wings and courtyards were arranged. She could navigate her way reliably from the eastern portions to the central heart and then to the western suites. She could reach the top of the tallest tower – just a dusty garret, otherwise empty.

She found another door into the demonic staterooms. And did *not* pass through it.

I won't be getting lost much anymore. Or, at least not for long. She might not know every corridor. In fact, she wouldn't, couldn't – not in three days of exploring. But she'd always know in what part of the castle she walked.

She found a jewel chamber very near to the study where she'd so fruitlessly thrown the paperweight.

It was like a tiny circular chapel, carved of rose marble. Dainty stone ribs curved up from the marble floor as delicate pillars and stretched to a low peak in the arched ceiling. Glass lamp globes, supported on butterfly wings, illuminated the space. Glass-fronted cabinets with polished brass mullions between the panes, and slanted white velvet shelves within, filled the walls between the stone support ribs.

It was so charming a space, it should have felt nice, lovely even. But the castle's dozing evil intruded here as it did everywhere. Fae was glad for the protective feel of her bow.

Fae wasn't very interested in the jewelry: tiaras, earrings, bracelets, necklaces, rings, brooches. Every kind of stone: emeralds, sapphires, amethysts, tiger's eye. She just didn't care.

But there was one case filled with watches.

Hefty gold pocket watches on long chains. Dainty silver watches on pendant necklaces. A tiny porcelain watch on a charm bracelet. And several more practical watches on short fobs.

She tested the cabinet doors, pulling on the handles. They featured keyholes, but weren't locked.

She swung them open.

The hinges clicked when they reached the full range of their swing. A puff of faintly perfumed air drifted out from the cabinet's interior – rose.

A plain gold watch with a white dial and the hours marked in black enamel drew her attention. The metal was smooth to her touch. The watch hung on a short fob of white leather with a gold brooch at the top, formed into a Celtic knot. She could pin it to the waist of her dress.

If it worked.

There was the question.

Would it be like the always-full birdbath in the conservatory? Never changing? Frozen in time?

The hands paused at one minute to twelve. Just like the clocks she'd seen. Would they refuse to move when she wound the timepiece?

Or would they be like the doors in the castle? The doors swung open when she pushed them. And closed when she pulled them shut behind her.

Would this watch adhere to whatever made the castle so dead?

Or would it change when she moved it?

A small watch key dangled on a silk cord behind the leather fob. It was tied to a tiny loop on the back of the brooch. Handy! You wouldn't lose it.

Fae opened the back of the watch. What an amazing arrangement of diminutive gears! They were beautiful! Representing such skill and cleverness on the part of the maker. A thousand times more intriguing than mere gems.

She placed the key over the winding-arbor – a tiny stem that fit inside the hollow on the end of the key – and started winding. Around, and around, and around.

There. That was enough.

She removed the key.

Tick. Tick. Tick.

She gave a small skip in place.

Tick. Tick. Tick.

Clear and crisp with a metallic tone. And the gears were moving.

She turned the watch over, the back still open, and watched as the minute hand s-l-o-w-l-y edged beneath the hour hand, pointed at the twelve.

Ding, ding, ding, ding, ding, ding, ding, ding, ding, ding, ding, ding.

This watch had a chime, musical, but quiet and clean.

Her eyes filled with tears. She impatiently brushed them away with the back of her hand. *I'm getting things back.* Bit by bit. Time. Memory. *Myself. I'll get it* all *back. Every bit.*

The watch had just chimed twelve o'clock, but that wasn't right. What time should she set it to?

She put the watch key on the setting-arbor and moved the watch hands to show ten minutes before two. It felt right, and she could always adjust it, if it wasn't.

She closed the watch back and pinned the brooch to the waist of her gown. The white fob and gold watch case looked nice against the white cotton.

She looked up to close the cabinet doors, and suddenly she was reliving a memory again.

In memory, Fae dozed in the hammock in a rose garden. The still, warm air encouraged the languorous ease of her body even while it brought a faint dew of sweat to her skin. The canvas of the hammock cradled her. The overwhelming aroma of roses – rich, spicy, and sweet – suffused the arbor where the hammock hung.

The arbor possessed three bays. The one in which Fae lay – the middle one – was sheltered front and back by close woven trellises supporting a heavy load of climbing roses. She could hear the drone of the bees, so loud it seemed they buzzed inside her ears rather than within the crimson and apricot petals nodding about her.

The arbor bays to each side of her opened onto the garden with shallow steps leading down to the gravel walks that surrounded three parterres filled with rose bushes. The trellis hid most of the garden from her sight, but she was familiar with its arrangement.

Before she walked to the rose garden, Fae had been swinging on the swing in the wilderness garden. So-called "wilderness." It was a highly cultivated expanse of meadows and beech copses traversed by a stream and designed to look like the work of nature.

One of the trees growing above a bluff, leaning out over the steep slope, had a swing tied to its strongest branch. A lovely swing with a comfortable wooden seat and great long ropes. When she pulled it back to the top of the bluff where she stood, sat on the seat, and let herself swing out away from the hill, it was glorious!

The ground fell below swiftly as the swing swept her down and away forever, then up and up for another aeon, and then back and back and back toward the bluff.

She'd been swinging on it all the afternoon. And been more than ready to nap when she sought the hammock in the rose garden.

The crunch of someone's steps on the gravel woke her.

She lay there sleepily wondering if a servant were bringing her a glass of lemonade with mint leaves floating in it. She could do with something to quench her thirst. Cool mint and tangy citrus would be . . . *mmm*.

The murmur of voices sounded from the garden: the deep tones of a man and the softer ones of a woman. A woman desiring to please.

Fae sighed. Not a servant with lemonade then. More likely a courting couple.

They came closer, no doubt aiming for the graceful teak bench located beyond the endmost parterre right below the trellis and Fae.

"Can you make someone fall into *kairos*?" asked the woman.

The man chuckled. "If you're clever about it."

"Really?" The woman was intrigued.

And Fae knew – with those clearer words – that the pair was *not* a courting couple. This was Milady and Fae's Uncle Aion. The two were friends, not lovers.

"How do you manage it?" pursued Milady. "Surely one must be relaxed in order to leave the ordinary flow of time; to leave *chronos*."

Fae heard the rustle of Milady's gown as she sank onto the bench. Then came a creak, as though Uncle Aion stood to one side and lifted a booted foot to rest it on the farther arm of the bench.

"Not at all," he said. "Relaxation isn't a pre-requisite for the experience of *kairos*."

"Tell me more," said Milady, almost purring.

Uncle Aion shifted, making the bench creak again. "You're thinking of the most common experience of *kairos*, meditation. Thinking falls away, tension falls away, and the moment of now fills the awareness. That's a very relaxed sensation."

"But not necessary, you say."

"Relaxation is not the heart of meditation, Dione. You know this."

Ah, yes. *That* was Milady's name. *Dione*. Fae never called her so. Had never been invited to make free of Milady's given name. But she knew it. She'd merely forgotten it, along with so much else.

"What would you say the heart of meditation is, then, Aion?"

"Focus," he answered.

"And how does that lend itself to forcing *kairos* upon someone?"

"It means you need not approach the task as a battle of wills." Uncle Aion snorted, very, very softly. "Invite your prospect to dinner and serve him an excellent meal accompanied by interesting conversation. Or partner her at a ball, if you dance well and she loves dancing. Offer any activity that's pleasurable and engrossing. It's the easiest thing in the world. Only boredom holds a person in *chronos*, weighing the dull minutes as they pass on the clockface. Pleasurable experiences partake of eternity. They are timeless."

"Yes. Yes, I see." Milady's voice was thoughtful.

"Is your prospect unwilling?" questioned Uncle Aion. "I thought she was disposed to trust you. To follow your guidance."

"She is, of course. But I need to be sure I prevail, if she should have second thoughts at the last minute. I need her – *we* need her – thoroughly severed from *chronos*."

"Removing someone from *chronos* is another matter."

"Oh?" Milady's voice sharpened. "But that's the entire point. She must be exiled from *chronos*. I thought you said that pushing someone into *kairos* was easy."

The bench creaked as Uncle Aion removed his foot from it. Standing straighter, perhaps? Fae couldn't see him or Milady, only hear them. What she was hearing chilled her.

Milady and Uncle Aion plotting against someone. Plotting to push her into *kairos* – not so bad; the flow Fae experienced while running or hunting was exhilarating. But plotting to exile someone from *chronos*? What did that mean? It didn't sound like they intended anything good.

Caught in Kairos

UNCLE AION'S FOOTSTEPS crunched on the garden's gravel. He must be pacing in front of Milady.

"The mind and spirit transition back and forth between *kairos* and *chronos* all the time, Dione. From rushing so as not to be late – *chronos* – to enjoying the symphony – *kairos*. From waiting for your friend's arrival – *chronos* – to engaging her in conversation – *kairos*. But, the body?"

Milady echoed him breathlessly. "The body?"

Uncle Aion's pacing footsteps stopped. "The body dwells always in *chronos*. Affected by the mind in *kairos*, yes, but not present there with it."

Fae stared fixedly at the velvety amber of the rose bloom tapping her cheek. She wished she were a bee and could crawl inside it, sleep within its silken warmth, sip its sweet nectar. She wanted to be anywhere but here, listening to cold cruelty spoken by her godmother and her uncle. How could they? She'd thought them kind, caring. But this dialog of theirs . . . Fae repressed a shudder.

"What can we do?" demanded Milady. "Can *you* do anything?"

"Oh, I think I might." A hint of laughter colored his voice. "Time is my realm, eternity, my pleasure. I think I might do anything. Or even something, Dione."

Fae's memory came to an abrupt end.

She shut the watch cabinet doors and staggered back to the corridor outside the jewel chamber.

Dear. Gods.

I'm in kairos. *This castle is* kairos. *Somehow my body has been expelled from* chronos *to dwell here with the rest of me.*

And Milady did it. With Aion's help.

But why?

Fae didn't know her Uncle Aion well. He'd always been a distant figure who visited rarely.

But . . . Milady! Fae couldn't remember most of her own history, including her history with her godmother. But she remembered her feelings for this caretaker well enough: trust, reliance, a little bit of fear, a longing for more affection from her, and admiration.

Milady wasn't the squishy godmother type. She didn't bake cookies or sing lullabies. But she'd cared about Fae. Wanted the best for Fae. Done her best to replace the mother that Fae had never known.

No, Fae couldn't remember her life or the events in that life. But she *knew* Milady.

How had her godmother's stern good nature and rigid integrity changed into active malevolence?

Fae saw nothing of the castle as she walked. And walked. And walked. Barely noticed the unpleasant rancor that underlay it. Realized where she was going only when she arrived at her bedchamber door.

Numbly, she went in and sat heavily on the side of her bed.

The rollicking suns in the cornice frieze did not cheer her. Nor did the beaming one illuminating the cloud castle on the ceiling.

She'd been betrayed by someone she trusted.

It felt awful.

She snatched a pillow from the head of the bed and clutched it, muffling her mouth in its softness. Was she going to cry?

No, she decided. She wasn't. She'd hold out for more information. Not that she'd believe Milady innocent without some pretty convincing evidence. But there was still more that Fae *didn't* know than there was of things she *did* know. And knowledge was the key out of her prison, she felt more and more sure.

I'll go find out. I'll hunt *down my answers.*

She paused before the mirror of her dressing table.

Did she *look* like a girl who deserved to be betrayed?

Thick dark hair pulled back in a simple braid. Gray eyes, slightly reddened, even though she had *not* cried. Pointed chin, a little wobbly. No circles under her eyes, though. That was good. And her lips weren't dry. Also good.

I don't deserve this.

No, she didn't look like a girl who deserved betrayal. But she did look like a girl who wasn't getting enough to eat. Did she? Really? Chin a little pointier, cheeks a little thinner, eyes and temples a little stretched?

Maybe. Or maybe not. She felt hollow *inside*, and scared. Which made her face look scared too.

I'll figure something out. She'd figured out a lot already. *I'm not giving up.* It wasn't her nature.

But she wasn't eating oatmeal for a late lunch. She wasn't going back on that decision. Not today.

She finished off the remaining four goblets of water.

Then she visited the water closet before she set off. That took her water supplies down to two and a half cannisters. She'd need to haul water tomorrow. But this afternoon, she was going to find that door in the gymnasium, come Hades or high water.

Hades? Did she have an uncle by that name? Or was she merely confusing a play with reality, like she had before?

Fae shrugged and strode off on her search.

She found a fencing salon, equipped with blades and fencing garb. She found a billiards room with comfortable leather armchairs, as well as the billiard table, cues, and billiard balls needed for the game. She found an orangery, empty of orange trees, lemon trees, or lime trees, although the gardener's nook was full enough of watering cans and such.

There were more salons and withdrawing rooms and surprise passages than she would have guessed, even on her first day when she'd described the castle as huge. But she didn't find either a gymnasium or the second arched, splintery door forbidden her by Milady.

She did find something even more interesting: a gallery of paintings.

It was so large it might have been a gymnasium, but it wasn't.

A vast floor of marble inlay – featuring large medallions of black and white and gold points – swept away from the double entrance doors. Tall, three-sashed windows, more than a dozen of them, marched along one wall. Between the windows, fluted pilasters and delicate plasterwork arabesques ornamented the wall surface. Gilded coffers formed the high ceiling.

Paintings and more paintings hung on the inner walls as well as on freestanding panels.

Most of them were portraits.

Fae walked over to a large canvas framed in heavy gold.

It depicted a frowning man with curling black hair – rather like Fae's – that bushed out in a mane, too riotous to fall below his chin. Gray eyes, also like Fae's. Neat, but curly, black beard.

He wore a Roman toga of a purple so dark it was nearly black, and sat upon a throne carved of black onyx. He held a tall, black scepter, in his hand, its base touching the floor, its tip shaped like a skeletal hawk.

Fae stepped closer.

Beneath the portrait, a plaque held writing.

"Hades, Ideal of the Unseen, the Quietus, and Dark Genesis."

Fae stepped back and looked up at Hades' portrait.

Well, his throne room was shadowy enough. But her question was: uncle? or mythology? No memory returned to answer it.

She moved on to the next painting.

It was one of the few landscapes, depicting a paved mountainside terrace, circular and surrounded by white stone columns connected by white stone lintels. Vines clambered up the columns and massed on the lintels. Sun shone on the whole scene, although a haze softened the mountains in the distance.

Had Fae been there? It felt familiar, but – as with Hades' portrait – no returning memory provided more information.

It was frustrating. Why would a cabinet of watches or the aroma of the stables trigger so much, while these more detailed artifacts evoked nothing?

The next painting – another portrait – seemed more promising. Fae recognized the lady. She wore her dark hair up, a complex mass of braids arranged becomingly and adorned by a thin gold tiara. Her brown eyes were lowered to gaze lovingly on the infant cradled in her arms. She smiled, and the baby smiled back at her. Her gown, in the draping Grecian style, was spring green and pinned at the shoulders with gold brooches. The baby's blanket was white.

This was Fae's Aunt Pallas with her youngest daughter, little Charis.

And now memory arrived.

Not as a vivid scene, the way the earlier ones did, but as facts and feelings settling in place. A *lot* of them.

This *was* Fae's family.

She did have an Uncle Hades. And an Uncle Nathanos. Many more uncles. And aunts. And a horde of cousins. There was a reason this gallery was so big! Was it big *enough*?

She started counting on her fingers: Hadrien – Leander – Nathanos – Xenon – Hades. Pallas – Kira – Sariah – Galilaia. And so on.

She gave up after a while, but she knew the answer to her question about the room size. No, it was *not* big enough. She'd gotten to a hundred and twenty-one before she stopped counting. She had a lot of relatives. And they weren't ordinary either.

That question – uncle? or mythology? – had a complicated answer. Or maybe it was a simple one, but it didn't feel simple to her.

The plaque under Aunt Pallas' portrait was similar to the one beneath Uncle Hades' portrait.

"Pallas, Ideal of the Great Mother and Giver of Nourishment.

Charis, Ideal of Grace and Loving Kindness."

Fae's family were descendants of the original Olympians. Were they gods? Were the original Olympians *really* gods?

Fae could remember questioning Milady on these points when she was very young and first learning about her inheritance. Milady confessed that no one truly knew, but that certainly members of their clan – the Theosian clan – could achieve results achieved by no ordinary mortal. And they lived longer. *Much* longer.

So the simple answer to "Uncle? Or just mythology?" was *both*.

The complex answer . . . Hades was special; different; even scary. As were all Fae's uncles, aunts, and cousins.

But – and this was important – Fae herself was not.

Milady had found her – a baby in a basket – at a rural crossroads, wailing. And taken her to Hadrien, insisting that Milady be allowed to keep the orphan.

Evidently Uncle Hadrien had hemmed and hawed a bit, making noises about locating possible relatives. But Milady prevailed, and Fae grew up under her "godmother's" supervision.

She'd often felt overshadowed by her magnificent cousins. She'd played with them. Quarreled with them. And envied them, the way children do.

Theophane memorized facts the first time she heard them. And could master gymnastic moves after but a few attempts. Eulalie seemed to know how to sculpt clay without being taught. Every horse in the stables obeyed and loved Helios as though he were the stallion of the herd.

Fae's cousins *were* special. Talented. Gifted with abilities that would only grow as they matured.

Fae herself? Not so much.

So she'd both envied them and looked up to them. And eventually found her place among them. They weren't bullies and good-naturedly accepted her as a playmate and a member of their clan.

Now . . . now she thought back to her conversation with Uncle Leander in his smithy and her perception that her aunts and uncles were limited.

Uncle Hadrien was the ideal of fatherhood, kingship, and force. She'd bet his plaque in this gallery – when she found it – would say just that. What if he wanted to follow someone else's lead for a change? Or bow to someone else's emotional power?

Fae had never seen him do so. *Could* he? If he wanted to?

Aunt Pallas embodied motherhood and nurturing. Her plaque *did* say so. Could she be selfish? Just once? Or must she always sacrifice her interests to those of her children? Did she even have her own interests? If she did, Fae had never seen them.

Her relatives – relations by adoption – were as trapped in their identities as Fae was trapped in this castle in *kairos*.

The Ideal of Fate

⁂

FAE MEANDERED PAST more portraits, checking to see whose likeness hung in the gallery, and if any did not.

There was Uncle Leander – with his neatly clipped brown hair and beard, his hazel eyes – depicted before a forge much more impressive than his smithy – hammering out a lightning bolt. Did he really forge lightning? Fae had a feeling he might.

Had Uncle Leander ever felt a yen to do something other than smithing?

There was Aunt Sariah. And, there, Fae's cousin Theophane.

Even portraits of her friends Philyra, Calanthe, Thalia, Zoe, Oranthe, and Lydia were present. Right. Friends *and* second cousins, or some such.

Milady's portrait depicted her wearing a white gown in the draped Grecian style, with silver shoulder brooches shaped as serpents. She sat on a tall stool, with ornately carved legs, in a limestone grotto. Coiling mists rose from a deep crack in the floor, and Milady's eyes were closed. Her face held the same sternness that Fae knew so well, although with a hint of ecstasy softening her features.

Milady's plaque read: "Dione, Ideal of Oracular Prophecy."

Fae felt a sense of shock – the positive recognition of old knowledge, and the unpleasant sensation of danger – reading the inscription. The oracle of the Theosians wielded power. Perilous power? Fae wasn't certain, but her godmother possessed the gift of prophecy.

There was no portrait of her cousin Apollo that she could find. And there were two portraits of people she did not recognize.

Tethys, a mature woman with long green hair and swathed in translucent blue veils, but little else, bore the identifier of: "Ideal of Fluid Power and Primordial Mystery." She looked powerful. And passionate.

Eris, a young woman with short silver hair, and wearing nothing at all save her creamy skin, danced within a starry void, the colored dust of nebulae placed to form a natural halo at her head. Her plaque said: "Eris, Ideal of Chaos, Strife, and Discord." She looked dangerous, wild, almost fey.

The gallery lay along the western side of the castle. The light from the windows was slanting at an ever increasing angle as the sun slid lower in the sky.

Fae's watch chimed.

Ding, ding, ding, ding, ding.

Five o'clock. She'd better go cook dinner.

Reluctantly, she moved toward the double doors. About to pass through, she noticed a painting on their immediate left, a landscape showing a many-towered castle with pointed red roofs and flapping blue-and-gold pennants. Pleasure gardens, lawns, and an orchard surrounded it. A carriage drawn by four horses approached along the splendid esplanade before the castle's entrance. The top of the carriage was folded down, revealing the bright blond tresses of the three women in it.

This was the home of Clan Theosis, but Fae hadn't lived there.

Visited, sure; brought there often by Milady. But she'd lived in Milady's lodge, some miles away.

Fae studied the painting. Castle Farnesse. That was its name. It looked as though it *could* be the castle in which she stood at this moment.

She looked around the gallery. Shaded her eyes and gazed out the window. The vegetable gardens lay there, richly colorful in the setting sun. Were this castle and Castle Farnesse one and the same? No knowing. At least, not right now.

Maybe this castle was a version of Castle Farnesse – which was why it felt familiar at times, and yet she didn't know it, didn't know her way around it.

Fae stepped through the doorway and hurried through the maze of corridors that eventually deposited her at her bedchamber. She felt tired. Once again she'd been on her feet from morning to evening.

She unstrung her bow and hung it and her quiver from one of the lamp brackets. The glass globe was lit, even though the bright sky and the golden light of early evening meant dark was some ways off.

She went to her cooking bay. All eight glasses of water were empty. And she'd drained her canteen more than twice during the day.

Good! She'd drunk enough.

She checked the stove-hose-fuel cylinder array for leaks and then lit the burner. She spooned *all* of the oatmeal into the pot, added salt, covered it, and started it heating. If she were going to skip lunch – as she had today – dinner needed to be substantial.

She touched her chin and cheeks.

Was she *really* growing thinner? She didn't feel thinner. But she had looked . . . peaked, in the mirror. That was worrying, but she refused to worry.

I'm the happy one. The cheerful one. That was part of why her cousins liked her so well. And she felt happy now. Or, at least, so relieved that it could pass for happiness. It was incredible to know at last who she was, what her life had been, where she belonged.

Many details remained missing – that felt true. In fact, she still did not know her own name. Her chosen name – Fae – felt more and more right, but it wasn't what her cousins had called her. At least, she didn't *think* so. However, the horrible, empty nothingness of her past, spotted by a few vivid memories and one nightmare – all she'd been able to recollect before – was gone.

I know who I am. I like knowing who I am.

The oatmeal was ready quickly, as was usual with well-soaked grains.

Fae left it to cool a nice long time. It smelled delicious, making her feel good about her skipped lunch. She really couldn't face oatmeal three times every day, but twice was working. Her meal appealed, and she would eat it all as soon as she could do so without burning her tongue.

She thought some more about her cousins, while she waited, perched in the hall before her dining "table."

Theophane had become more and more serious as she grew older, less playful. She seemed to think she was right about everything, and corrected everyone. Even her father, Fae's Uncle Hadrien. Was it because of her pre-destined role as the "ideal of strategy, heroic endeavor, and practical knowledge"?

Eulalie had lost her youthful certainty as she left childhood behind, along with her enjoyment of outdoor pursuits. She became a bookworm who sculpted and wrote poetry and obeyed her mother. With protests, to be sure, but yielding obedience despite that. Was the change because she was the "ideal of innocence and daughterhood"?

Fae grimaced, not liking where her thoughts were taking her, and tested the oatmeal.

It was cool enough now, and it tasted scrumptious. She loved what salt did for it.

By the time she was finished eating and washing up, her watch said it was quarter past seven. She studied the darkening sky through her bedroom windows. Soft, dusky gray banded the horizon, shading to pearl white and then a clear turquoise. The first star pricked out in the deep cobalt overhead.

Had she set her watch correctly? If this were late summer?

It would be later, she thought.

She nibbled her lip, and reset her timepiece for a quarter after eight. It chimed as the minute hand passed the twelve.

Ding, ding, ding, ding, ding, ding, ding, ding.

She wound the spring. There. She'd compare watch time to sun time again in the morning.

For now . . . she'd better get ready for bed. She didn't know exactly when the lamps went dark. And she needed to know. Needed to be in her bed before the happy suns on the cornice frieze turned into spiteful imps. Before the cloud castle became a fortress of smoke, the abode of the demon who loved hatred.

She shuddered.

Her white gown remained fresh, just as had the aqua one yesterday. She wished *she* stayed fresh, and then changed her mind when she considered what that might mean. *I'm alive. And living creatures do not stay fresh.* Not without bathing.

Fae wondered if she could rig a bath somehow.

She bet she could. If she dragged some of the supplies in the gardener's nook up to the conservatory and the birdbath.

Tomorrow, she started to promise herself. *No, not tomorrow.* She was down to one and a half full cannisters for drinking, cooking, and washing. Tomorrow she'd be hauling water and searching for more food. And more information. She wanted to fill those remaining gaps in her memory.

She pulled a nightgown on over her head, a dusty blue one, and tied the neck strings.

Walking toward the water closet to clean her teeth, Fae realized that she'd forgotten to start another batch of oatmeal soaking. Her Aunt Pallas had taught her to cook, thank goodness. And over Milady's strong objection. But Fae had never kept house or cooked regularly.

She sighed – there was a lot to keep track of – and glanced out the bay window.

Shadows filled the court, and the blue of the sky shone deep and luminous above. Three stars pricked out. She had a little more time. Didn't she?

At least she seemed to be good at the washing up part of housekeeping. The big mixing bowl was clean and ready for more oats, water, and a dollop of vinegar. She covered it with the dish cloth and then entered the water closet for teeth cleaning and using the commode. Which took her water supplies down to a little less than one cannister.

Definitely, she'd be hauling water first thing after breakfast.

She scurried back to her bedchamber, eying the lamps anxiously. They showed no signs of extinguishing, but would they give any sign of it ahead of time? They hadn't before.

She climbed into her bed and pulled the covers up to her chin. Made it!

And then noticed that she'd not taken her braid out to brush her hair.

She resisted climbing back out of bed for a while. Her eyes grew heavy with sleep, and her mattress felt so good. She was tired. But the center braid was an uncomfortable lump behind her neck whenever she lay on her back.

She really should follow her usual routine. She'd brushed her hair every night when she readied herself for sleep in Milady's lodge. She would brush it here, too. Being herself was part of winning her freedom here.

Sitting at the dressing table and giving the hundred strokes of the brush that Milady claimed were healthful, she felt almost like she were at home. Her bedchamber in the lodge was nothing like this one, but the routine was soothing.

She rebraided her hair in two pigtails, tying each with a blue ribbon that matched her nightgown. As she straightened the hand mirror, the comb, and the hairbrush on the dressing table, the lamps went out.

And it was worse, far worse, than she'd remembered.

Away from the protection of her bed and the gryphons on its headboard, the scorn of the goblins pierced her like rose thorns, while the hatred of the demon bludgeoned her literally to the floor. She bruised her knees, falling off the dressing table stool, and crouched there, unable to move.

Her body was unharmed, aside from the knees. She could see it was so. But the illusion of harm increased. Had she blood gushing from her mouth and a spear sprouting from her chest, she could feel no more wounded. The pain pinned her.

✑

Oh, why hadn't she hurried more?

Why had she fallen for the comfort that came from her routine?

I must get to my bed.

Yes, but how was she to accomplish it when she couldn't stir an inch?

A tickle of fire singed her left forearm, then raced in a blaze to her shoulder, the sensation excruciating, even though she saw no hint of actual flame.

She screamed, a full-throated shriek of agony.

For just an instant after her scream, the pain abated, and Fae flung herself to her feet, racing for the bed.

As she reached it, the torment returned; but when she fell, she fell on her mattress. The pain switched off, like her camp stove burner when she closed the fuel regulator.

She burrowed under the sheet, the blanket, and the quilt, and burst into wracking sobs.

Never again, never again, never again would she risk the darkness unprotected. Twice was two times too many. Oh, gods!

She didn't notice when she stopped crying or when she crossed into slumber, but her next awareness came as she dreamed.

In her dream, Milady sat on a tall stool in her oracular grotto, but she was the demoness of nightmare, not the ideal of the daytime gallery of paintings.

Fae struggled to awaken, to escape the advancing dream.

Sleep held her fast.

Milady's black, demon horns sprouted from her brow and encircled her head like an abbreviated tiara, the tips pricking upward just past her ears. The red centers to her eyes rolled up, half hidden by her eyelids. Her face strained, wrought by unpleasant awareness.

She wore the traditional draping gown in the Greek style, but its folds were satin black, not white.

The mist seeping from the crack in the grotto floor possessed a green noxious hue rather than its normal pale white. Nor did it smell slightly of egg, wholesome in a way. Did it bleed from a crypt for the dead, to generate that penetrating scent of rot?

Fae fought again to wake up – fruitlessly.

Milady opened her lips to speak, and her split tongue undulated within her mouth like wrestling snakes.

Fae shuddered.

Milady's hands, previously clasped in her lap, rose into the air, her arms writhing like the tongues within the palisade of her teeth.

Her voice, abnormally deep, emerged in fluid syllables that meant nothing.

"Owl lay, lee owl, wohl nee awl, gaul. Nee ay, lee ohle no, gee zay, lee gohl nohne."

Milady swayed, and the rhythm of her guttural speech quickened, then passed into intelligible words.

"She who lay in the crossroads,
　She who bore the spindle, the rod,
　　and the knife in her swaddling bands,
　She who received our mercy,
　She is fate's ideal.
　Beware her!
　She brings death.
　Beware her spindle!
　Thus far does the thread stretch and no further.
　Beware her rod!
　Thus far does the rod measure and no further.

Beware her knife!

Her cut is the moment of ending.

No dynasty lives forever.

She shall be the Theosian bane."

Milady yelled – a deep bellow of alarm – and fell from her stool.

The grotto disappeared into darkness, and Fae felt the muscular, sinuous movements of large snakes massaging her limbs and back. She would have screamed, but her nightmare did not allow it. She endured it, horrified, terrified.

FOURTH

Thumbing Her Nose

A SMOOTH PRESSURE encircled her legs, then wound around Fae's waist and upward.

The largest serpent was climbing her.

Her ribs crushed in, stifling her breath.

Then the snakes passed away from her, and she felt herself floating in water. Pure water. Cool water. Healing water. She tasted its sweetness on her lips, like honeyed violet petals.

I'm safe.

When she woke, it was morning. Sunlight streamed across the blue silk of her quilt, flaming on the crimson knots and gleaming on the silver swans and golden stars.

She snuggled her cheek against her pillow, savoring its freshly laundered smell and the caress of its soft white cotton.

I'm safe.

And she was. The rest of her room showed its daytime face: merry suns in the cornice frieze and guardian sun on the ceiling, the rancor of the unseen goblins and the enmity of the invisible demon blunted by the light.

She scrambled out of bed and raced for the water closet down the hall.

After she washed her hands, she decided to cook breakfast before she dressed. She'd be hungry, ravenously hungry, if this place allowed it. There was a wobbliness in her limbs, a hollowness to her torso. Not hunger, but discomfort.

I need food.

She rolled her nightgown's blue sleeves up. The ruffles and ribbons at the wrists might catch fire from the stove burner otherwise.

She went over the cooking checklist in her mind. *Check for leaks. Start the fuel gas flowing. Ignite the burner.*

The cooking oatmeal smelled absolutely divine. *Mmm!*

Once it was ready, it tasted as good as it smelled.

She ate it all. *Mmm, indeed!*

Then she washed up the breakfast things, filled the eight water goblets, and her canteen.

She started her dinner oats soaking.

That took the last of the water. She was all out.

I'd planned on hauling water this morning, she reminded herself. But it still felt risky to be without it.

She chose a dove gray gown from the everyday wardrobe. It was of a plainer cut than the others she'd worn – with a simple scoop neckline and a flaring skirt. Lacing criss-crossed the back, from the tips of her shoulder blades to her waist. Tone-on-tone embroidery – gray on gray – formed a vine-like pattern from neckline to hem. Fae slipped it on over her head, snugged the lacing, and tied it. She checked herself in the dressing table mirror.

I look older. Was it the gown? Was it the pallor in her face – not enough to eat? Or was she growing older in *kairos,* even as it felt like no chronological time were passing at all? What if the three days she'd lived in *kairos* were really three years in *chronos*?

I can't do anything about that.

I can go get water. Which I need to do.

She brushed her hair out, rebraided it in a single plait, and fastened it in a coronet around her head. She wound her watch. Twenty-three minutes past eight o'clock. That felt about right. The sun streaming in through the windows was strong, the way it got in full morning, well past dawn. She wouldn't change the watch setting.

She tied the aqua hair ribbon around her wrist.

Water, she reminded herself.

She took all six empty cannisters upstairs at once, one at each elbow crook, two gripped in each hand. The handles bit into her flesh uncomfortably, but she was going to have to make many trips to get the full cannisters back down to her cooking bay. A little discomfort to make only one trip up was worth it.

After using the shoulder yoke to carry four just-over-half-full cannisters to the head of the staircase, she had an idea. Why not top up two of the cannisters *after* she got them to the cooking bay instead of leaving them just-over-half full? She wouldn't need to lift them once they were there.

More water is good, she decided.

At the bottom of the stairs, using the cart from the stables was so much easier than straining under the shoulder yoke. *I wonder if I could find another cart to station in the conservatory?*

She'd keep her eyes open, but wouldn't go looking right now with the current job unfinished.

Milady would never believe how responsible she was being. *I was more happy-go-lucky before all this happened.* She sighed.

She made sure the two cannisters she intended to fill to the brim were placed where they wouldn't get in her way. Then she poured the contents of the other two cannisters into them.

Her guess that each was a-little-over-half-full hadn't accounted for their wide necks. This was good, because it meant the now-empty pair of cannisters were all-the-way empty. She wouldn't be carrying any water back *up* the stairs.

She moved briskly through another round of filling four cannisters (the two remaining in the conservatory and the two she'd brought back to it) and conveyed them to her cooking bay.

Little godlings, but hauling water was grueling work!

She topped up two more cannisters, then made one more round to half-fill the last pair.

When she was done – four fully-full cannisters and two half-full ones – she went to her room and flopped on the bed, massaging her cramping fingers and wriggling her sore shoulders.

Was it better to work hard and have water enough for maybe three days? Or would it be better to haul water every day, but less of it? Before being trapped here, she would have answered *less* every time. After watching her eyes grow dark circles and her lips crack with dryness . . . that changed things. Changed *her*.

In any case, the chore was done now.

She gazed at her ceiling. Was there the hint of a face in the painted sun illuminating the cloud castle? Maybe an echo of the cheerful faces in the suns on the cornice frieze? She squinted, scrutinizing the mural more closely.

Sweet Marionya! That was the demon face that appeared each night by moonlight.

And now that her eyes had the trick of the angle, she could

perceive the smoke fortress within the bastions of the cloud castle, and even the goblins on the sun frieze.

She dove under her quilt, trembling.

✍

She'd hidden in her bed her first day here. It did her no good then, and it did her no good now.

The daytime ghosts of the sinister images, latent within the happy ones, held none of their nighttime powers. Only the ordinary waspish sniping – that she was used to – nipped at her. She had to get moving.

You've experienced their worst, Fae, she told herself. *This is nothing. Get on with finding the second godmother door.*

It was hard to pry herself out from under the covers. Her head knew she could take the petty sniping. It was more than the nothing she'd called it, but bearable. But her heart remembered the agony they'd delivered at bedtime, only yesterday.

Breathing fast, she extracted herself.

She stood still for a moment, proving to herself that she could. Then she slung her bow and her quiver over her shoulders and whisked herself into the hallway. Which wasn't really any better. The goblins were everywhere in the castle. At least she didn't have to see their cruel faces though.

I wonder if I'll be able to enjoy my room and the happy suns again? It seemed a loss. She already possessed so little to bolster her spirits.

But I have me! That'll have to be enough.

And it was. All the way down the hall, she indulged in the vine step of Greek line dances, returning to herself, being the "happy one" that her cousins called her. That *she* called herself.

Crossing an enclosed bridge, high above a paved interior courtyard, Fae found herself in an older, medieval part of the castle.

Windows were smaller with round arches at their tops. The thick walls were half-timbered – heavy beams filled in with wattle and daub – or else formed of huge rough gray stones. Massive piers supported the ceilings of large spaces such as the great hall and the place of arms where the knights would have assembled.

Almost, she wished she could see them, in their bright polished armor with their vivid plumes on the helmets. They'd be magnificent.

Almost. But she'd fallen out of time once, and landed here. She didn't want to do it again.

In one of the dark corridors high on the outside wall, she spotted a puddle filling a deeply uneven area of the floor. Apparently the roof leaked there. Just down the hall from the puddle, a small rectangular door opened onto a tiny vestibule. A second door behind the first gave onto a garderobe.

The walls were of gray stone, also the slanting ceiling and the bench with its circular hole.

The warm breath of summer blew through the opening, bringing the aroma of peaches and mown grass with it. Fae could see an expanse of river rushes below, growing on the bank down to a stream.

Dear. Gods.

She was on her knees in an instant, stretching a hand to the outdoors, feeling the sun on her skin and the brush of wind-stirred air.

Oh, oh, oh, if only the opening were larger. If only the stone seat were wood that she could batter to pieces. A brief inner vision of herself clinging to a rope of bedsheets, escaping the castle via a medieval toilet, made her giggle even as she wished it were possible.

But it wasn't.

She examined the stone seat more carefully. No, of course it hadn't been used in centuries. Who would choose such an unsanitary solution, with plenty of modern water closets on hand? The stone was clean. She hadn't been wallowing in ancient muck.

On the other hand . . . she eyed the arrangement speculatively. She'd been drinking from her canteen religiously; it was empty. Which meant her bladder was full. And uncomfortable.

She hadn't been squeamish about such things when hunting in the woods. She wasn't about to begin now.

I want to be fully myself, she decided. Surely one use wouldn't do much harm to the ground below.

Although there was no need to eschew modern comforts when they were available.

She scampered back to the more modern part of the castle to a water closet there. It might be missing water – it *was* missing water; she checked – but it boasted a full stock of loo paper and soap and hand towels. She pattered back across the bridge and set the soap and hand towels down by the puddle. She refilled her canteen. Then she took the loo paper with her into the garderobe. And emerged triumphant a moment later to wash her hands with soap and dry them.

Hah!

She felt liked she'd thumbed her nose at the evil powers imprisoning her here.

So there!

♉

The Theosian Doom

⁂

SHE FOUND A GYMNASIUM on the floor below the garderobe.

It had probably been a salle de guerre originally, where the castle defenders practiced swordsmanship and other hand-to-hand combat skills. Later inhabitants had placed a floating wood floor over the stone one. Oak wainscoting covered the lower portion of the walls to head height. Whitewash brightened the rugged stone blocks above where the wainscoting ended. A long line of horizontal windows near the beam-supported ceiling allowed sunshine to stream in.

Fae could see dust motes sparkling in the rays of light. It was just like her memory . . . of the second door! An instant later she saw it, there in the shadows under the balcony that ran below the windows.

Small with a pointed arch, splintery, and unpainted, just like the first one she'd found in the tower.

More boldly than in her earlier encounter, she marched over to this door and turned the knob. The scritch of its inner spring sounded as the knob turned, but the door didn't budge. Did some strong bolt on the other side hold it closed? Likely it was merely locked. The plate below the knob held a keyhole.

Like the tower landing, the gymnasium felt warm and welcoming, the spite of the goblins held at bay.

Fae gathered her courage and aimed a kick at the unyielding door. Maybe she could force it open.

The wood quivered; that was all.

Fae growled in frustration. She really should stop trying physical solutions in this place. Except that some things *required* physical solutions. Like eating and drinking and peeing. But escape was apparently not to be begged, borrowed, or stolen from doors or windows or garderobe holes.

Fae snorted.

It was a mental puzzle, just as she had suspected for some time.

As she turned away from the obdurate door, memory caught her.

In memory, Fae had been summoned to Milady's record room in the lodge.

The lodge was so very different from the castle, with clean lines to its spaces and little ornament. Milady's record room took this difference to an extreme. Its floor, walls, and ceiling were finished in straight, narrow boards of grayish brown. Even the muntins between the panes of the double French doors featured this dull material.

None of the dainty whites or dark mahoganies or walnuts for Milady. Nor the elaborate moldings and coffered ceilings. Yet the lodge was not austere. It was . . . subtle.

Fae preferred it herself, but this heart of Milady's domain – her record room – exuded her authority in a way that made Fae nervous.

When Fae entered the room, Milady stood up from the chair behind her desk – very tall and stern in her fitted black velvet gown. Milady termed her working surface a desk, but it was little more than a large table with a stand for her fountain pen.

"I have something to tell you," said Milady. She gestured to the two wooden armchairs – uncushioned – in front of her desk.

Fae was barefoot. She crossed the satiny smooth floor to the firm pile of the carpet where the furniture was grouped. Dappled light sifted in through the skylight over Milady's desk and the French doors beyond it. The room was dim, sheltered by the shade of the tall oaks outside.

One door stood cracked open to an intimate terrace. Birdsong came through the opening, cheerful in the quietude. Fae didn't feel cheerful. Why had Milady summoned her? Not for discipline, which would be daunting enough, but something more serious.

Fae sat. The seat of the chair pressed against her thighs, the spindles of its back dug into her spine.

Milady lifted a teapot from the tray on the small table between the two chairs and poured hot mint tea into two mugs. The scent curled into the air mingling with the pine aroma of Milady's potpourri.

Fae accepted her mug and sipped. No honey in it, just straight tea, but it was good; warm on her throat, fresh and cooling to the taste.

She gazed around the room, familiar because she'd sat here many times before, discomfiting because those summons usually dealt with her transgressions.

A lattice of pigeonholes took up one whole wall, housing scrolls of oracular ritual, all of them old, many of them ancient. The oracles of the Theosians went back a very long time.

Bookshelves covered the other three walls, their shelves filled with slim volumes bound in covers of tan, beige, lilac, and gray. Their pages recorded Milady's prophecies and those of all her predecessors.

The history contained by this room was daunting. Fae felt daunted. *How appropriate*, whispered an inner wiseacre voice.

Milady shifted in her chair. The black velvet of her gown rustled, drawing Fae's attention. Milady leaned forward as though to touch Fae's hand, then drew back.

Was *Milady* uneasy? Fae studied her godmother's face: pale skin, steady gray eyes, nose slightly aquiline. She looked calm, as always, but underneath the calm . . . lay some other feeling that Fae could not identify.

"I've been away for some months," said Milady.

Fae nodded. Indeed, Milady had returned just the day before, after an absence of nearly a year.

"My journey was on your behalf."

Now that, Fae had *not* known.

"Yes, milady?"

"I have learned the thing I've been pursuing all these years."

It was true that this had been Milady's third long trip, apparently all three taken for the same reason. And none of them had started with the prelude that Fae remembered concerning the necessity that a door remain unopened. That had been the play in which she and her friends played roles, not real life.

And yet . . . some portion of the exhortation, "You must never open this door, nor allow any other to do so," held true, even though Fae didn't see how that was so.

"About me, milady?"

"About you," confirmed Milady. She paused, studying Fae's face in turn. "This is not an easy thing, child."

No, Fae had gathered that from the moment of her summons. The maid servant had been anxious in a wholly unusual way. "What is it?"

"We – your uncles and I – thought you a villager's child. We were wrong."

Fae's stomach sank.

She'd initially disliked that she was the only ordinary child among her cousins. But that was then, when she'd first understood their difference, when she was little. She'd come to accept their difference, and then to embrace it.

The possibility that she'd need to relinquish her ordinariness now did not appeal.

"Who am I?" she whispered.

"You are the daughter of my sister, Themis."

Milady had a *sister*? And Fae was Milady's niece? A Theosian?

"It's n-n-not true!" Fae stuttered.

Milady straightened in her chair, looking down her aristocratic nose at Fae. "You're displeased?" Her voice was cool.

"I'd – I'd grown used to my ordinary origins."

Milady's voice warmed. "Very wise, child, but now there's no need for your humility."

Ugh! Fae hated it when Milady condescended to her.

"But there is a problem," Fae challenged her. "No?"

"Themis was the ideal of cosmic order and justice."

"Was?" Fae wondered. What happened to justice when it's ideal was no more?

"We've not seen my sister for more than two hundred years. We know not whether she still lives or whether she has abdicated her duties." Milady tapped the wooden arm of her chair with one forefinger. "Clearly she was living fourteen years ago, when you were born."

"How can you be certain that I am her child?" Fae didn't want it to be true. She would be squeezed into an identity that wasn't hers, that cut off parts of who she was. Like Theophane. Like Eulalie. An inexorable process that there was no resisting. She didn't want it. Passionately didn't want it.

"I found my brother Iapetus, also long lost. And he recounted his last encounter with Themis. She was heavily pregnant, soon to give birth."

"With some other child, not me. You should be searching for that baby!"

"Oh, I have, but you are that infant. The timing is exact."

"I'm not!" Fae was beginning to panic.

"Why do you resist your heritage? It is a glorious thing."

It wasn't. It was a horror.

"It feels all wrong." A teardrop rolled down Fae's cheek.

Milady reached out her hand to caress Fae's face. Milady's voice turned warm and loving, the way Fae had always wanted to hear it. "Moira. Dearest."

Fae's sinking belly turned to ice. *That* was the name her godmother – and her aunts and uncles – called her. Not Fae. *Moira,* for "bitter," because being an orphan was a bitter thing.

Milady had further revelations to share.

"We named you well," she continued. "Better than we knew."

Yes, they had. But not for her foundling state. It was being a Theosian that was bitter. Except Milady did not think so. She thought being a Theosian was wonderful. Why then did she approve the name?

"Moira has another meaning," said Milady.

"I still think you're wrong." Fae wasn't going to surrender without a fight. She gulped the rest of her mint tea and stood abruptly. "I bet a hundred ordinary women gave birth to a hundred ordinary babies on the day that your sister had her daughter."

Fae started to pace the room, angrily, forward to the French doors, back to the shelves behind her and Milady's chairs.

Back and forth.

Milady's smile deepened. "You see? You feel the truth of it already, that Themis birthed a girl. That you are that girl."

"I'm not!"

Back. And forth.

"I also found my oldest sister, Tethys."

Oh, gods! Milady's reunions with her siblings were beginning to feel like a noose around Fae's neck. Gymnasium Fae thought, *I am Fae.* She refused to be Moira. The Fae in this memory recalled that the painting of Tethys hung in the portrait gallery of the castle. She couldn't pretend her aunt didn't exist, as she was tempted to do with her uncle, Iapetus.

"Tethys served as midwife to our sister. She saw you born. And she followed Themis' instructions after."

Fae stopped pacing directly in front of Milady's chair.

She was rude. "Shut up! Don't say it! I refuse my heritage!" she yelled.

Milady actually laughed, low and melodiously.

"Tethys placed you in a basket and wrapped your signifiers in your swaddling bands: the drop spindle for spinning the lines of fate, the rod for measuring them, and the knife for severing them. *You* are the ideal of fate, dear Moira. And Moira's other meaning *is 'fate.'*"

"I'm not!" Fae's protest was louder than before.

"You were found in a basket at a crossroads with the spindle, the rod, and the knife wrapped in your swaddling bands."

"You never told me that before. About the signifiers." Fae felt desperate.

"We thought you a weaver's child. And, as you grew, you did seem quite ordinary."

"I'm still ordinary," Fae insisted.

Milady was looking down her nose again. "Why would you want to be, when you could be extraordinary." Milady sniffed. "Even were you ordinary, it's too late."

"What do you mean?" Fae cried.

"Have not you bathed in the Achillean Springs with your cousins? Their waters are transformative."

There were no mirrors to reflect Fae's face, but she felt pale.

Milady continued her explanation. "Mortals have become immortal with enough immersion in the springs." She tilted her head. "You've envied your cousins often enough. And it didn't seem fair to deny our foster child the advantages conferred on our natural offspring. We allowed matters to take their course."

Fae grew abruptly calm. Whether innate or conferred, it seemed there was no undoing what was done. She was Theosian.

She slowed her breathing. Her panting gasps were doing her no good.

"You have more to tell me," she observed.

Milady swallowed. "Yes."

Fae sat again. "It is worse," she guessed.

"You are the ideal of fate, and we Theosians are fated. My last prophecy – a year ago, today – declared you to be our doom. Just as a mortal's life is spun, measured, and cut, so is our Theosian rule spun, measured, and cut. You are our bane, Moira."

Yes, that was worse. Much, much worse.

"What can I do?"

Milady reached out again, and this time her fingers rested on the back of Fae's hand.

"I hate to ask it of you, child. Your well-being is our ill, and our well-being is your ill."

Why was Fae not surprised? Had all her life been flowing to this moment? From loss to acceptance and happiness, then renewed loss and grief segueing into more acceptance and happiness.

Here was the next loss. She sensed it.

I'll accept it, as I have accepted loss before. I'll grieve, but then I'll find happiness again.

"Tell me," she urged. "I'll do it. I owe you and my uncles everything. I'll save you as you saved me."

"Dear Moira." Milady was moved. "Dear child. This will be harder for you than all else."

"Then I'll learn to make it easier."

"I fear that you cannot. Do you understand what we Theosians are?"

Fae shook her head.

"The ideal of any quality found in the world – motherliness, inventiveness, oracular prophecy – is embodied by a Theosian ideal."

Yes, Fae understood *that*. "Aunt Pallas. Uncle Leander. You."

Milady smiled graciously. "Yes, that is right. And every instance of that quality in the world and its people connects back to the ideal, like the strands of a web connect to the spider at its center. We ideals hold the web secure within ourselves. With the web secure, the world and her denizens remain secure. And we ideals manifest our powers."

"You foretell the future, milady."

"I do. Just as Leander builds marvelous inventions. And Hadrien's leadership commands our obedience." Milady inclined her head. "You understand well. But do you also understand that while a Theosian is born, an ideal must be claimed?"

Fae's brow wrinkled. What *did* Milady mean?

"I thought not." Milady's voice grew very cordial. "A Theosian holds her ideal for a very long time. Centuries, perhaps millenia, but not forever. Eventually she releases the burden for another to take up. And all that is required for that transfer of power is consent. The elder ideal consents to the relinquishment of her task, while the new ideal consents to undertake the task."

"That's all?" Fae was surprised. It seemed too simple.

"That's all," confirmed Milady. "But that is the heart of your sacrifice, dear Moira."

Fae was still confused.

"You are the ideal of fate. The younger ideal of fate in the process of consenting to take up your duties from three elders who bore them together and now relinquish them to you. But you must not complete the transfer. You must renounce your powers. Withdraw yourself from them and from the world, allowing your elders to either keep the powers of fate or pass them to another heir. Only then will Clan Theosis be safe."

Fae frowned. "How shall I do that? When I cannot even feel these supposed powers?" Her doubt returned full force. Milady had to be wrong. Fae had no powers. She was ordinary. Beautifully ordinary.

Milady bit her lip. "You must grow retiring. Withdraw from your cousins. Withdraw from the woods. Withdraw from life."

Fae's lips parted. "I must die?"

"Oh, no, no, no." Milady hurried to reassure her. "I could not consent to that. You are my sister's child and the daughter of my heart. You must live, but you must become cloistered, solitary. Live as might a hermit."

"I must leave here?" questioned Fae, bewildered. "Find a cave somewhere and make that my home?"

Milady's face lightened, and she actually laughed. "Goodness, no! You'll remain here, of course, with all the comfort I can give you.

But . . . no more hunting, child. No visiting with your friends. You must occupy yourself with reading and meditating and thinking. Drawing and sculpting, if you wish. Writing. Designing and building mechanisms, perhaps. Solitary pursuits."

Fae's belly felt hollow all over again. Everything she loved would be taken from her. Was that not a definition of death?

She felt frozen. Like cold stone. This couldn't be happening.

Milady drew Fae onto her lap, cradling her adopted daughter in her arms.

When Fae started to cry, she felt Milady's tears fall, too, hot on the back of her neck.

Together, they wept for a long time.

The Labyrinth

WITH DIFFICULTY, Fae pulled her attention out of the past.

She felt a little weepy, but she also felt angry. Her godmother could have done better than that, surely. If she loved Fae as much as she claimed, wouldn't she have fought harder for Fae's freedom? Instead of crumpling the instant her *precious* – Fae gave the word great sarcasm in her mind – oracular powers indicated a problem.

Fae compared this memory – her godmother weeping – to her memory of Milady in the rose garden, cunning and sly. Which was the real Milady?

Fae didn't know, but she could no longer accept the weeping Milady on faith.

Only in the play *The Race of Atalanta* had Milady uttered the words, "And you must never open this door, nor allow any other to do so." But in real life, she had guided Fae to shut herself away from the nighttime, with its star-spangled sky and its moonlit woods. In real life, she had encouraged Fae to hide away from the daytime, with its sunshine and the jolly games with her cousins.

I closed all the doors in my life, and my godmother manipulated me into doing it.

She wished she'd been less trusting. Her choice to withdraw had been wrong; she was increasingly certain.

She looked around her at the gymnasium, liking the safe feeling of the space. What was it that made it feel so comforting? The sunbeams making the dust in the air sparkle? The strength of the medieval bones of the place? Those were silly questions. The simple absence of the pinching, gnawing goblins explained its peace perfectly.

She wondered if she could sleep here, instead of in her bedroom. Would it still feel safe in the night? If it didn't – if the goblins and the demon achieved their full potency – she'd never get back to the protection of her gryphon bed, never survive till morning.

She walked to the archway connecting the gymnasium to the corridor beyond. There was no door, just a simple opening to step through.

She paused, reflecting.

The memory of Milady's dire revelation possessed a codicil.

Fae had gotten the gentlest horse in the stables out – foregoing saddle and bridle – and ridden bareback from the lodge to the castle, seeking Leander.

She'd found him not in the smithy, but in his studio, drawing plans for a new invention, a geared lift connected to a steam engine that would turn the gears and raise the platform.

Large northern windows cast even light on his slanted drafting table as well as illuminating the piles of odd parts – metal tubes, sheets of copper, boxy steel housings, and so on – that filled the shelves and bins in the generous space. It smelled of machine oil.

"Uncle Leander," she'd said, a catch in her voice, as soon as she set eyes on him, bent over his work.

He finished the line he'd started, set the drafting pencil down, then turned and stood.

"Sweetheart, what is it?" The concern in his face started her crying again.

He drew her over to his drafting stool and seated her on it – her back to the table to protect his work from her tears – then stood next to her, his arm warm and solid around her shoulders.

She told him everything.

His shock showed in his eyes. Despite it, he kept his habitual soothing demeanor and listened, asking sensible questions, making suitable comments. But he didn't have a better answer.

At the end of their conversation, he took both her hands and looked seriously at her.

"Sweetheart, I cannot advise you to disobey your Aunt Dione. *She* is your guardian. But let me tell you this: find some way to stay true to who you are. Find some corner of yourself to keep. If you must shut the door on the outside world, do not shut the door on who you are."

It was good advice. She was grateful still that he'd given it. But it had not been enough. She hadn't found a way to follow it.

She'd pulled back from all the activities that gave her pleasure, that gave her life meaning.

Not all at once. She couldn't do it.

When the sun was calling her, she went out sometimes to enjoy it.

When her cousins invited her to play hide-and-seek in the woods, she joined them.

When the moonlight was too beautiful to resist and there were baby fawns to watch, she roamed the night.

Milady forbade her nothing.

But Fae knew what the consequences would be to her family, if she did not withdraw, if she did too little, too late. Disaster. Unspecified, but disaster nonetheless. She saw it in Milady's eyes every time she indulged in an old happiness.

So Fae was happy less and less.

And away from the outdoors that she loved, she felt cut off from her inner self as well.

She experimented with activities new to her. Maybe she would like watercolor painting. Or playing the harp. Or doing solitary Patience games with playing cards.

She even tried writing poetry.

Her friend Calanthe found her at it one afternoon, calligraphy pen in hand.

"I can't believe you're indoors on a day like today!" complained Calanthe. Her freckled face was flushed, and her short red hair looked particularly spikey.

Fae sighed. She *wanted* to be outdoors. "You know why I'm here."

"Yeah, our idyllic duties – *and powers* – will pass away, and Clan Theosis will dwindle. Or some such. Unless *you* immure yourself in solitude. Hah! I don't believe it."

Well, it was more serious than Calanthe implied. Their idyllic powers wouldn't just pass away. They'd be torn away, doing damage in the tearing. But some days Fae didn't believe it either. Today she did. She looked at the pen in her hand and the parchment on the writing desk. Ugh!

But she had to do something. Wandering from window to window gazing longingly outdoors was worse than writing dreary poems about being trapped or imprisoned or held captive.

Calanthe took up her litany. "C'mon Fae! Come play battledore and shuttlecock with me on the tennis lawn. It'll be fun. Aunt Pallas would even say it was good for you. 'Move your limbs, child,' she'd say. C'mon Fae, do!"

"I can't," said Fae.

"Yes you can," insisted Calanthe. "What are you writing anyway?" She snatched Fae's paper from under her pen and read a line. "'Fae, you must stay alive. See to your physical sustenance first of all. No provision has been made for you.' Ugh! No wonder you grow melancholy. I'll show you what's best for this drivel!" And she tore the paper right across: once, twice, thrice. "Hah!"

She started to tug Fae out of her chair.

Milady's cool voice from the door of the room interrupted her. "Calanthe, dear, I know you mean well, but you make this harder for Moira, not easier."

That was Milady's daunting tone, but Calanthe refused to be daunted. "Aunt Dione, just look at this!" She held up the torn strips of paper. "Fae's in a funk. You have to do something!"

Milady accepted the sliced poetry, casting her eyes over it. "Dear me, Moira has indeed grown pensive." She scrutinized Fae. "Yes, perhaps Calanthe is right."

Milady folded each poetic line into a tiny square and then tucked them into the reticule hanging from her wrist. "Take a break from your seclusion, child. Tomorrow will be soon enough to resume it."

Fae didn't need to be told twice.

Outside on the lawn, with the springy grass under her feet and the sun warming her skin, she felt free. The swing of her arm holding the battledore turned her in dizzy circles. Seeking the shuttlecock when it bounced into the sky blinded her momentarily, but was so much better than the dim mildness of inside. And joining Calanthe's laughter was best of all.

But when it was over, returning to solitude and the indoors was painful. Her longing to be out with her friends grew stronger, not less. And she felt as though she were turning into a ghost of herself.

Where was that corner of herself that Uncle Leander had spoken of? Her essential core. Where was the way to stay true to herself? She'd not found it. Never once in that long removal from the people she enjoyed most and the activities she participated in with them.

But now, in a castle with rooms from all the ages, untied from *chronos*, cast footloose into *kairos*, she'd returned to herself. And she was never letting that go. Never again. It was a price too high to ask anyone to pay. And she refused to pay it.

I'm me! I'm myself! I've touched the breeze through a privy seat!

That started her laughing.

What would Milady say, if she knew Fae had embraced the stone where people of the past once sat to poop?

I don't care!

She started to dance across the floor of the gymnasium.

Vine, and vine, and vine.

Kick, step, kick.

Her bow and her quiver of arrows bounced on her back.

Vine, and vine, and vine.

Spin, step, spin.

It felt good. It felt glorious. It felt like who she was. *I'm not following anyone else's solutions after I get out of here.* If there were problems, she'd devise her own solutions. In fact, she was devising her own solution right now.

Her watch chimed when she left the gymnasium.

Ding, ding, ding.

Three o'clock.

I'm going to look for the third door. I'll bet it holds the most important memory of all.

She barely noticed the return of the flat, eroding feel of the goblin-haunted castle. All her attention focused on completing the next segment of her quest to put together the full puzzle of her past. Therein lay her escape.

The third door wasn't in the medieval part of the castle. She searched it thoroughly.

She found the great chamber where the lady of the castle would have slept. Her canopied bed, with massive dark pillars at the corners, was curtained in a rich red brocade, the pattern showing a unicorn cavorting in a flowery mead.

Such a stately private space.

She found the solar with its extra complement of windows and chairs with backs, against which the lady might relax during those few moments when she was not busy with her responsibility for overseeing the smooth running of kitchens, butteries, pantry, sewing room, and washroom.

Did the lady of a medieval castle have any leisure?

She found the oratory, the small and private chapel for the lord and his family. The tender expression on the portrait of Saint Marionya over the altar there brought on the desolate feeling from when Milady wept with her. Milady had *never* looked at Fae that way.

I wonder who my real mother was. Was she really Themis, the ideal of cosmic order and justice? Fae hoped Milady was wrong about that, just as she'd been wrong to shut Fae away from life.

Fae left the medieval wing just as her watch chimed five o'clock.

Ding, ding, ding, ding, ding.

She wasn't on the enclosed bridge. She'd discovered another connection between the newer annexes and the old section: a circular stone vestibule, with a serpent-guarded apple orchard carved in bas relief on its curving walls. One doorway opened onto the medieval bottlery, where wines would have been stored. The other doorway led into a stone passage with matching bas relief panels, these depicting nymphs dancing in the orchard.

At the end of the passage stood a stone door with a pointed arch – the only door, aside from the two wooden ones she'd discovered, with that shape. It was much larger than the wooden ones, and black scorch marks marred its surface.

As Fae drew nearer, she could see cracks in the stone as well. What had happened here? No other structures in the castle showed damage like this.

The passage didn't deadend at the door as she'd thought, but turned left. At its farther shadowed end, two smaller corridors branched away, and a dainty spiral stair of stone rose to the next floor.

Fae turned to the scarred door in front of her.

It had no handle, but there was a narrow slot in one side through which light shone.

Fae placed her hand in it, gripped the edge, and pulled, leaning back with her full weight.

Slowly the great stone portal swung open.

The smells and sounds of a dovecote hit her first, the contented broody murmur of settling birds and the warm scent of their feathers. More faintly, behind the feathery smell followed the odors of the outdoors: mown hay, crushed apples, fresh loam.

Next came the light, broad swathes of sunshine blinding her.

She stepped inside, blinking and shading her eyes.

The space had once been a large chapel, but its shattered roof lay open to the sky. Great ribs of stone rose from the tall, ragged walls through the space where once they'd supported a soaring vault. Cracked niches in the walls, empty now of statuary, provided shelter for the dove flock. The niches of the wall in shadow – the western wall – stood empty, but those of the sunny eastern wall housed dozens of restless birds. The sun was slipping down in the western sky. A few doves flew up to perch on the lofty ribs of stone. Their soft gray plumage brightened in the sunlight.

Urrrrrrr, urrrrrrr, murmured the doves nesting in the niches.

Twooo, wooo, called those roosting on the stone ribs.

Stone rubble, dust, and bird droppings obscured much of the floor. It looked as though a vast boulder had been flung against its center, shattering the point of impact and creating radiating cracks in the stone. But no mass of rock occupied the site of the blow, just the broken fragments of paving. Close by the door, where Fae stood, a clear spot revealed an abstract mosaic in tones of tan, pale ecru, pale blue, and white.

Fae closed her eyes and breathed in, slowly, luxuriously, savoring the aromas of the outdoor world and the feeling of being out of doors.

The sun shone directly on her head, not through glass.

The breeze ruffled her hair.

Faint hints of pollen tickled her nose.

Abruptly, she knew what lay under all the debris: a labyrinth.

Not a maze. Mazes were for losing yourself in. In a maze, one wandered between hedges or walls or even pleached trees, hoping at each intersection of the paths to turn aright, guessing where the heart of the confusing knot might lie. If you were unlucky, you might stroll all the afternoon. Unless you gave up and requested aid from the custodian standing on a platform to one side.

This castle was a maze. Except it had no way out. And no custodian to ask for help. She repressed a sob. *None of that. You* are *getting out.*

But the design on the chapel floor was not a maze.

Labyrinths were for finding oneself. They were laid out as stepping stones on a lawn or colored wools in a carpet or patterns of mosaic in a marble floor. The pattern was formed of one long, carefully looping line. It never crossed over itself, but turned and turned again, forming quadrants of a square or a circle.

You walked the pattern slowly, gently breathing in as your right foot stepped forward, breathing out as your left foot moved ahead. When you reached another quadrant, you switched, breathe out on the right foot, breathe in on the left.

By the time you reached the center, you were calm. You rested there in meditation. And when you were ready, when you had found your own center, you followed the pattern back to its entrance point, breathing in, breathing out.

Fae had walked this chapel labyrinth at close to midnight.

Milady had come to Fae's bedside when Fae could not sleep.

Fae had lain on the simple white-draped mattress listening to the crickets sing beyond the open window, watching the shadows cast on her gauze curtains by the rising moon, lengthening. She tossed. She turned. She wished she'd joined her cousins in playing Capture the Flag that evening. She wished she'd gone skinny dipping with Calanthe after the sun set. She wished she'd done anything but spend the whole day moping around Milady's lodge.

I hate my life.

She gave her pillow a vicious thump.

And then Milady was there, laying a cooling hand on her heated brow.

"Dearest, can you not sleep?" she'd asked.

"Who could?" muttered Fae.

"I know." Milady's voice could sound so sympathetic sometimes. Even while her face remained cold and distant. Fae could not see her face in the dark.

"I believe I've found another solution," Milady breathed.

Fae sat bolt upright in her narrow bed. "What is it?" she demanded.

"A ritual."

"To do what?"

"If done properly, done soon, it will remove your Theosian essence. You will no longer be the ideal of fate."

"Do it now. Tonight!" Fae demanded. With relief in reach, she couldn't bear to wait through the rest of the long hours of darkness. Through another dragging day on the morrow. And another unending night after that. How long might she have to wait? She didn't want to wait *at all*. "Do it now!" she repeated.

Milady laughed, low and exultant. "It might be done tonight. Now, if you wish."

Fae thrust the bedclothes back and stood up in her nightgown. "I'm ready," she said.

"Very well then. Come!"

Fae pulled on riding boots. They saddled the horses themselves, and at the other end of their two-mile ride to Castle Farnesse, they stabled their mounts without help.

Uncle Aion awaited them in the darkened chapel.

Votive candles, their small flames dancing, lined the path of the labyrinth pattern on the floor. More candles flanked a high, narrow table set at the labyrinth's center.

"She is willing?" Aion asked Milady.

Fae pulled her riding boots off.

"She is willing," answered Milady.

Fae was having second thoughts. Uncle Aion's face looked sinister with the flickering light illuminating it from below. He refused to meet Fae's eyes.

Milady met Fae's eyes with her own, but her gaze was strangely intent.

"Moira, wait here. When I beckon, start walking the labyrinth. Keep your gaze on your steps. Intone the syllable 'rhohm' with each step. Can you do that?"

Fae nodded. It was all beginning to feel like a dream. She'd awake in the morning in her narrow bed, facing yet more of the anxious boredom that had grown ever since she'd learned of her true identity. *Was* this a dream? Or had she been drugged, to produce the peculiar mental lethargy taking hold of her?

Maybe it was just the result of too many nights without sleep, following on too many days of worrying that she wasn't doing it right. Wasn't pulling away from her fateful powers as she must. Imagining dear Aunt Pallas riven from her baby and dying. Because of Fae. Seeing Uncle Leander crushed on his own forge, because Fae had snipped his thread of fate unknowingly.

Milady and Aion walked straight across the labyrinth, utterly ignoring its presence. That shocked Fae. It seemed . . . wrong.

She stared at her feet. She heard Aion's voice begin a rhythmic chant: *rhohm, lohm, gohm, trohm.* Milady's voice joined his, but in melodious counterpoint, not in unison. *Alaliyah nuwherawon malaysias!*

Fae looked up.

Milady beckoned, and Fae started the labyrinth.

"Rhohm!" for the right foot.

"Rhohm!" for the left foot.

Fae's dreamlike feeling increased. She watched her steps.

Somewhere in the middle, Milady's song changed from unfamiliar words to words that meant something.

"Chaos burns in the icy void.

  Colors turn to ash.

  Chaos spins in the blackest void.

  Touch implodes to absence.

  Chaos sings in the silent void.

  Time unhooks from time.

  Chaos writhes in the fathomless void.

  Unmaking the anchors of chance."

Fae had arrived at the center of the labyrinth, the hem of her nightgown nearly catching fire from the candles beside the tall table. Milady stood at its head. Aion, at its foot.

"Lean into me," whispered Milady.

Fae felt her shoulders taken by her godmother, while her uncle supported her knees. Together, they lifted Fae onto the table.

The two celebrants took their places again at the head and the foot.

Fae stared at the shadowy ceiling of the chapel, feeling dizzy.

Milady's voice rang out.

"Three is for change. Four brings completion. Fae, daughter of Themis, have I your consent?"

Fae's throat felt tight. This would not end well. "You have it," she whispered.

"By the darkness," rumbled Aion.

"By the wounding light," belled Milady.

"From *chronos*," said Aion.

"To *kairos*," said Milady.

"In sorrow." That was Aion.

"In blood." Milady's tone was vicious.

And then Milady's hands came into Fae's field of vision. They seemed to grip a knife, and yet only empty air lay within the encircling fingers.

Milady's hands plunged down.

Only when that knife of nothingness entered her own breast did Fae see a shimmer of opalescence – transparent – in the shape of a blade.

She felt cold. She felt hot. She felt betrayed.

An instant later, she unfurled. Meteorically, impossibly vast. Beyond the sky. Beyond the sun. Beyond the Milky Way that she once had watched through Uncle Leander's telescope.

She traveled in an explosion of light, agonized by joy, soothed by love, ecstatic with the sense of coming home. She floated, arriving at a singularity, bathed in radiance.

When her eyes drifted closed and she slept, her remembering transitioned from memory into vision. Fae could see herself slumbering in the light, a smile on her lips, and hymns sounding around her. Her nightgown drifted up to her knees, revealing a blister on the inside of her calf, where her boot had rubbed the bare skin.

The light intensified, turned golden, and faded out.

Fae lay sleeping in a bed with golden gryphons at its head, and a blue silk quilt – with crimson knots, silver swans, and gold stars adorning it – over her.

The vision faded like the light, and Fae fell to her knees in the ruined chapel. A chapel ripped asunder by her departure from *chronos* into *kairos*.

Now she knew it all, from beginning to end. In all its faithlessness and perfidy.

Dear. Gods.

❧

Bleeding

✤

FAE DROPPED HER HEAD into her hands. She *had* consented to her exile. Yet she had also been betrayed. Milady had lied to her about the purpose of the midnight ritual. But had Milady lied about everything? Fae didn't think so.

The danger to her clan was real.

Were Fae to become the ideal of fate, the ideal embodied by each of her kin would be ripped away, damaging – killing? – the holder.

In the weeks before she'd retired into complete seclusion, Aunt Pallas had offered twice as many hugs as usual and stroked her hair. Eulalie had bit her lip, every time she set eyes on Fae. Uncle Hadrien had looked at her as though she were his personal dilemma. And Uncle Leander had invited her into his workshop every time he had something interesting under construction, instead of waiting for her to wander in randomly.

Her family knew the danger. They did not speak of it, but of course the elders had witnessed Milady's oracular prophecy.

Did Fae need to stay here? Stay in *kairos* to protect the ones she loved? Instead of struggling to escape it? It felt awful to even consider reversing her declaration that she would find her own solutions.

I can't decide this now.

The whirring calls of the doves, strengthening, made her look up.

Shadow had crept across the rubble-strewn floor and started climbing the sunny eastern wall.

Fae watched the shadow's edge approach the sill of the lowest niche. The birds there were agitated, pecking at one another, tumbling over one another. The shadow touched the scratching talons of their feet. They grew abruptly still.

Fae could hear her watch ticking.

The shadow flowed upward, claiming the birds' downy breasts, their sleek-feathered necks, their dainty heads. They stared out across the chapel, utterly without motion, something sinister in their stances. They looked less like doves, more like hawks. Their niche fell completely into gloom, and the shadow approached the next niche.

The hawk-like birds took flight in a burst of wing flaps, aiming for the sky. When they passed into sunlight, their differences shone clear: charcoal-gray plumage, muscular bodies, hooked beaks, stronger talons tucked for flying.

Uneasily, Fae lifted her bow off her shoulder and took it in hand, then nocked an arrow.

She'd lost the birds in the sun.

The next batch of doves-turned-hawk took to wing, their niche engulfed by shadow.

Fae backed toward the chapel door.

Three diving hawks erupted from the sky, talons outstretched to rend their prey.

Fae didn't even have to think.

Twang, swoosh, thunk.

And again.

Twang, swoosh, thunk.

The two leading hawks dropped to the floor with her arrows in their breasts.

The third scored her cheek with its left talons before veering away, climbing to renew its attack. She felt blood dripping down her face. One scarlet droplet fell to the floor.

Fae dashed forward. A good archer didn't leave her arrows behind.

She snatched up the bodies of her attackers. They were heavy, still warm. But they were hawks no longer; they had returned to their dove form. Their feathers felt silky smooth against the palms of her hands.

The wing beats of another flight of hawks sounded. The screech of a diving bird pierced Fae's ears.

She dodged back.

The buffet of wings extending at the bottom of a hawk's dive brushed her head. Reaching talons flashed in her periphery. The hawk had missed.

She darted through the chapel door and turned to lean her shoulder into it, forcing the stone portal closed. The sound of wings filtered through its hand slot.

She was safe.

The dead birds were leaking blood. *Fae* was leaking blood. It spattered, scarlet on the white stone floor. She transferred both birds to her left arm, cradling them against her body, still gripping her bow in her left hand. She pressed the back of her right hand against the burning cuts on her cheek.

She felt stunned.

Thank the gods I had my bow.

She'd seen a golden eagle kill a wolf once. These hawks hadn't been so large as an eagle, but with three of them on her – or more; she remembered the wing beats of another wave of the birds launching themselves – yes, they could have slain her.

She started to shake in reaction.

Not now, Fae, she told herself. *You have dinner to cook.*

She looked again at the hawks-turned-dove on her left arm. They really were doves. And dove flesh, unlike hawk flesh, was edible. Maybe she could reduce the increasing pallor she'd been seeing in her face in the mirror. Cook up a meal of more than oatmeal.

Fae knew how to prepare game birds for the pot. The first time she'd plucked and drawn a pheasant had been overwhelming. And messy. But that was long ago. She had the routine down pat, and doves were so small they were easy.

She pressed the back of her hand harder against her cheek. Had the cuts stopped bleeding yet?

She had a lot of work to do, if she were going to prepare and then braise the doves. She released her hand from her cheek and felt another droplet of blood run down the skin. Head wounds bled a lot.

I can walk and apply pressure at the same time, she decided.

She used the back of her hand, remembering that she'd handled the birds with her palms.

The question was: how to get to her part of the castle from here? She could retrace her steps through the medieval wing. But that would take her all around Robin Hood's barn.

I bet if I try this little spiral stair, it will pop me up near the gun room, and I know my way from there.

That proved to be quite right, but it was a bit of a hike.

In her cooking bay, she left the doves on one of her improvised shelves and entered the water closet to wash her hands twice with lots of soap and water. The two cuts on her right cheek had stopped bleeding. She was lucky. They were shallow, almost superficial, and didn't require stitching. She rinsed them with fresh water and then went hunting in the nursery down the hall for bandages.

A basket in its armoire held strips of gauze and a small scissors, but she couldn't find a way to tie the gauze that didn't either cover her eye or feel really uncomfortable.

It's stopped bleeding. I really don't need bandaging.

Especially since the nursery supplies included a tub of basilicum ointment. She smoothed some over her cheek. That would help prevent infection.

Now it was time for a kitchen run.

She brought back a stack of large bowls, a cutting board, a square of oil cloth, a slotted spoon, and two very sharp, small knives. Then she laid out her tools.

She'd need one bowl for the entrails and the feathers. She filled it with a ladleful of water to keep the fluffiest of the feathers from drifting. Another bowl for the head and feet and bones. She filled this one half full with water and added a dollop of vinegar. And a third bowl for the meat she intended to eat, which she also filled with water, but no vinegar. Instead she scraped a goodly amount of salt from the salt lick and stirred it in well.

There wouldn't be time to soak the meat in the brine for as long as would be best, sealing the pores and thus helping it to retain its moisture. But even a little bit would help.

She spread the oil cloth square on her work surface and started plucking feathers. It went quickly, as was usual. Dove feathers came out easily. The trick was to be gentle, so as not to tear the skin. When she was done plucking, she scooped up the feathers, discarding them in the bowl she'd filled with the ladleful of water. She rubbed the revealed skin with her thumbs to remove any remaining fluffy pin feathers.

She examined the bird. It really was a dove, not a hawk.

She shivered, imagining the chapel at night, the entire flock roused and seeking prey, their talons outstretched at the base of each dive. Hawks were properly diurnal, but the birds in the chapel evidently partook of the castle's differing daytime and nighttime aspects. Except that the doves' transformation occurred at the first touch of shadow, rather than awaiting the dimming of the castle lamps.

She wondered if there were other predators in the darkest spaces of the castle. The unlit kitchens by night. The stables. The wine cellars. What might lurk there? Skeletal horses? Or vampire bats? She shuddered.

I'm safe now, she reminded herself.

Next came the drawing of the birds. She used the smallest knife to remove the feet at the knee. And she removed the head, cutting at the base of the neck below the crop. She tossed heads and feet into the bowl of acidulated water. Then she sliced down one side of the spine from the neck, all the way down and then on around the vent. This was the most delicate part of the whole business. She had to be careful not to penetrate beyond the skin and pierce the entrails. Then back up the spine on the other side.

She gripped the spine bone at the neck and pulled up. Beautiful! The guts came with the bone, just as they were supposed to.

She separated the pieces: bone to the bowl of acidulated water; entrails to the bowl of feathers; and heart, liver, and gizzard to the oil cloth. Then she drew the other bird.

She checked over her work. Yes, both carcasses were free and clear of innards, but they could use some rinsing.

She prepared a fourth bowl of water and rinsed the carcasses, hearts, livers, and gizzards. She set them on the cutting board and wiped the oil cloth down, shaking her towel over the bowl of discards. Amazing how clean the towels stayed. Just like her dress, trapped in *kairos*.

Her watch chimed.

Ding, ding, ding, ding, ding, ding. Six o'clock.

Thank goodness her watch and all the castle doors moved, as though some fraction of *chronos* adhered to them. She imagined being trapped all these days in her bedchamber, unable to open the *kairos*-closed door. She'd have died from lack of water. Although it was handy about the linens. She looked down at the skirt of her dress. Two downy feathers clung to its gray folds, but there were no bloodstains, despite Fae's wounds and the clutching of two dead birds to her ribcage.

She shook her head, smiling. Living here was so very strange. And she *didn't* want to stay here. That was the truth. Did she have to?

In her mind's eye, she saw Eulalie nailed to a cross. Milady flayed alive.

Oh! Gods! The images horrified her. This was why she'd agreed to Milady's ritual. The people she loved were in danger. She hadn't been sure that her seclusion was enough to protect them. What if it were not?

She took up the second knife and sliced the first gizzard in half. There was the gravel-filled interior. She picked at the inner membrane with her fingernail and peeled it away with the gravel. She tossed the membrane and gravel, rinsed the gizzard flesh in the rinsing bowl, and peeled the other half. And then did the gizzard from the second bird.

She deboned the carcasses and diced the meat, tossing the bones into the acidulated water. Except for the sturdier wishing bone from the larger bird. Milady had always pulled it with Fae, when they ate roasted fowl. And Fae had made many wishes. She seemed to win the pull. Often. Was that part of being the ideal of fate? Ugh!

She scooped the diced meat into the salty water, then minced the hearts, gizzards, and livers, and added them to the brine.

There. The prep was done!

She dumped the bowl of rinse water and then scrubbed it, the cutting board, the knives, and her hands. Thank goodness for a sink that drained. Pouring fresh water was pain enough. If she'd had to carry and dump the dirty water also, that would have been worse than irritating.

She did need to do something with the bowl of discards. The entrails were beginning to stink already.

But I know just what to do with them.

She ferried the bowl to the garderobe in the medieval wing, dumping the contents through the hole in the seat. The warm evening air blew in. She wished she were outside. And then fled across the enclosed bridge. The castle lamps were lighting, but the medieval wing was lampless and beginning to be gloomy. Who knew what skulked in its shadows?

She'd been so sure that whatever Milady's ritual brought, it couldn't be worse than her empty lonely days, alone in Milady's lodge. Or the interminable lonely nights. And she'd been wrong. Very wrong.

Her seclusion had been a barren, awful thing. That part was right. But the servants had brought her meals and clean clothing. Milady had visited her, however briefly. She hadn't retired to a hermit cave, the fancy of her imagination when Milady first explained the necessity for her withdrawal. She wasn't entirely alone as she was in this castle of *kairos*. She could have changed her mind – if she'd wanted to.

And she'd wanted to.

That was the real reason she'd agreed to Milady's ritual.

I just couldn't stand any more. I had *to have a change, no matter what it was.* So she'd chosen to walk the labyrinth and hold still for Milady's knife. Even when she'd seen in Uncle Aion's face that she would not get what she was hoping for.

Deepest Tragedy Looms

BACK AT THE COOKING BAY, the lamps gave the space a cozy glow, while the sky outside the window deepened.

Had she made a mistake? Agreeing to Milady's ritual?

No, she decided. *I hate this place. I hate everything about it. But I am doing something here.*

Oh, not the feeding and watering of herself. Although that was part of it. She was pushing toward some sort of solution, some sort of resolution. She sensed this was true, even though she didn't understand how or what the hidden progress meant.

She checked the stove for leaks, started the burner, and began heating a small amount of fresh water with a dash of salt.

I'm not giving up on saving my family. But I'm not going to stay here either. I'm going to escape.

Staying in *kairos* would be like withdrawing to Milady's lodge. Not the right choice. Not a true solution to looming danger.

Her breath puffed out in a sigh of relief. She hadn't realized how tense she'd become. How worried she'd been that she would decide staying put was best. How scared she felt that saving her family meant sacrificing herself.

I will find my own solution.

That felt good. Incredibly good.

And for the first time, she had another thought: *why must I do all the saving? why can't they do some of it?*

Why not, indeed?

I've been taking it all on my shoulders, and that's ridiculous and unfair.

She felt a spurt of anger zing through her.

If she could commit to finding her own solution, surely her very talented aunts and uncles and cousins could work on finding theirs as well.

The water in the pot was boiling. She added a little more salt, then scooped the meat out of its brine with the slotted spoon, transferring it to the cooking pot. She turned the burner to low and looked at her watch. Half after six. She'd add the oats in five minutes. She didn't want to overcook the dove meat. That would make it tough.

She'd emptied her canteen only twice today, so she sipped at one of the eight water goblets while she waited for the meat to cook. The steam rising from the pot smelled *delicious*. Savory and rich. If only she'd had a little butter and some herbs. That would have been divine. But just the salted meat would be good. Very good.

She checked her watch. Thirty-four minutes after six. Not quite time, but the meat had lost its redness. She spooned in the soaking oats, quenching the bubble of the broth. She turned up the burner. And started sipping a second glass of water.

The water was warm, not cool the way she liked it. But it was clear and clean and fresh, not stale. Its simple liquidity soothed her mouth and throat.

Her stew started to bubble. She turned the burner down again and checked her watch. Two more minutes.

The patch of sky visible above the courtyard had acquired that deep, deep turquoise of late evening. Fae wished she were out under it, playing tag with her cousins or just wandering through a meadow alone. Anywhere not indoors.

The stew smelled magnificent, an incredible blend of savory meat and fragrant oats.

She turned the fuel regulator closed (to keep the connector hose empty), and the flame went out.

She set her improvised table: napkin, spoon, water goblet, and a small bowl of scraped salt.

So what am I going to do tomorrow?

What was her next step in devising her own solution to being the ideal of fate? Finding the third door, yes. That was necessary, and she would look. But she might not find it. The looking she could control. The finding? Well, she'd find nothing, if she didn't look; but the finding was something she influenced, not something she controlled.

She spooned half the stew from the pot into a bowl. Thank goodness she'd brought a whole stack of bowls up with her. Eating stew off a plate – even a plate with a deep rim – was not the best. Although the oats had thickened it nicely. She admired the deeper hue the meat had given the mixture. She inhaled the aroma, mellow and meaty. Was it cool enough? She took a half spoonful and blew on it.

She tasted it.

Mmm. The rich flavor spread across her tongue, seeming to penetrate straight from her mouth into the rest of her body, assuaging that uncomfortable sensation of gauntness that she experienced instead of hunger.

She carried the bowl to her table and set it down, sat, and spread the napkin over her lap. She sipped her water and took another bite of stew. *Mmm!* There was a chunk of meat in this one, flavorful and tender.

I'm going to survive, she realized. *Even if I'm here for months and months.* Water and oatmeal and meat would sustain her. And she wouldn't be so silly as to do her hunting in the evening, when the doves turned to hawks. High noon would be the safest time. When the doves were merely doves.

She ate all the stew. It was delicious. Every single bite of it.

By the time she finished the washing up and other necessities – including the washing of her own face, carefully avoiding her basilicum-smeared scratches – she'd used an entire cannister of water. Prepping the birds for cooking had used a lot, but she could not regret it. Meat would keep her strong.

She set another batch of oats soaking for her breakfast, and added another dollop of vinegar to the soaking dove bones. She covered both bowls with hand towels, and examined the wishing bone she'd set aside. It was clean of meat. She put it on a plate and set it close to the glass of the window. Extra light would help it dry.

She checked her watch. Quarter to eight o'clock. She wished she'd paid attention to the time last night. When did the lamps dim? Not at eight, surely. That was too early.

I'll be in bed by nine. Before nine. She never, never, *never* wanted to be at the mercy of the goblins in the moonlight. The goblins and the demon.

I'll be mindful of the time tonight. I'll know *what the hands of my watch read when the lamps fail.*

But she had a few more things to do, before she could climb between the sheets.

She shook the fuel bottle she'd been using to cook. The liquid sloshed inside. There was a fair bit of it left; it was still quite full.

But she'd used *some*. Maybe a fifth. That was worrisome. She might have food for months and months, but she didn't have fuel for more than . . . how long?

Let's see . . . she'd been in *kairos* four days, but only started cooking the second day. She'd cooked dinner that second day, breakfast and dinner the third day, and the same today – the fourth day. Five meals. Which meant – she did some quick arithmetic – she had twenty meals left in this bottle and twenty-five in the second bottle. Twenty-two-and-a-half days worth.

I'll figure it out. I've gotten this far.

The sky above the courtyard outside her cooking bay had deepened to velvety dark blue. A sprinkle of stars beckoned from on high.

She set the fuel bottle down and went to clean her teeth. The minty freshness of the tooth powder heartened her. *I'm getting out of here long before a month goes by.* She lifted her chin and smiled at the mirror over the wash basin. Was there a little more color in her cheeks? Her eyes less haunted? At least the cuts from the hawk talons looked healthy under the grease of the basilicum ointment. The narrow scabs were red, but no inflammation reddened the surrounding skin.

She rinsed her mouth and exited the water closet, walking along the lamplit hallway to her bedchamber. The warm cheer of its furnishings welcomed her. She barely noticed the goblin rancor that overhung the space, just as it did all of the castle. Was she becoming inured to it?

She loved the robin's egg blue of the wainscoting and of the striped wallpaper above the panelling. She loved the rosy hue of the red oak floor and the oak furniture – wardrobes, dressing table, writing desk. And she loved the golden gryphons guarding her bed best of all.

Maybe the simplicity of Milady's lodge wasn't her preference after all. It was Milady's. Maybe Fae liked furnishings that were . . . quirkier.

I do, she decided.

She chose a nightgown of cream cotton embroidered with blue daisies. The dove gray frock she'd worn all day was fresh and clean, as usual. Fae herself was even less fresh.

I know what I'm going to do. I'm going to take a bath!

She'd promised herself that last night and recanted. This time she'd go through with it. Tomorrow morning, she would bathe.

She unpinned her hair from its coronet around her head and unbraided it. After one-hundred strokes of the brush – she counted – she plaited it in pigtails.

There. She was ready.

She checked her watch, lying on the dressing table. Half after eight. She was in good time.

The sheets of her bed felt even softer than usual, the mattress, even comfier. She was so tired. *So* tired. She snuggled her left cheek – the uninjured one – into the pillow. *Mmm.* Her eyes felt so heavy.

She was long asleep when the lamps finally dimmed.

And she dreamed.

In her dream, she saw her cousin Eulalie at work in a medieval garderobe. Not the one Fae had found in the daytime, but similar. This one's stone walls and ceiling and seat were red in hue, not gray. Eulalie wore another tunic and pants with cutwork lace at the hems, fashioned from primrose yellow linen. A bulky coil of knotted sheets lay on the floor at her feet. She wielded a chisel, working to enlarge the privy hole.

Chink, chink, chink.

Chink, chink, chink.

If one could laugh in a dream, Fae would have laughed.

So Eulalie was going to escape *kairos* by dangling from a medieval garderobe. How clever of her to seek out a chisel with which to make it feasible. That possibility had never occurred to Fae.

Fae studied the chisel cuts in the stone. It might take Eulalie weeks to make the hole large enough for her to climb through, but she *would* do it.

Yet something was wrong. A sense of foreboding gathered in the small space, the way it can in a dream. Or in a moment of waking intuition. Disaster awaited Eulalie's final chisel stroke.

The dream shifted, and Fae saw her Uncle Leander at work in a large place of arms. Just as Eulalie's garderobe wasn't identical to Fae's, so Uncle Leander's place of arms was different from that in Fae's medieval wing. The stone walls were creamy and speckled, and a crudely carved frieze of prancing horses encircled their upper reaches.

Uncle Leander was assembling a trebuchet, a monstrous medieval machine to fling chunks of rock with great force. He'd already collected a pile of suitable missiles in one corner, and his trebuchet was nearly done.

Fae's sense of looming disaster grew stronger. When her uncle battered the exterior wall down with his creation, what would enter through the gap?

Nothing good.

Her dream shifted a third time to show her the interior of a ruined tower. It was square, with lofty walls of rough stone blocks. A fragment of stair hung far above, and the roof was missing altogether. Fae's cousin Theophane clung to the rocks halfway up, positioned near a corner. A massive coil of rope – with grappling hooks attached – was secured to Theophane's back. When she reached that crumbling walltop, she'd have a prudent way down the outside.

Fae felt dizzy watching her. If Theophane slipped, there was no one belaying her. She would fall to her death.

But . . . this was Theophane, the athletic prodigy. No, Theophane would not fall.

Why did Fae feel so uneasy?

On that walltop, when Theophane's passage over it opened some barrier, doom would arrive.

Fae's dream shifted yet again.

The scene unfolded in a vast underground space with natural cavern walls of unshaped granite, and a low, rugged vault overhead. Somewhere beneath this castle's deepest foundations. A river of translucent green water emerged from a low, natural arch to flow along one wall and then exited through a much smaller arch on the other side of the grotto.

Fae's Uncle Nathanos – he of the curly gray hair and beard, who loved the sea – stood naked and waist-deep in the river near the exit arch. The muscles of his powerful torso and corded arms flexed as he lifted a huge block of stone into place, the beginnings of a dam to turn the river into a lake.

Fae shivered. What would happen when that lake pressed and pressed against that foundation wall? What would enter when that wall came tumbling down?

Her dream shifted again.

Aunt Pallas, garbed in a spring green gown of the draping Grecian style she favored, was watering a massive clump of bamboo. The plant grew from a stone trough, one in a long row of bamboos lining the outside wall of a conservatory. Their roots already bulged the inner stone of the trough. What were they doing to the outer wall? And what would happen when those strong, probing roots tore it apart?

Catastrophe. Calamity. The doom of Clan Theosis.

Fae's dream flowed onward, showing her cousin after cousin, aunt after aunt, and uncle after uncle – each of them engineering escape, each of them provoking deepest tragedy.

Why had the oracle named Fae the bane of the Theosians?

Each and every one of her kin courted disaster.

FIFTH

What Is the Next Right Thing?

⚘

FAE JERKED AWAKE, sweaty and gasping, the distress of her nightmare still gripping her.

It was morning. Early morning, with cool light streaming in, and the pale pink sky of dawn visible outside the windows. The red oak of the room's floor and furnishings showed a less rosy hue under the thin sunlight, and the robin's egg blue on the walls lost some of its warm brightness.

Fae huddled the sheets and blanket and quilt up over her shoulders to her chin, soft and cozy.

She wasn't really cold, but she felt chilled nonetheless.

She scrutinized the merry suns in the cornice frieze. Were they less merry without either strong daylight or cheerful lamplight illuminating them? Did the cloud castle on the ceiling also display a less welcoming aspect?

I didn't waken in the night. Why, I wonder?

She glanced up at the golden gryphons guarding her bed. They shone, fierce and resplendent as always, undimmed by the weaker light.

She pondered her dream. Eulalie and Uncle Leander trapped in *kairos* like herself and working toward freedom like Fae was.

Theophane and Uncle Nathanos and Aunt Pallas doing the same. All of her family using their gifts and inclinations to attack the castle that imprisoned them.

A short laugh puffed out between Fae's lips.

Why was I ever worried about them? They're far more resourceful than I.

And yet … she was worried. Her dream felt true. It was more than the interpretations her sleeping mind attached to her daytime experiences. In a hundred other pockets of *kairos*, her relatives engineered their escapes. And disaster waited on their success. Unspecified disaster, but disaster nonetheless. Did it wait on hers as well?

No. But why? She worked toward escape as assiduously as they. Wouldn't the same outcome prevail?

She knew it would not. Felt it deep in her bones. But why?

Because they attack the physical castle, while I attack its puzzle.

Was that true? Hadn't she merely solved the puzzle of who she was and where she came from? How was that solving the *castle's* puzzle?

Because solving her own puzzle *was* the castle's puzzle.

Yes! Like the ringing of a gong, the rightness of that rang true.

Her cousins – and aunts and uncles – all sought exterior answers. They'd framed the problem logically and were constructing logical, and physical, solutions. Fae had done the same when she smashed a castle window with that paperweight and failed to achieve anything.

Would her kin fail similarly?

She thought not.

They didn't walk the labyrinth. I did. Their prisons are less impervious than mine. And . . . if I escape, so will they.

Were they truly imprisoned? Or was Fae's dream just a dream, with no bearing in reality?

She shook her head. The pillowcase under her rustled.

No. Milady was the ideal of prophecy. She would not prophesy falsely. It was Aion who was the ideal of time.

A sudden sour certainty flooded Fae's belly.

Aion, who had conspired with Milady in the rose garden. Aion, who had presided over Milady's ritual sacrifice of Fae in the chapel. At the very center of the labyrinth.

Aion knew!

Fae bounced upright, angry.

He knew. That was the origin of the look on his face during the chapel ritual. *He* had destined Fae and all her kin to be imprisoned in *kairos.* Her dream was more than a dream. Fae and Eulalie and Uncle Leander and Theophane and all the rest were trapped. Even Milady. Fae had seen her also, attempting an oracular trance to escape. But Aion . . . was *he* entangled?

No, she thought not. Fae had not seen him in any of the many scenes of her dreaming. He went free, to fulfill whatever his aim might be.

I must get free.

Disaster loomed if she didn't. Disaster loomed if any of her family managed it first. Victory arrived only on Fae's escape, if she could tread the maze to its exit. And the key to the maze relied on intuition.

I'm getting up!

The light had strengthened, acquired a more golden hue. The sun was up, and the sky blue. Her bedchamber wore its familiar, merry aspect. Beneath it, the subtle biting of the hidden goblins took on a familiarity as well. *Aion.* Of course, Aion. The goblin contempt bore Aion's supercilious character.

Gah! She should have recognized it days ago. Or at least the moment she remembered who she was in the portrait gallery. But she hadn't.

I know my enemy now.

Unless, just as Aion pulled Milady's strings, there was yet another puppetmaster behind Aion.

Fae yanked her covers back and sprang out of bed.

Mulling and pondering would only go so far. It was time for action.

✑

She wound her watch. Half after seven o'clock.

She brushed her hair afresh, braided it in a single plait, and wound it around her head in a coronet. She doffed her nightgown, but dressed only in undergarments: camisole and pantalettes.

I'm going to bathe, as I promised myself I would.

Really? Shouldn't she be hunting that third small, splintery door? Sleuthing to discover the solution to the castle's maze?

Yes, she should.

That was the logical answer. Just as Theophane's tower-climbing and Uncle Leander's trebuchet were logical. And would bring only disaster.

Intuition, she reminded her critical inner voice. *The logical question isn't the right question. And the logical answer is no answer at all.*

Intuition had guided her to the first godmother door. And the second. But getting free of *kairos* wasn't so simple as opening a door. Or even finding one. From the moment she'd awakened on her first morning in *kairos,* she'd been engaged in a complicated dance of gathering . . . what had she been gathering?

Most of all she'd been reclaiming herself. Her memories. Her good cheer. Her determination.

But the food and water she'd found were equally important. And the godmother doors.

No one element was supreme over all the others. She needed the whole dance, not just a step here or a pirouette there.

Right now this moment, she wanted to find the third godmother door. And she *did* need to find it. She was sure of that. But intuition whispered that a bath must come first. Perhaps the third door was unfindable without cleanliness. Or perhaps it could not be opened. Or perhaps some other condition could not be met that was necessary for her release.

She could recollect all too well her very first step through her bedchamber door into the hall. Intuition had directed her toward the darker end of the hall. Where – unbeknownst to her then – the kitchens lay.

The dark had worried her.

She'd turned away from it. And ended up in the demonic wing.

She would not make that mistake again.

Despite the fiber of her will pushing her toward action, she would bathe. Evidently, in this moment now, bathing *was* action. At least, it was the choice she needed to make.

Fae sighed.

Very well. No sleuthing. No searching. No hunting. Not this morning.

She smiled at herself in the mirror. *C'mon, Fae! Was that so hard?*

Well, it was hard. But she was learning.

In the mirror, the cuts on her cheek looked much better, healing. *Good.*

She got up from the stool. Time to get on with it. The sooner she bathed, the sooner she could do whatever came next after that.

Emerging from her bedchamber, she found the hallway in shadowy gloom. It didn't possess the eastern windows that her room did. She drank all five goblets of water that remained from yesterday. *Mmm*. Lukewarm, yes. But clean and liquid and *good*.

She visited the water closet to wash her face, reapply basilicum ointment, and use the commode. The glow of its happy, lemon-yellow panelling encouraged her to replace her impatience with enthusiasm.

I'm the cheerful one, she reminded herself.

She cooked breakfast – oatmeal, as always – and ate it. *Mmm*. Fragrant and substantial and *good*. She couldn't help wishing she had butter. Or honey. Or both! But the oatmeal was ever so much better than nothing at all. Even though she felt no hunger, the strange, thin, gaunt sensation that had come after a day and a half without food – her first interval in *kairos* – had been unpleasant. Alarming.

She filled and drank two more glasses of water. Then she filled the other six goblets and her canteen. She washed up, and set another bowl of oatmeal soaking for tonight's dinner. She returned to her room to tie the aqua ribbon around her wrist. She mustn't forget about drinking enough water.

Her physical wellbeing was part of the puzzle she was solving.

Now. That bath.

She trotted to the orangery in the west part of the castle and rummaged in the gardner's niche there. A huge, oval trough of galvanized tin used for mixing compost and soil would serve as her bathing tub. The coil of rubber hose would transfer water from the birdbath in the upstairs conservatory into the tub; she used the branch lopers to snip off a six-foot length. And a bucket might be handy for emptying the tub when she was done.

Right this moment, she couldn't imagine being clean. She could smell her unwashed state without even trying. She needed to soak and soak and soak, before she'd be really fresh. Plus scrubbing with the handsoap from the water closet.

She noticed a burlap bag of potting soil in one corner. The loamy smell of it reminded her of being in the woods after a spring rain – fresh and fertile. *I bet my Aunt Pallas discovered bags and bags of this stuff in her castle. That's how she started the forest of bamboo she was growing.*

Recollecting her dream restarted the feather of anxiety in her belly.

Hurry up, Fae.

She put her shortened hose and the bucket into her tub, then started dragging it behind her, the handle at one end grasped in her fingers.

It was light, but the far end scraped along the stone floors like fingernails on a chalkboard. And it clanged as she towed it up the first flight of stairs.

Clang, clang, clang.

Then came another interval of fingernail scraping through a hallway. And then another flight of stairs.

Clang, clang, clang.

And then yet more hallways.

In the conservatory, she set the tub near the birdbath and took the bucket out of it. She arranged the hose, coiling it to fit in the birdbath and immersing it entirely. Moving quickly, she held one end under the water while pulling the other over the lip of the basin to fall into her bathing tub. Would it work? The way Uncle Leander had described this little bit of practical genius? Siphon, he called it.

Fae waited a moment.

No water flowed.

✎

Her shoulders slumped. She wanted a bath, definitely. But even more importantly, she had to *have* a bath. Preferably without having to fill the tub ewerful by ewerful. That was the next right thing.

She studied the hose. It seemed so improbable that water would flow from the opening of the hose uphill to where the hose passed over the rim of the birdbath. But Uncle Leander had said it would. And she believed Uncle Leander on anything mechanical.

Wait a minute . . .

She'd skipped a step, hadn't she?

What, what, what . . . ?

Ah! She had it.

She coiled the hose under the water again. Bubbles rose, the air leaving the interior of the hose. That part of the procedure was right. She spread the palm of her hand flat against one end of the hose, and then gripped with her fingers to press the rubber edges firmly against her skin. She had to keep that end sealed. And she had to keep the other end underwater while uncoiling the hose enough to get the sealed end into her bathing tub and below the water level of the birdbath.

It felt like she needed at least three hands, maybe four.

But she managed it.

Crouching – holding her breath – and holding the upper end of the hose submerged, she released the lower end.

Water spouted from it into the tub.

"Yay! Uncle Leander was right!"

Were these the first words she'd spoken aloud? Her voice sounded strange, but she wanted to get up and dance her triumph. Except she needed to keep her hand on the upper end of the hose. She could feel that it would fall out of the birdbath, if she let it go.

Her watch, pinned to the waist of her camisole, chimed.

Ding, ding, ding, ding, ding, ding, ding, ding, ding. Nine o'clock.

Holding the hose, she stood cautiously. Would the birdbath remain full under this more extreme draining of its contents? It seemed so.

The tub took a while to fill. A good ten minutes, in fact.

Fae wanted to throw her undergarments off and leap in the moment it was ready. All that water awaiting her looked *so* good! But she wasn't quite ready. She'd found bath towels and wash cloths, along with a basket full of soap bars, in an upstairs linen closet, but she hadn't yet brought them to the conservatory.

And there was one other problem.

She needed her bath, but she also wanted to start simmering the dove bones to make a broth in which to cook the oatmeal for her dinner. She didn't think she should leave the stove burning unsupervised, at least not at first.

Well . . . there was a fix for that.

With one longing glance at her full-to-the-brim tub, she departed to gather more supplies: the bath towels, wash cloths, and soap (the obvious); and the camp stove, stew pot, and bowl of soaking dove bones (completely unrelated and unobvious). On a second thought, she dragged one of the flower stands – one with two shelves – up to the conservatory as well. If her bath sloshed, she wouldn't want to douse a floor-situated stove burner.

She set her auxiliary kitchen near the wall of the conservatory, but not too near. The line of drain tiles circled the entire space, and she needed the flower stand to sit straight, without a leg tipping into the drain openings.

She poured the bones and their soak water into the stock pot and added more water. She started the burner going, placed the stock pot on it, and covered it. Would the burner take the weight of so much water? It was such a delicate, spidery-looking thing. But sturdy. Well constructed. She'd felt the thin supports give a little as she settled the pot on them, but they held.

She set her bath towels on the lower shelf.

Then she doffed her camisole and pantalettes and climbed into the bath.

It was cool, like the soothing water of her dreams, and refreshing. She sank down in the water, letting it cover her shoulders. *Mmm.* This was bliss. This was perfection. This was as good as she'd hoped it would be.

Although she couldn't still her niggling desire to be up and doing.

Somehow, walking felt like it might accomplish something. Bathing felt . . . self indulgent and lazy.

C'mon, Fae. Getting clean is just as much of an accomplishment as walking from point A to point B. Which was true. It even *felt* true. It was just that moving felt better than being still when she was anxious. And she *was* anxious. Anxious that Uncle Leander might let fly with his trebuchet while she lounged in her bath.

Stop it, she told herself.

When she saw steam puffing out from under the lid of her stock pot, she got out – dripping. Her skin pricked up in goosebumps as the water evaporated off her in the warm air, but she didn't feel chilled, in spite of the cooling sensation. She felt alive. Intensely here. *Real.* It felt good.

Maybe she was accepting that this was what she had to be doing here and now.

She turned the stove burner down as low as it would go without extinguishing altogether and removed the pot lid. She skimmed the froth forming on the surface of the broth. Those were impurities that needed to be removed. She dumped them into the now empty soaking bowl. Then she replaced the lid on the pot, aslant to allow a small vent, and climbed back into her bath.

Mmm. It was just as glorious as when she'd immersed herself the first time.

She kept an eye on the stock pot. It looked like she'd gotten the burner heat just right, and the lid positioned just right. Steam rose gently through the vent, but the pot did not boil over. She felt some of her worries ebbing.

Be here now, Fae.

With a sigh of surrender, she gave herself entirely to enjoyment of her bath.

Another vivid reliving of memory overtook her.

Sacred Waters

◈

IN HER MEMORY, she was very young. Five? Six? She stood naked and waist-deep in flowing, bubbling water amidst a grove of green, leafy maples and hickories. The water was silky smooth and cool. It bubbled out from beneath several large craggy boulders in the spring, stirring bright pebbles and sand along the bottom.

Fae's cousins shrieked and splashed nearer the center of the spring, ducking one another in a game. Their nurse sat on the mossy bank, smiling fondly. Behind Nurse, Milady stood next to the peeling white bark of a lone sycamore trunk.

"Immerse yourself, Moira," instructed Milady. "Bathe your face, then plunge down, all the way under."

But little Fae – "Moira" – paid her no heed.

The murmur of the rushing waters and the rustle of the breeze-stirred tree leaves enchanted her senses. Beneath her feet, the sparkle of the pebbles – cream and rose and glinting ecru in the dappled light – drew her gaze. The fresh scent of the air just above the moving water – so clean and clear – beguiled her nose. She moved to a deeper spot in the spring and bent her head to taste the water. Cool and faintly sweet. *Mmm.* A stray beam of sunlight slipped through the tree canopy and dazzled her eyes. The gentle current pushed against her shins.

Milady's instruction faded into insignificance, overlain by the marvel that was the Achillean Springs.

Fae raised her arms and lifted her knees, dipping down, immersing herself wholly, eager to feel the caress of the waters all over her. Like silk, like flower petals, like gentle rain. All those and more.

Underwater, someone clasped her hand and pulled her to the surface. Theophane, also young, maybe eight. Her face glowed with excitement. "C'mon, Fae! You can swim! Come play!" And she dragged Fae into the clump of her cousins where the water was too deep to permit standing.

Fae swirled her hands and circled her feet, staying afloat and enjoying the buoyant sensation. She didn't really listen as Maia – the oldest of them – explained the rules. The springs were too enticing.

Then her cousins were diving away and calling and laughing. Fae joined them, enthralled by the rapture of quick movement through quiet ripples. It was like bathing in liquid light. She splashed and dove and swam. The rules of her cousins' game didn't seem to matter much. The game was just an excuse to soar through the water and enjoy. It was glorious.

The white stone walls of the conservatory, light flooding down from the glass panes over head, pulled her awareness out of memory.

Returning to herself in a compost tub next to a birdbath wasn't as subduing as she expected. She could not curvette like a young porpoise, true, but this water felt just as marvelous. Like liquid light, indeed.

If only the glass of the conservatory roof did not divide her from the blue, blue sky and its breezes. If only Aion's malice – the true origin of the goblin nipping – did not fill this space.

So Milady really had bathed Fae in the Achillean Springs. And changed her thereby.

Fae could remember it now: the greater strength in her body, its increased resilience to bumps and bruises, her heightened vigor. Each time she came out of the springs, she felt different, more able. More like her cousins.

If she were really the daughter of Milady's sister – Themis – should she have been so profoundly affected? Had her cousins, the offspring of Theosians for sure, felt the same?

Fae wondered.

When she'd stumbled upon the portrait gallery during her third day in *kairos* and remembered who she was, after two days without such knowledge, it had felt wonderful. Like she'd retrieved it all. Like all of her memory lay open to her probing, limited only by the normal haziness and small forgettings brought by the passage of time.

But she'd not recollected her first experience of the Achillean Springs. No mere passage of time should obscure such a memory. It gleamed bright and vivid now, a beacon undimmed. Yet, before this moment, she'd only known that she *had* bathed in the springs, known without recollecting. There were pieces of herself, of her identity, still missing. She could no longer feel their absence, but she *hadn't* gotten everything back.

With that conclusion, another memory enfolded her.

She was much younger, too young to walk. She lay wrapped in blankets on someone's lap. The space around her was blurry and dim, lit by flickering golden light, perhaps the flames of a low fire in a hearth?

Fae's concentration was all for the immediate, focused on things close by. The soft warmness of her beige wrappings. The gentle firmness under her. The smell of damp wool. And the murmur of motherly humming just above and behind.

"Lullalay, lullalay, lullalay, my sweeting. Lullay, lullay, lullay."
Her voice was low and sweet, filled with love. Her hands, strong and
skillful and tender, lifted Fae's tiny arm from the nest of blankets and
stroked it with a warm damp cloth.

"Lullalay, lullalay."

She dried Fae's arm and hand, and then enfolded them again in
the coverings.

"Lullalay, sweet sweeting."

She washed the other arm and hand, recovered them.

"Lullay, lullay."

She washed Fae's head and face, then her shoulders.

Fae was being bathed, bit by bit, carefully, so as not to chill her or
scare her.

This woman loved her very much.

Mother, thought Fae muzzily. Was she Themis? Or Tethys? Or
someone else altogether?

The skin on the careful large hands was work roughened, but the
woman was very, very gentle.

Mother. This was Mother. No nurse would care so much.

Strong sunlight in Fae's eyes brought her back to the conservatory.
The sun had risen above the rim of the conservatory wall to dazzle
her. She blinked and squinted. She lifted her hands out of the water.
The pads of her fingertips were wrinkled with their long soaking. It
was time to apply some soap.

Not to her hair. She'd pinned it up for a reason. It didn't need
washing more than once a week, and she didn't want to get it
unnecessarily wet.

She climbed out of the tub, dripping on the tile floor and shivering slightly. The warmth of the sunlight was welcome after the cool of her bath. She splashed her face, then worked up a lather with the bar of soap between her hands. It smelt faintly of lavender and felt creamily smooth on her palms. She applied the lather to her brow, nose, cheeks, and chin, working in small circles. She could hear Milady's instructions in memory: "Use the gentlest of pressure and never stroke downward, child. A lady doesn't want to encourage wrinkles."

That made Fae smile.

Milady always knew the right way to do something, and she loved telling her friends and family the proper method and why. Aunt Sariah and Aunt Kira often exchanged glances of faint exasperation when Milady expounded. But they also took her advice. As annoying as Milady's tendency to instruct might be, she was usually right.

Fae had always taken Milady's bossing as the way her godmother showed caring. Milady didn't hug and kiss or utter caressing endearments. She certainly never *said* she cared. But year after year, she'd shared her ways of living and doing with Fae.

Had it all been so that Fae was firmly under her thumb when the crisis came?

Fae scooped up another double handful of water from her bath and rinsed her face, letting the soapy water spatter on the floor. She wanted to keep the bath water clear for her final all-over rinse.

She picked up the bar of soap from the floor and started lathering the rest of her. The lavender scent of the soap rose around her, and the creamy lather felt light and soft on her skin. The soap itself was slippery, slippery, slippery. She dropped it twice. *I bet it's pure Castile.*

Milady said that any soap but Castile was far too drying to use for anything but household cleaning tasks.

So had Milady spent all those years of effort and attention on Fae merely to control her?

Or had she really cared about her adopted daughter?

I'll have to ask her when I see her next. That was the only way to know for sure. Fae would ask. And when Milady answered, Fae would study Milady's face. The true answer wouldn't be in Milady's words. It would rest in Milady's eyes.

The pondering of whether she were loved ought to hurt, but it didn't. Fae felt curiously free, as though the truth would heal any wounds when she learned it.

I won't be caught in kairos *forever.* Fae was sure of that, in this moment now, as she bathed. *I will find or create my freedom, and when I do I'll return to* chronos *and ask Milady my question.*

Fae stood covered in lather, foamy and white, as though the lather were a garment.

She looked dubiously at her bath tub. If she simply climbed in, the suds would overwhelm the clarity of the water too quickly. *I know. I knew that bucket would come in handy.* She grabbed the bucket and filled it. Stepping away from the tub and the birdbath, she poured it over her shoulders and back. The water sluiced down, carrying the soapy lather with it to the floor, then flowing across the mosaic pattern toward the drain tiles near the wall.

Fae rinsed with another bucketful and then climbed back into the tub. Her clean body felt wonderful, buoyed up and supported by the water. *I did it! I bathed!* Each small victory in this place felt significant. As though she were the Count of Monte Cristo, scraping stone with a pot handle to escape.

The final soak in the bath removed the last traces of soap from Fae's skin, and she emerged, glistening in the sunlight flooding down. She dried off with a bath towel, then wrapped it around her, fluffy and warm.

She checked her stock pot.

The liquid simmered gently, giving off a savory, meaty aroma. The level was a little lower in the pot, but not a lot.

I bet I could leave it to simmer while I search for the third door.

It wouldn't boil over. It wouldn't boil dry, unless she left it overnight; which she wouldn't. And the conservatory was all tile and stone. Nothing to catch fire, if the unthinkable should happen: a bird crashing through the glass roof and knocking the burner over, or something like that.

Yes, she would seek that door.

What about the tub? Should she leave it full, ready for another bath?

The water held only a trace of soap scum, but it wasn't clear the way the water in the birdbath was. She doubted *kairos* would keep it clean, since it had not been already full when dragged into timelessness.

Fae sighed. Oh, well. Filling it really hadn't been that hard. And she could use the same shortcut for emptying it.

The siphon worked well when she placed one end of the hose in the tub and the other end on the floor, pointed toward the line of drain tiles. It was like magic, watching the water level drop in the tub, while it flowed through the hose and then on across the floor. When only a few inches of water remained in the tub, Fae simply tipped it on its side to empty it. Clang. And the water rushed out, a wide liquid sheet, running down to the drains. Easy peasy.

She smiled.

There.

She collected her undergarments, took one last look at the well-behaved stock pot, and returned to her bedchamber. It was overly warm from the sun shining all morning through its windows. Was Aion's malice stronger here than elsewhere?

Impatient to get going, Fae dithered in front of the wardrobe. She was tired of wearing dresses. She'd doffed Milady's taste in furnishings, deciding she preferred quirkiness to simplicity. Maybe she could also discard Milady's choice for Fae's garb. But dresses were all her room's wardrobes offered: ball gowns in one, morning dresses in this one.

I'll check the contents of some of the other bedchambers today. And wear not-a-dress tomorrow.

She chose a gown of pale yellow – so pale, it was almost cream – with small white flowers embroidered all over it. The dress had the same scoop neck and back lacing of the gray one she'd worn yesterday. She liked the bohemian style better than the more tailored pintucks and collars of her earlier choices.

She glanced down at her bare feet.

Milady herself wore shoes, elegant velvet slippers or trim suede ankle boots. But she'd never said a word about Fae's preference for going shoeless. That was curious. Milady had opinions – and instructions – for nearly everything else. Why nothing about shoes? Or the lack thereof?

Fae's watch chimed as she pinned it to her dress waist.

Ding, ding, ding, ding, ding, ding, ding, ding, ding, ding, ding. Eleven o'clock.

She settled her canteen on one shoulder, her bow and quiver of arrows on the other. She checked her wrist. There was the aqua ribbon, somewhat damp and bedraggled. She hadn't removed it for her bath.

She stepped through her bedchamber's door, pausing in the small vestibule between it and the hallway. Where to? The third door? That had been her stated aim.

No. I'll seek what is important, what matters most. The final piece of the puzzle that will set me free.

The urgency she'd wrestled down earlier surged again. She needed her freedom now, now, *now*. But panic and rushing wouldn't procure it. She couldn't let urgency overwhelm her.

Easier said then done, but if she couldn't *feel* calm – and she couldn't – she'd pretend to be so.

She closed her eyes and swung around in a slow circle.

Into the Darkness without a Light

⚶

WHEN SHE OPENED her eyes, she saw the coffered wall of the vestibule right at the end of her small nose. She laughed. Evidently she hadn't turned exactly in place. Lucky she hadn't bumped that little nose before she stopped.

She headed for the castle kitchens. Logically, it made no sense, but it *felt* right. Hurray for intuition!

The kitchens were cavernous as usual, dimly lit from the arched windows near the low, vaulted ceiling. Fae revisited the side door with its shallow steps down from the kitchen floor and its bricked in doorway.

The milk cannisters were gone from their shelf, all six congregating in Fae's cooking bay, but three of the shoulder yokes remained on the other wall.

There was nothing here of further use. And yet . . . there was something. Fae closed her eyes and put her fingertips to the wall beneath the lowest hanging shoulder yoke. She felt for the first step with her foot, found it, and stepped up, eyes still shut. Then the next step. And the third.

The wall plaster was rough under her touch. And there was the corner. Fae followed it, walking without seeing, trusting the level evenness of the floor, and trusting the guidance of her fingertips.

Her hand passed across one of the plank cellar doors with its iron straps and hinges, then another.

The light through her eyelids grew abruptly dimmer.

She opened her eyes.

She was standing behind one of the massive piers that supported the low, vaulted ceiling. On the other side of her, two shallow steps led down to a narrow passageway disappearing into darkness.

She peeked around the pier. The kitchens were still there with all their countertops, tables, cabinets, hanging pots, and unused cookware.

She looked down the dark passageway.

That was where she had to go.

She pondered fetching a candlestick from somewhere.

No. I need to go into the darkness without light.

She bit her lip.

Then the image of the chapel by candlelight came to her.

Light was not always safety. She would take her own strength as her safety. Not a candle.

I can always turn back, if it gets too dangerous. Or I get too scared.

Heart beating fast, she moved to the steps and down them, her fingers tracing the wall. The plaster ended after just a few feet, giving way to rough rock, like that of a natural cave, and then to bare earth. She could feel the feathery ends of roots protruding from the cold, dry, packed soil.

The smooth stone flooring lasted a little longer. Then that too gave way to packed earth.

She could see nothing. The cool smell of earth surrounded her. The passage turned and twisted, but stayed level.

She ought to be scared, but she wasn't. The pounding of her heart was not fear, but excitement.

She kept walking, feeling the compacted earth beneath her feet and the feathery root tips against her fingertips. She went on, and the absolute blackness around her softened, then turned to gray. There was light ahead.

The floor transitioned to stone, then the walls. She could see. She was walking through a passage of gray-grained natural granite. Then the rough rock changed to smooth paving and dressed stone walls. The stone walls acquired a plaster finish. She turned one last corner and emerged in a small hexagonal chamber. A dark wood bench ran around it. A faceted crystal dome roofed it. Fae could see the blue sky and the sun, repeated in the facets the way a kaleidoscope repeated its colored disks into a pattern. The wall to Fae's right held a door. A small arched door of splintery wood with a tarnished bronze knob and escutcheon plate.

The third door.

Fae sat on the bench opposite the door – splashed in sunlight – and studied it. It looked just like the other two.

I will open this door and pass through it.

Somehow.

But not immediately. Without even testing it, she knew this door was locked. And that opening it – and the other two – was necessary to her freedom.

The beating of her heart slowed. Like the spaces adjacent to the other two doors, this one was free of Aion's malice. She relaxed against the rough plaster behind her and breathed. Her bow dug into her shoulderblade. She felt happy. Finding this third door was key.

She could feel the memory associated with this door pressing to overtake her.

She resisted it.

One more time through Milady charging her to guard this door unopened felt . . . unnecessary. Uncalled for. Unwelcome.

I won't.

She knew what Milady had said in that long-ago performance of *The Race of Atalanta*. She knew what the painted theatrical door had looked like: bearing a rendition of her cousin Calanthe, with her short, spiky red braids, and costumed in golden armor. Fae didn't need to relive the scene. Didn't want to.

With her refusal came the certainty that she must escape soon. Before her aunts and uncles and cousins broke open the bubbles of *kairos* holding them and allowed the unmaking of chaos to flood in.

She had dreamed truly last night. The danger was real. She had limited time.

Reluctantly, she left the pocket of peacefulness in the pavilion around the third door.

Aion's malicious nipping grew ever stronger as she moved through the darkness of the twisting passageway. It reached its full intensity when she emerged into the barren castle kitchens. She squared her shoulders. *I am used to this. I can ignore it.* And she could. But it was wearing. Everything about this castle in *kairos* was wearing.

She scanned the shadowy space with its dim gleams of indirect light.

I'm done here. Her next "important thing" – whatever it was – lay elsewhere.

The aqua ribbon on her wrist teased her eye.

Blast! Had she drunk any water this morning? Any water at all?

She cast her thoughts back. During her bath, she had been so caught up in the pleasure of buoyancy and getting clean, so immersed in the water on her outsides, that she'd forgotten about water on her insides. And then she'd been so pleased with her determination to follow her intuition – straight to the third door, as it chanced – that she'd forgotten everything else. Had she even remembered to soak oats for her supper? She'd have to check. How could she? How could she forget the most basic and most important action of all: drinking water.

She'd learned that lesson on her first day in *kairos*.

And forgotten it several times since, most completely today.

All her hatred for the castle rushed back. Its isolation – *her* isolation – hurt her heart. Aion's sniping hatred – present in every space except around the three godmother doors – gave her cramp of the soul. And the unnatural absence of hunger and thirst – and who knew what other necessary physical prompts – endangered her life and health. She hated this place. Hated it. Hated it. *Hated* it!

She stamped her foot, hearing its muffled thump against the stone paving, feeling the coolness of the floor against her bare sole, feeling the impact of her stamp traveling up her leg bones.

Be sensible, Fae, she told herself.

She didn't feel sensible. She felt angry. Like she couldn't take one more iota of this dreadful place.

But she uncapped her canteen and started drinking. The liquid on her lips – dry lips – felt lovely, and even lovelier in her mouth, on her throat. She drained the entire canteen, savoring the moisture returning to her body.

There. That was better. Much better.

Three sieves hanging on hooks drew her attention.

I'll need a sieve to remove the bones from my broth.

She lifted all three down and nested them, then started toward her cooking bay. Had she started her supper oats soaking? Or had she forgotten? Fae hurried upstairs.

She'd not forgotten.

The bowl full of oats and water and a dollop of vinegar sat on her plant stand "counter," covered and right where she'd left it. The relief of it – that she'd not been completely forgetful and irresponsible – passed through her body like a wave.

She refilled her canteen and saw the two empty water glasses beside the six full ones. *That's right!* She'd drunk five glasses of water remaining from yesterday, and then two fresh ones with her breakfast. She'd not been so very irresponsible after all.

But she had forgotten about drinking water for a considerable interval. From nine o'clock to – she checked her watch – to half after one. Four and a half hours. It was not so much the four hours that worried her. It was the forgetting. This time it was merely four hours. But the next time she was absorbed in something of importance, how long might her forgetting last then? And if she could forget water, could she also forget other things? The memories she'd been retrieving so slowly?

Did *kairos* continuously erode the things of *chronos*? Or did it merely – ha! *merely!* – do so all at once, when her body had entered *kairos*?

No doubt Aion could answer that question. Fae could not.

She trotted up to the conservatory to check her stock pot.

There it was, sitting trimly on the low-burning camp stove, steam rising gently from the vent between the lid and the pot. The savory aroma was stronger, more concentrated, deliciously rich. *Mmm.* Supper would be yummy.

She surveyed the conservatory.

The tub still lay on its side, but it and the black and white mosaic floor were bone dry, all moisture evaporated by the sun shining through the glass panes above.

She smiled and did a quick dance step.

Ha! She wasn't doing so badly. She'd made mistakes, yes. But she'd fixed them. Milady might think you had to be perfect, but Milady was wrong.

The thought gave her pause. And sparked a new idea.

Did Milady really strive for perfection? Fae thought about all Milady's directions and instructions and cautions. Yes, Milady hated mistakes. Poor Milady.

How odd it felt to be pitying Milady. Perfect Milady. Controlled Milady. Hemmed in Milady.

Had Milady betrayed Fae?

Or had Milady been betrayed?

Fae shook her head, closed her eyes, and spun in place. A little more vigorously than when she'd stood in the vestibule of her bedchamber. She had a good deal more room here.

It felt good: the spinning.

She laughed and spun again; then stopped. *Whoa!* She was dizzy!

She waited for the tipping sensation to subside, then inched forward a step. Stopped. What if she ran into her stock pot? Knocked it over? Burned herself?

Okay. Intuition *and* prudence. She let her eyelids open the tiniest crack, just enough to see the mosaic floor, no more.

She moved forward. There was the tub on its side. She walked around it.

And now she was passing out one of the three doors. Which one, she didn't know.

She let her eyelids fall closed all the way and reached out her arm to brush the wall with her fingertips. The marble was cool and oh-so-smooth. Its surface dipped into shallow niches as she walked, raised itself in corrugated pilasters, and turned at precise corners.

She went on. And on again.

The light coming through her closed eyelids dimmed. Had she left the many-windowed corridor outside the conservatory?

She took three more steps and opened her eyes.

She'd turned down a short passageway without windows. Behind her lay the light-filled hall. Ahead of her in the passageway was an arched door of marble, similar to the one downstairs that entered the shattered chapel with the hawk doves. This door was smaller and in good repair. Delicately carved marble moldings, like lace, fringed the passage and framed the door.

Fae took her bow from her shoulder and nocked an arrow.

She'd learned from the hawk doves that the castle could deliver immediate and acute dangers as well as the longterm insidious ones.

The door opened in.

She pushed on it with her upper back, bow and arrow ready to be raised, aimed, and fired.

The door was heavy. It moved easily on its hidden hinges, but slowly, ponderously.

The instant the opening was large enough, Fae stepped through it and whirled, raising her bow.

Her eyes darted.

Where was the target? Where was the enemy? From where did danger approach?

✑

Be Who You Are

⁂

THIS CHAPEL WAS SMALL and intimate, a confection of lacy marble and stained glass depicting floral garden borders. It must lie on the eastern side of the castle, because the afternoon sun did not slant through the gold and rose and spring green of the windows. The light gleamed mild and dim.

Half a dozen marble pews filled the space between the door and the altar table. Blue velvet cushions softened their seats. Runner carpeting – floral wool to match the windows: rose and spring green and dusty blue – covered the marble floor at the side aisles. An embroidered tapestry – more flowers – draped across the marble altar, its curving legs unconcealed, two tall candles in gold sticks atop its flat surface.

The portrait of a golden-haired woman adorned the wall beyond the altar.

Fae lowered her bow and relaxed the tension on its string.

Silken banners with embroidered mottoes hung from the pointed vault of the ceiling.

A lilac banner with white writing read: *Each step toward justice requires sacrifice, suffering, and struggle.*

Dusty blue words on gold silk: *Justice denied yields poverty.*

Cream satin with a rose inscription: *Law and order exist to promote justice.*

This chapel honored Themis, the ideal of cosmic order and justice.

Fae studied the painting behind the altar. Shining gold hair swept up in a smooth chignon. Draping gown in the Greek style, its folds, immaculate white. Golden balance scales hanging from one hand, golden scepter in the other. And her face . . . alive, but calm; blue eyes gazing very straight; yet tenderness about her firm lips.

Was this portrayal a vision of the real Themis, as seen by the artist's eye? Or did she originate from the artist's imagination?

Was she Fae's mother? With her straight, classical nose and her oh-so-blue eyes? Her lovely cheek bones? Her arching eyebrows? Her perfectly proportioned lips?

Fae thought about her own face as seen in her dressing table mirror: small snub nose, straight bows, gray eyes, curling dusky hair. *Was* she Themis' daughter?

She replaced her arrow in its quiver, slung her bow back over her shoulder. She stepped forward, leaning her hands on the back of the backmost pew. The scrolling curve of the marble felt cool and smooth under her fingers.

Memory – intense memory – took her.

In memory, she was infant Fae once more, wrapped in beige swaddling, held in the arms of her mother, the woman who had bathed her so lovingly. Her mother's gown was beige linen and worn, but her cradling clasp felt secure and safe. And her face bent toward Fae's. Faint crow's feet marked her temples. Laugh lines framed her mouth. Her lips were pale, her gray eyes tired. But love illuminated her, shining in every line and curve.

She kissed Fae's brow and murmured, "My little Faith, my darling

Fae, my sweet daughter. Mmm." And she kissed Fae again, on the crown of Fae's head this time. Once, twice, and thrice.

Infant Fae cooed.

Fae in the chapel to Themis felt tears sting her eyes. *Mother.* That had been her mother. With Fae's gray eyes and Fae's pointed chin. Tired and worn and mortal. Not an ideal of anything. Not a Theosian at all. Ordinary. But incandescent with motherly love.

She would never have let me go.

How then had Fae been separated from her? How had Fae come to lie in a basket at a lonely crossroads?

I want her back, the lady with the gentle hands, the loving voice and face. The lady who held me close and cherished me.

Instead she had . . . well, right now she had no one at all. But for years and years she'd had Milady, severe and reserved. Aunt Pallas, warm and kindly, but absorbed in her own children. Aunt Kira, gentle and generous, but reclusive. And Aunt Sariah, bossy and strict.

You had Uncle Leander, she chided her spurt of melancholy.

Yes, Uncle Leander. Calm, practical, and caring. Always present when she needed him. She could see him now in her mind's eye: neat brown beard and mustache, closely clipped brown hair, and steady hazel eyes. Strong, lithe muscles, less burly than you expected a smith to be. Uncle Leander.

She missed him. Missed him dreadfully. If he stood by her side at this moment, she wouldn't feel so alone and so affected by the goblin nipping. *Aion's* nipping rancor. So sad for the mother she'd never known.

Be who you are, he'd always told her.

She was mortal by birth, but Theosian by nurture. All those immersions in the Achillean Springs. All the instruction from her aunts and from Milady.

Had she become the ideal of fate, as Milady believed? Or as Milady *said* she believed?

Fae didn't feel fateful.

How could she be spinning the course of lives – mortal and immortal – measuring their spans, and cutting them short without any awareness of it? That made no sense.

Why had Milady decided on seclusion as the solution to Fae's supposed powers. Why not training? Why not practice? Why no trust in Fae herself?

I loved them. I loved even Milady. Even if Milady didn't love me. I would never have harmed them.

Was that true? She'd watched Theophane grow ever more proficient in the arts of war and strategy, the ideal overtaking her cousin's more playful attributes. The same with Eulalie, who lost her merry conviviality to increasing solemnity and solitude.

Would the role of the fate have erased Fae's essence? Molded her choices into fateful ones instead of loving ones? Maybe.

Be who you are.

Right now, she had a choice.

Right now, she could be the Fae trained by Milady to be knowledgeable and skillful. She could be the Fae encouraged by Aunt Pallas to be outgoing and kind. The Fae taught by Aunt Kira to be thorough and precise. (Those had been hard lessons; Fae wasn't naturally precise at all, but the reverse.) She could be the Fae forced by Aunt Sariah to be stubborn.

A giggle escaped her lips.

She would always remember Aunt Sariah's astonishment when she discovered her niece experimenting with a lotion of mud and honey, because Fae had read in an old folk tale that the combination conferred invulnerability, and Fae was tired of the splinters she seemed prone to at that time.

Red-faced Aunt Sariah berated, while stubborn Fae resisted feeling either punished or wrong.

Fae was all those things: skillful, knowledgeable, outgoing, kind, thorough – although only marginally precise – and stubborn. She'd acquired those qualities, but they *were* hers.

And then there was her innate character: cheerful, open, prone to wonderment, and lively.

Uncle Leander liked her for who she was. He always had.

If Milady were Fae's foster mother, then surely Uncle Leander was her foster father.

That was a new thought. She'd lost a mother – her birth mother – but she'd gained a father. It felt good.

I can be Uncle Leander's Fae. The Fae who laughs and dances. The Fae who is curious. The Fae who likes making friends.

If she had a choice – and she had a feeling that being in *kairos* was all about making a choice – she would be the Fae born to a mortal mother and the Fae who had learned from Theosians. The ideal of fate she would reject.

She lifted her chin and wiped the residual tears from the corners of her eyes with her fingers.

She looked around at the chapel. What an overly precious place! White and lacy and pristine, too restrained, too proper. Ugh!

Fae turned to go.

Just as she crossed over the chapel's threshold, abrupt recognition seized her.

She called me Fae. Short for Faith. Oh!

It felt good. Really good.

I know who I am.

❧

She sipped from her canteen as she walked through the short passage to the sunnier hallway. She paused by the conservatory, inhaling to savor the aroma of rich broth emanating from its doorways.

What was the next right thing to do?

She'd learned to feed herself in *kairos*. She'd found all three godmother doors. She'd discovered her true identity. But something – or some things – still remained undone. Some action or knowledge or moment of truth that would set her free.

It was so *frustrating* that nothing was straight forward or obvious here.

At any moment Theophane would rappel down the outside of her tower. Or Eulalie would wriggle through the enlarged privy hole, dangling from her knotted sheets. Or Uncle Nathanos' river would burst that foundation wall and bring the whole castle down around his ears.

And all Fae was doing was taking baths and spinning in circles. She gritted her teeth.

C'mon, Fae. Stop finding fault. The bath was *right*. It had brought the most precious memory of all – the memory of her mother bathing infant Fae. And the spinning had enabled her to find the third godmother door.

Was something trivial – like hunting for more practical clothes – the next right thing?

A small shock of recognition rippled through her.

Apparently that *was* the next right thing.

Very well, she'd start searching. Maybe she'd discover a critically important detail. Come to think of it, she'd discovered so much of what she needed by accident. Why would the final details be any different? Just because she felt more time pressure now, more urgency, didn't mean the rules of *kairos* – whatever they were – had changed any.

She turned down another hallway, impatiently, almost at random.

And started opening doors.

The first revealed a canopied bed decked out in ruffly pink; drapes and table skirts of the same.

She shut the door. No point in even checking the wardrobe. It would be all frills and furbelows.

The next few rooms were similarly useless: floral lilac print, gauzy blue, lacy white. No, no, and no.

The mint green room with murals depicting willows overhanging a brook appealed to her, but its built-in closet held frocks with sashes sewn for a ten-year-old.

A quirky room with gold-tasseled ottomans of scarlet leather and bright niches tiled with turquoise, indigo, and apricot enticed her to linger for a bit. It smelled of cloves, and a crimson-lacquered cabinet displayed a collection of carved jade elephants and sandalwood monkeys. But the chest at the foot of a brilliant green divan held only long tunics of purple or fuchsia and matching flowy pants. No.

Choosing her clothes was part of deciding who she would be. And deciding who she would be – *being* who she would be – was essential to solving the puzzle that trapped her in *kairos*.

She kept searching.

She caught sight of her aqua ribbon bracelet often – reaching to open all those doors – and remembered to drink.

Her watch chimed four. *Ding, ding, ding, ding.*

Her canteen was empty.

One more room, and then I'll go shut off the stove burner and let the broth start cooling.

She turned into a short, straight passage with teak wainscoting that ended in a window overlooking a pear orchard. The leaves had that dusty look they get in late summer, and Fae could see the pears forming on the branches. The sunlight shone golden and slanting. She wished she were out there, strolling under the trees. Or playing tag with her cousins. She could almost hear them calling and laughing.

A paneled teak door on her left led into a bedchamber that reminded her of the rooms in Milady's lodge: simple lines, subdued colors. The furnishings were all of teak; clean-lined chairs and side tables, four-poster bedstead. The drapes and hangings depicted autumn forest scenes, stylized stags and does half-glimpsed through the muted ambers and golds and bronzes of the foliage.

Fae felt like she'd come home. Milady's lodge had *been* home since her infancy. It might not be to her taste – it wasn't – but it *was* familiar; comfortable.

Smiling, she opened the doors of the plain teak wardrobe.

Yes! Tunics and more tunics on the hangers, all of them in reasonable hues: dusty blue, sage green, soft taupe, cinnamon brown. And stacks of supple leggings on the shelf over the clothes rod. Perfect!

She gathered a handful of tunics, the hangers clutched together in her grip, and then stopped and laid them on the bed.

No. *I'm going to do this thoroughly. The way Aunt Kira taught me.*

The Wishing Bone

SHE STRODE all the way back to the conservatory. She'd come quite a ways, opening doors. The smell from the open doorway was absolutely amazing. So rich and savory.

Shadow claimed the entire eastern wall and all of the floor. The blue flame under the stock pot glowed in the dimness.

Fae lifted the lid. A cloud of steam puffed out. Mmm. The broth had reduced, coming only halfway up the pot. That was good. It would be more flavorful, more intense.

She turned the regulator knob where the connector hose attached to the fuel bottle.

The burner flames went out.

In a bit, when the broth had cooled, she'd transfer everything – stock pot, stove array, and tinderwheel – to the cooking bay. Although . . . she could dump the skimmings from the broth now. They looked nasty, all congealed and cold in the bowl.

She ferried them to the medieval garderobe, poured them through the hole. Then scooted back to her cooking bay to wash the bowl and the spoon in the water closet across from it.

Next she took the ball gowns out of the second wardrobe in her bedchamber. Every single one. Gods! They were awful! White gauze spangled with silver. Gray silk adorned with seed pearls. Sky blue velvet dotted with crystal solitaires.

Well, okay. They were pretty. But she just wasn't fond of big, poufy skirts and low necklines and all the formal, fanciness that went with balls.

She lugged the dresses down the hall and past her cooking bay to a box room with shelves and shelves of things in storage . . . and an untenanted clothes rod. *Ha!*

It took four trips.

Then she emptied the wardrobe floor of dance slippers, and the wardrobe shelves of stockings and petticoats.

Finally! Its clothes rod and surfaces were bare.

She returned to the autumn-hung room upstairs and started carrying tunics down. Then leggings. Then ankle hose and moccasin boots. She pounced on the breastbands and knicker briefs unearthed in a back corner. Yay! These sparer undergarments were so much more comfortable than bulky camisoles and long pantalettes.

It was half after five by the time she finished.

She put her bow away properly – hanging with string slack – and the quiver of arrows, as well. She liked having a weapon any time she entered unfamiliar areas of the castle, but it wasn't a helpful adjunct to cooking.

In the conservatory, the bone broth had cooled to nearly room temperature.

She carried it downstairs and then returned for the stove and tinderwheel.

She poured the broth through a sieve to remove the bones and picked out the small fragments of meat to use. Then she returned the liquid to the empty stock pot and added the meat pieces and the soaking oatmeal. She lit the burner and started it cooking. The aroma was divine, the fragrant oats blending with the savoriness of the reduced stock. *Mmm.* When she sprinkled salt over it and sat to eat, it was even more amazing. This was her best meal yet.

I'll have to go hunting tomorrow. I need more meat.

The rest of her evening routine sped by smoothly: wash up, tidy up, ferry the spent bones to the garderobe, and set oats for breakfast soaking.

She tested the wishing bone still drying by the window panes. It felt springy, but not spongy – exactly ready for pulling. And how would she manage that? She didn't want to pit right hand against left.

The sky was darkening to luminous cobalt. As she watched, the first star of the evening bloomed, bright and clear, an emblem of hope.

She brought the wishing bone with her into her bedchamber.

She could tie the bone to one of the gryphon's talons. But she and the gryphons were on the same side. It felt wrong to divide winner and loser between them.

She studied the catches on the window casements. Now there were her enemies: window catches that wouldn't open. She wanted *them* to lose.

The dressing table held ribbons by the dozen. She selected a peach one and tied it snuggly around the lower end of one half of the wishing bone. The surface of the bone felt dry, almost splintery. The ribbon felt very smooth, but its threads caught a little on the bone. That was good. It wouldn't slip off.

She made another knot in the ribbon, just an inch away from the knot securing the bone. Then she tied that knot snug against the handle on the casement catch.

Nerves fluttered in her stomach. Who would win? Fae? Or the castle window? And would it matter? At all?

I want to win.

She took the end of the free half of the wishing bone between her right thumb and forefinger.

The fluttering in her stomach grew.

She tightened her grip and pulled.

Snap!

Half the wishing bone came free in her hand, a small spur from the other half attached.

I won, I won, I won!

She danced a short jig, bone held high while she pranced around her room.

This was silly. She knew it was silly. But it still felt great. She wasn't even worried about the coming of dark and the dimming of the lamps. Although . . . *prudence, Fae, be prudent.* Yes.

She set her winning bone fragment on the dressing table and brushed out her hair, then braided it in two pigtails. She donned a spring green nightgown with white ribbons at its neck and wrists. For a wonder, she was almost as fresh as the clothing she put off. This time. Baths were a fabulous thing!

A trip to the water closet to clean her teeth and use the commode.

And then bed. She placed her wishing bone half under her pillow. And fell asleep so fast it was like the plunge of a meteor. She'd meant to think about all that she knew and all that she suspected, to devise the next step of her escape from *kairos*. But her eyelids never grew heavy; they simply closed, and she was out.

Spirals of light – gold and rose and opalescent pearl – coiled in the darkness behind her sleeping eyes. The golden helix twined with the rose one, and the pair tangled with the curving opalescent strand.

Fae was dreaming.

A soft curl of peach light arose to dance with the mingling threads of glowing color, and then another of pale yellow.

More swirls and more, until they formed a roiling whirl, a tornado of rainbows.

Fae's breath quickened in her dreaming. The chromatic tempest was building toward something.

A coil of electric silver burst from the void, sizzling up and around the cyclone of light, and the spinning mass coalesced into . . . Eris, the ideal of chaos, strife, and discord.

She danced in the star-spangled void, slim and unclothed, her creamy skin dusted with scintillas of brightness, her short silver hair gleaming in the light of galaxies. Her smile of exaltation communicated anger and malice, as well as elation. She was dangerous in her power.

As she danced, she traveled. Her pirouettes turned into skips, and she leapt from star to star, from nebula to nebula.

The velvet blackness of the night faded to gray and then to dusk. Eris was skipping along a dirt road with shadowy hillsides rising above it, their rough grasses barely visible in the gloom. The road entered a cluster of cottages. Warm hearth light shone out from their windows, flickering on whitewashed walls and the ruts in the road.

Eris opened the splintery wood door in the very smallest cottage – just one room.

The door was arched and unpainted. Just like the godmother doors in *kairos*.

Fae's heartbeat sped up.

Inside, a large loom filled half the space, with baskets of spun wool grouped around its framework. A crude round table stood before the hearth, two stools drawn up to it. A bed lay along the far wall.

Perhaps the bed was a wealthy family's discard, cast off only when it grew too shabby and creaky. The scrollwork on the headboard and footboard showed fine craftsmanship, but the finish was dull, worn away. A welter of patched sheets and blankets lay untidily over the woman sleeping there. A weaver, by the looks of her.

The weaver woman's skin was pale, so pale. Crow's feet marked her temples. Laugh lines framed her mouth. Her gray-streaked dark curls fanned across her pillow. She wore a stained nightgown.

Mother! She was Fae's mother!

And she was not sleeping.

Her eyes lay shut, yes, but her breast neither rose nor fell. No twitch stirred her still fingers or limbs in dreaming or sleeping restlessness. She lay in death, not slumber.

Mother! Mother! Mother!

Almost did Fae's horror and grief break her from this vision. She knew she was dreaming and struggled to awaken, but sleep held her fast.

An infant's wailing sounded in the cottage.

In a rush basket on the floor beside the bed lay a baby wrapped in beige blankets. Black fuzz covered her scalp. Her eyes were screwed shut in her crying. One little fist emerged from her wrappings, tight clenched in distress. Fae, baby Fae.

Dreaming Fae struggled again to wake and failed.

Poised in the doorway of the cottage, Eris, the ideal of strife, smiled. A nasty smile.

She directed a calculating look at the baby, then strode forward. She plucked a birchwood drop spindle, an ash measuring rod, and a small, sharp knife from a shelf beside the loom, and crossed the room to the bedstead. She dropped the items into the basket with the baby, gathered the hinged handles in one hand, and lifted.

The baby quieted with the motion.

Swinging the basket, Eris exited the cottage.

No one stopped her as she sauntered through the hamlet. The road lay empty, the cottagers inside.

Once past the last straggle of buildings – a smithy, a chapel, and a cooper – her pace increased. From a stroll to a stride to a skip. The baby seemed to like the swing of her basket. She made no sound.

The dusk cloaking the road grew deeper. Eris crested a shallow rise, then followed her route around the curve of a hillside. The terrain flattened, and she passed through a cluster of birches. Their leaves rustled on a movement of air too faint to be called a breeze.

In the fields on the other side of the trees, the way arrived at a crossroads.

A signpost with two arms marked the intersection. In the darkness, the lettering on the arms was barely legible. The one pointing back in the direction from which Eris had come read "Brixhill." The other, pointing right, said "Askern."

Another basket lay at the base of the post; a very fine basket woven of wicker.

Eris skipped up to it and stopped with a flourish.

Another girlchild lay within. Her blankets were soft and pure white. The tools lying on her blankets, products of luxury: polished tigerwood for the drop spindle, bright brass for the measuring rod, and chased silver on the hilt of the small knife.

This baby was older than the one occupying the rush basket gripped in Eris' hand. Her blond hair had grown long enough to form ringlets all over her head. Her dark eyes were wide and wondering, studying Eris' face as the ideal leaned over the basket.

The baby cooed.

Eris snickered, lifted the basket with her free hand, and set down the other basket.

Whistling, Eris skipped away into the night.

Below the signpost, baby Fae had fallen asleep.

The clouds in the night sky drifted away, and the constellations wheeled. The Spinner trundled above the horizon, standing tall with her spindle dropping away into the abyss, spinning a thread oh-so-long.

Was there a woman visible behind the net of stars? Her graceful arms outstretched and her gaze intent?

Then came the Drawer of Lots to join the stately dance of the sky, bending, her fateful rod flanking the thread of the Spinner, measuring, measuring, measuring the apportioned length.

Infant Fae's eyes opened, staring into the dark, too young to focus on the stars. Her baby face tightened, precursor to a wail.

Did the women behind the pattern of stars look down in pity as they progressed through their fateful tasks? Dreaming Fae could see them, less ghostly than before, spinning and measuring, shaping the lives of all living.

The late moon, a mere crescent, rose with the Cutter. Moonlight glinted on the sharp knife, poised at the end of the Alloter's measuring rod. The blade would flash, the thread would fall, a life would end.

The diaphanous forms of the Fates were solid now, their perfect limbs ready to cast doom into *chronos*, their faces showing a strange mix of grief and joy.

Baby Fae's mouth opened to emit a thin wail.

The night turned, the moon climbed, and the Fates labored, spinning and measuring and completing.

The infant cries grew stronger, more urgent.

Dreaming Fae fought to waken.

The night sky lightened to gray. The stars faded, and the Fates vanished.

A thin line of pink appeared on the horizon.

Infant Fae's shrieks diminished to whimpers.

The pink ribbon of sky expanded and turned golden. The sun rose over the hills, painting the grasses vivid green.

A woman wearing a gown of black velvet strode along the road which the signpost labeled Askern. A black hood concealed her hair. A short black silk cape fluttered from her shoulders.

Milady.

The infant's whimpers had ceased, but Milady seemed to hear them still. She hurried toward the crossroads, breaking into a run.

Then she was beside the basket, falling to her knees, scooping the baby up in her arms and holding her close, pain clenching her face, a tear dripping from beneath each closed eyelid. Did she love the baby so much? Already?

Milady sank back on her heels and fumbled in a pouch at her waist. She extricated a milk-filled glass bottle with a rubber nipple and repositioned infant Fae in her arms. The baby snatched eagerly at the bottle with her little lips, guzzling the milk in great sucking gulps.

Oh! Oh! Oh! Dreaming Fae felt relief so strong it hurt.

Milady knelt in the crossroads until the bottle of milk was empty. She returned it to the pouch, shifted the baby to her left arm, and stood. Gracefully, she bent to lift the basket in her right hand, and then marched briskly away toward Askern.

The pink sky had turned to clear blue, and the twitter of meadowlarks filled the air.

As Milady's striding form receded in the distance, the scene shifted to the interior of a cottage. It resembled the one from which Fae had been stolen: whitewashed walls, small windows with circular glass panes, heavy beams supporting a low plaster ceiling. But the feel of the place was altogether different. Sparkling clean whitewash, rather than stained. Carved floral garlands adorning the ceiling beams in place of rough splintery woodgrain. And neat doorways leading into other chambers rather than the limited one-room space of Fae's birthplace.

The three ideals of fate sat around a round polished oak table, watching as a little girl with curly blond hair lifted a bowl of milk to her lips and drank. The other baby from the crossroads. Fae knew it the way one knows things in a dream.

"Today we will teach you the cutting," said the Spinner. "Sharp and swift for mercy or slowed-but-certain to grant time for farewells. Or fumbled and dragging to inflict suffering. All are needed in their time."

The Cutter nodded.

The little girl's eyes widened.

And the scene shifted again.

Dreaming Fae floated in the Achillean Springs by night.

Bubbling water caressed her limbs. Overhanging hickory limbs made a shadowy lace against the starfield of the night sky. The call of a nightingale sounded amongst the trees, liquid and rippling.

Fingers pinched Fae's nostril's closed while a hand closed around the back of her head and dragged her beneath the water. Milady's hand?

Sleeping Fae labored to struggle, her limbs heavy and unmoving, but dreaming Fae acquiesced. The water closed over her face, and she drifted downward, bumping against the sand at the bottom.

The hand of the unseen person behind her held her there, underwater.

The coolness of the current brushed over her skin, soothing and gentle.

The pressure in her lungs built and built.

When it became unbearable, the fingers pinching her nostrils opened, and dreaming Fae gasped, inhaling water by the lungful.

It didn't sting the way water should. It didn't strangle. It didn't provoke convulsive coughs.

Like evening air, warm and soft and pleasurable, it slid through her breathing passages and flowed out through her arteries, flooding her body with ease and strength.

The hand steadying Fae's head relaxed and departed. Fae hovered in the current.

The water turned golden, turned to light. Fae floated, bathed in divine radiance, an eddy of joy swirling through her.

The ghostly forms of the Fates began to coalesce in the streaming light.

Before they solidified, Fae awoke.

LAST

No Time Left

STRONG SUNLIGHT touched Fae's closed eyelids. She turned her head, eyes still shut, and snuggled her cheek into her pillow. The scent of fresh linen drifted up from it. *Mmm.* She felt drowsy and relaxed. Cozy softness – her sheets and blankets – cocooned her. Only a bedchamber on a morning when everyone slept in could possess the warm, sunny quiet surrounding her. She wanted to drift there until noon, dozing and waking until Nurse came to chivy her out.

Her eyes flew open on the thought.

Squares of light marched up the blue and white striped wallpaper, topped by two curving triangles at the peak, sunlight through a window turning the white stripes golden and the blue stripes bright.

There would be no nurse coming for Fae in *kairos*. She was alone in this place.

She turned onto her back and scooted to sit propped against the headboard. The carved claws of the gryphons dug into her shoulders. She adjusted her pillows. The wishing bone she'd placed under them scratched her hand. She pulled the bone out and stared at it, trying to push away her drowsiness through sheer force of will.

Scenes of last night's dream flowed through her thoughts.

Her throat tightened and grew hot with suppressed tears. She'd suspected her birth mother was dead, but seeing it was so . . . hurt.

Dreams in *kairos* seemed different from dreams in *chronos*. More true? She'd never dreamed prophetically – or oracularly – before. Although the nightmares of Milady as a demon were likely more symbolic than literally true. But the dreams of her family trapped in *kairos* felt accurate. And last night's dream – of Fae's abduction by Eris and Fae's rescue by Milady – felt like history rather than fable.

It was just that . . . she'd barely retrieved those early memories of her birth mother – bathing Fae, murmuring endearments to Fae – and it hurt to have the certainty of her death follow so hard upon them.

She stroked the rough surface of the wishing bone.

I will win. I will.

Milady's face in the dream – the moment when she'd held baby Fae close for the first time – flashed in Fae's mind.

She loved me once. Does she still?

Fae shook her head.

Stop it, she admonished herself. *You'll find out. Right now you've got a rescue to organize.*

That much was true.

The languor remaining from her night's sleep fled. A sense of urgency rushed in. Urgent urgency.

Uncle Leander might not have fired his trebuchet yesterday – he couldn't have done, because she was still here, and here was unchanged. But she *didn't* have unlimited time. She wasn't sure she had any time at all.

She'd gone to bed last night because she had to. She needed her gryphons to protect her from the agony the night time castle inflicted. She'd gone to sleep only because exhaustion claimed her. She'd wanted to think and plan.

Today . . . today she *had* to escape *kairos*. *Had* to.

Except she still didn't know how. Was it even possible?

Yes. She'd *make* it possible.

She didn't know how she would do it. She doubted she *could* do it. But, damn it, she was going to try, and try a lot harder than she'd managed to so far. Her determination felt almost fierce.

I will open the godmother doors.

The thought came from nowhere – heralded by no train of logic – but it felt right, all the way down to the heels of her feet.

She'd had days of randomly exploring the castle, of cooperating with serendipity, of enduring *kairos*. Days of cooking and eating and cleaning up, necessary as those were.

I'm going to go study the first godmother door I found and I'll figure something out.

The goblin nibbling of spite flared in her awareness. She'd been ignoring it, but it didn't go away, ever. Except in the spaces before the godmother doors.

Ha! Exactly!

She thumped out of bed, hurrying.

Wishing bone on dressing table. Dash to water closet for face washing, commode using, hand washing. Back to room to dress.

Go! Go! Go! her urgency hammered.

She couldn't move fast enough to match the pace that her disquiet demanded.

Opening the wardrobe of tunics and leggings should have been exciting. If she weren't in such a rush. They were so much more *her* than all the dresses. Which would she choose?

But she *was* in a rush.

She grabbed the first thing to catch her eye: a pale taupe tunic with acorns embroidered all over it in sepia brown. And some sepia brown leggings to match.

She was tempted to simply throw the clothes on her body and run, but she didn't dare. Proper care of herself – dressing, grooming, eating, cleaning up – was part of the dance that would free her.

She brushed her hair out, rebraided it in one plait, and pinned it up in a club-style bun on the back of her head.

Ha! I'm not a princess, not a goddess, not anything more than mortal.

The practical clothes and practical hair felt *good*. Felt *right*. Felt like she was ready for action.

She wound her watch – quarter after eight – and pinned it to the waist of her tunic. Then hurried through breakfast.

She had the routine of cooking and washing up after it down to a routine, but the eating of it would never be commonplace – even when she was frantic to get *on*. Watching her face grow pale in the mirror had been scary. And the oatmeal smelled so *fragrant*, tasted so *good*. Especially with salt.

She set oats soaking for dinner, just in case today was *not* the day for her escape.

But, gods, it *had* to be the day for her escape. Tomorrow would be *too late*. Hell! This afternoon would be too late!

She finished off the four full water glasses from the day before and refilled them, filled her canteen, and then debated about bringing bow and arrows.

I'm only going to the first godmother door. No dove hawks there.

No, but what if she really did open it? She'd go through. And then what?

She strung her bow and hung it and the quiver over her shoulders.

There.

She ran.

Essence of the Ideal

UP IN THE TALLEST TOWER, the godmother door looked just as it had when she first stumbled upon it. Small arched shape. Dull, dry, splintery wood. Tarnished knob and escutcheon plate. Maybe the sunlight through the arrowslit in the little round chamber slanted in a different direction across the flagstone floor.

But the air felt warm and still smelt of cinnamon. And Aion's goblin spite remained absent.

Fae took a deep breath in of relief. She'd gotten here in time. Now she just needed to figure out how to *open* the door. As though there were any "just" about it. She *wished* there were!

She turned the knob. *Scritch, scritch,* went the inner spring. She tapped on the splintery wood. She shoved against it with her shoulder.

No, physical force was not the answer. Her aunts and uncles and cousins were trying that in their bubbles of *kairos*. The castle was a mental puzzle comprised of self and history and imagination. She needed to *think*, not flail. It was tempting to flail.

Calm, calm, she told herself.

She removed her bow and quiver from her shoulders and sat down on the floor opposite the door, leaning her back against the rough plaster wall.

If this door were a mental puzzle, what could she do mentally to get through it?

If she thought the right thought while turning the knob, would it open?

If she closed her eyes while turning the knob, would it yield?

If she stepped forward with eyes closed, envisioning it open, would she pass straight through it as a ghost?

None of those possibilities seemed right, but . . . she might as well try them. She was here to be stubborn and try everything and anything.

She reshouldered her bow and arrows, and attempted all three.

No. None of them worked. Not even when she tried a dozen different thoughts – *I am strong, I am powerful, Uncle Leander loves me, I can do this,* etc. – while turning the knob.

Fae doffed her weaponry and sat down again. The stone floor felt warm against the backs of her thighs. She stared at her adversary.

Peaked arch.

Splintery wood.

Tarnished knob.

Weird keyhole in the escutcheon plate.

Her chin came up. Weird keyhole. Keyhole. What did that keyhole remind her of? It really was oddly shaped, like a very, very narrow diamond, one point just below the shank of the door knob, the other point a good two inches below that.

Sweet Marionya! She had it!

It bore the same profile as the regulator control lever on her stove array.

She scrambled up, grabbed her bow and quiver, slinging them on as she went, and raced down the twisting stairs. Down and down and down.

Great gods, great gods, great gods! Was this really it?

Back in her cooking bay, she checked the regulator lever, attempting a counterclockwise spin. No, it was already closed. Good. She unscrewed the connector hose from the stove burner. Then she detached the hose from the fuel bottle. The springed pop-up closure on the fuel bottle clicked shut.

She scrutinized the lever, a narrow diamond with the shaft at its broadest middle part.

Oh gods, oh gods, oh gods. It *looked* right. It looked *really* right. Would it *be* right?

She ran back through the maze of castle halls and up the spiral stair in the tallest tower, arriving breathless in the circular room with the godmother door.

Her hands were shaking so badly she couldn't get the regulator lever into the keyhole. Was it too big? No, it was just her jittering hands. She steadied herself, and the lever slipped in.

She turned it clockwise.

The lever – in its off position – began to unwind, turning to its on position. The regulator hose clicked against the door knob as she turned it.

Click.

Click.

The regulator lever reached its on position and stabilized.

Fae pushed against the resistance in the lock.

S-c-r-i-i-i-t-c-h.

The tumblers turned over. *Clunk.*

Oh gods, oh gods, oh gods.

She removed the regulator lever from the lock, clutching it in her left hand.

She turned the door knob – s-c-r-i-i-t-c-h – and felt the latch slide free.

She pushed.

And the door swung open, its knob slipping out of her astonished hand.

The dry, sneezy scent of ground pepper blew through the archway on a cool breeze.

She could see a carved granite ledge extending on the other side of the opening. And then the door swung far enough that she could see more.

A dizzying abyss gaped beyond the ledge, no floor in sight below, no rooftree in sight above, just the vast night sky from one extreme to another, spreading darkness begemmed with stars and nebulae and galaxies, infinitely wide, infinitely deep.

The cool, pepper-scented breeze caressed her cheeks.

A sudden chorus sounded, chilled silvery voices singing wordlessly.

Fae felt potent, expanded, sovereign.

Like an empress ruling her empire.

A goddess engaged with her world.

A force like gravity, undeniable.

She could step through this door. She would take no harm. This was her heritage as one who had bathed in the Achillean Springs.

Stepping forth across this threshold, she would come into her own, growing mighty.

But she would not be Fae any longer. She would be the ideal of fate, apprentice to the Spinner, the Alloter, and the Cutter.

Fae shuddered. This was all that Milady had destined her for. This was all that she herself had repudiated. To claim her divinity, to lose her humanity. No! A thousand times no.

She stretched to reach the door knob, to seize it, to slam this door shut.

It was beyond her grasp. The door had swung open, all the way open, lying flat against the outside wall of her bastion.

Fae bit her lip.

What was this doorway really?

She stared at the glittering stars in all their shining glory.

Must she pass through the door to obtain her freedom? Or was there another purpose to it? She'd resented Milady in *The Race of Atalanta* for telling Fae in the role of Diana that she must keep the door shut, allowing no one to pass through it. Shutting the door would feel like shutting herself away from life, just as she'd done at Milady's behest.

Yet walking through it was unthinkable.

If Fae would not shut the door, but would not go through it either, then what?

Would something on the other side come through to Fae?

She listened to the singing voices, high and cold.

She felt the cool breeze and smelled the peppery aroma.

What *was* this?

The essence of the ideal. Deep and beautiful and part of her. But not all of her. A well at the foundation of her being into which she might dip at will, but not drown in.

The ideal of the daughter, the foundling, the puzzle solver, the child, the woman – all the many roles a mortal might inhabit, for a time.

Milady would have shut Fae away from all these with her dream of Theosian grandeur.

Fae herself had shut the door on these possibilities, when she retreated to solitude in Milady's lodge.

But now . . . Fae welcomed them in. Hello, life. Hello, uncertainty. Hello, risk. These were hers. They were precious.

Fae inhaled and bowed.

The breeze faltered, then resumed.

The chorus swelled, then steadied.

And Fae turned, going back down the stairs of the tallest tower, leaving the door open behind her.

At the bottom of the stairs, she drank from her canteen. She'd forgotten to loop the aqua ribbon around her wrist, but she remembered to drink.

The liquid, liquid water felt good on her throat.

Could she still hear the heavenly choir? Feel the fresh breeze? Smell the peppery scent?

No, but she would remember them for always, for whenever she needed to access the ideals of her humanity, to be a little bigger than herself.

Aion's nipping malice was back. She straightened her shoulders and threaded the castle corridors back to her cooking bay to replace the connector hose between her stove burner and its fuel bottle. She couldn't recollect what the keyhole in the second godmother door looked like – had she even noticed in the first place? she didn't think so – but she knew it didn't have the same shape as the first one. Heck, it might not even pose the same kind of puzzle. Maybe she *would* have to think the right thought or envision the right image while turning its knob. She had no idea.

Her watch chimed.

Ding, ding, ding, ding, ding, ding, ding, ding, ding, ding. Ten o'clock.

Time to get on with it. The feather of urgency – stilled by the magnificence of the ideal cosmos – stirred within her again, with more than her own longing to get out of here. Was she losing the race to beat her relatives to a solution? Losing her window for escape?

Oh gods!

Her stomach felt cold.

She raced for the gymnasium in the medieval wing.

Arriving, the goblin nips of Aion's malice fell away as she entered the space. Its floating wood floor felt lovely under her footsteps, so much warmer than the stone of the hallways, more resilient, almost friendly in its texture.

The morning sun shone through the ribbon of windows high on the outside wall, dust motes winking in the beams of light. The tall oak wainscoting glowed golden, and the plaster above the wood gleamed white. But the shadows under the balcony were deeper.

Fae walked straight to the godmother door in the shadows.

There it was: small with its pointed arch, dull splintery wood, tarnished knob and escutcheon plate.

She studied the keyhole. Indeed, it was different than the one on the door in the tower: two narrow slots extended vertically – up and down, not side to side – from a round center hole, like a traditional keyhole for a very, very old key. Only the keys from ancient times bore double flanges instead of a single one.

What would fit that keyhole? She doubted this door posed a purely abstract puzzle. It required a specific physical key, just as the first one had. But what?

She thought about the contents of her dressing table, especially the smaller items: hair clips, combs, tiny nail scissors, rings, even the wishing bone she'd left on its surface. That was silly. And none of the less ridiculous things possessed the shape of a double-flanged key.

Did this require an actual key? Maybe it did. In which case, had she seen any keys in the castle?

Hanging on the wall in the kitchens next to the wine cellar door, there was a massive iron one – the length of her hand from its bow to its pin and single flange – but she couldn't remember any others.

Except... keys, keys, keys... where had she seen a whole collection of them? She *had* seen them. Somewhere, somewhere, some –

Hah! She had it!

The cabinet in the jewel chamber with all the watches. Nearly every watch behind those glass doors had been paired with its key. But those were decidedly the wrong kind of key. They had no flanges at all, merely a shank with a shaped hollow at the end that fit over the winding-arbor and setting-arbor of a watch.

She fingered the watch key that hung behind the fob of *her* watch and drew it out where she could see it. Yes, it was just like most watch keys, diminutive, with the precision-formed hollow in one end for the watch arbors. But the other end – the end she held in her fingers to turn the key – *that* end possessed two thin semi-circular flanges to give her fingers leverage. Flanges that looked just the right size to fit in the keyhole of this door! *Hah again!*

She fumbled with the knot in the cord that secured the key to the back of the Celtic brooch that pinned the watch to her tunic. The knot didn't want to come loose.

C'mon Fae. That was Aunt Kira's remembered voice in her head. *Do this properly!* Fae smiled ruefully and unpinned the watch.

Holding it in her left hand while she picked at the knot with her right, she still made no headway.

Alright, alright, alright.

She stepped out from the shadows under the balcony, removed her bow from her shoulder, and sat down on the floor. She needed both hands for this.

The knot was at the brooch end, the cord passing through a loophole between the two finger flanges. Once she got the knot undone, the cord slipped easily out of the loop.

She scrambled to her feet and inserted the flange end into the door's keyhole.

It fit! It fit! It fit!

She felt like dancing and gave a small hop. But, oh, the shaft emerging from the keyhole was *so* short. And *it* had no flanges to give her leverage. She pinched the metal tightly between her fingers and turned.

The shaft slipped against her finger pads, not turning at all.

She needed something to grip with. A tool of some kind.

Where, where, where – ?

Hah! She had it again!

Leaving her bow, watch, and the lonely cord on the floor behind her, she dashed out of the gymnasium, seeking the gardener's nook all the way on the other side of the castle.

She ran the whole way, sprinting through the hallways and bounding down the stairs.

There on the gardner's bench were some pliers – a gripping tool – right next to branch lopers, a limb saw, and a stack of copper plant labels.

Fae seized the pliers and ran back to the gymnasium. Through the corridors, up the stairs, across the bridge – the whole meandering route.

The clutter she'd left on the gymnasium floor confronted her. *Right.* This wasn't the moment to get sloppy.

She tied the cord back onto the watch brooch in a bow – easy to untie, when needed – and pinned the fob to her tunic. The ends of the silk cord stuck out from behind the white leather. She slung her bow back over her shoulder. Only then did she approach the godmother door and the watch key protruding backwards from its key hole.

She opened the jaws of the pliers and clamped them around the key shaft.

Then she turned them, keeping them firmly pressed closed with her grip on the handles.

S-c-r-i-i-i-t-c-h.

The key turned and the lock's tumblers turned with it.

Clunk.

More prudent than last time, Fae set the pliers on the floor and pulled her bow off her shoulder.

She turned the door knob – *s-c-r-i-i-i-t-c-h* – then shoved the door open and nocked an arrow all in one swift motion, standing poised to shoot.

Mystery and Intuition

☙

CLOSE-GROWN TREES met her gaze, bright moonlight filtering down through their leaves – so bright that the shadowy leaves showed bright green edges in the night.

The threshold of the doorway extended out into a granite ledge, but the forest floor, a dappled pillowy reach of moss and ferns, lay only a few inches below the stone. Fae could step easily down, if she wished, and stroll among the rough-barked tree trunks.

If she wished.

The forest was beguiling, a rustling, living presence that called to her. In the distance sounded the ripple of water flowing gently over stones. A bird trilled, low and murmurous, like a smoky flute. The scent of moist loam and growing green things drifted into the gymnasium.

Fae lowered her bow, slung it back over her shoulder, and replaced the arrow in its quiver. She stepped right up to the threshold plate, drinking in the shifting dapples of the moonlight, the natural melodies of breeze and water and birdcalls, the resinous aroma of pine and the sweetness of honeysuckle. Mmm.

What *was* this? A forest that was more than mere woodland? More immense, deeper, richer.

It was mystery, she realized. Mystery and intuition and magic. The realm of the mother, the maid, and the crone. In this forest, she would come home to herself in a way wholly different than through the godmother door into the cosmos. Through this door into the trees, she would become the huntress, fleet of foot and keen of sight, steady of hand, sagacious in all the ways of the wild. She would travel into the heart of fear and find ecstasy there.

It drew her. It drew her for all the right reasons. And all the wrong ones.

She *was* the huntress in her innermost essence. There was a reason that her happiest moments, her most exalted moments, and her most wretched moments had all occurred in the woods around Milady's lodge. Fae belonged among the oaks and the hickories with her bow in her hand, an arrow nocked. But –

She was a human hunter.

If she stepped into this archetypal forest that summoned her so strongly, she would leave her humanity behind her as surely as if she had consented to become the ideal of fate. Instead of the combined roles of spinner, alloter, and cutter, she would take the role of Diana of the ancients – the ideal of the huntress.

She teetered, swaying first toward the trees beyond the door, then back toward the castle gymnasium behind her.

Forest or fortress?

Huntress or human?

Diana or Fae?

The memory of her mother, her oh-so-loving mother, murmuring her name, drifted across her awareness. "Faith, my darling Faith."

❧

"I am *Fae!*" She cried the words aloud and spun away from the door, barreling across the gymnasium floor, almost falling into the hallway beyond.

She'd left her watch key behind her. How would she wind her watch?

But she didn't dare go back for it. If she reached an arm and a shoulder through that godmother doorway into forest, to swing the door knob and its key hole within her reach, she'd never remain on this side of that exit. She'd step over that threshold, never to return.

Fae shuddered as she ran.

Her love of the hunt, her skill as a hunter, her embrace of the mysteries of animal awareness – immediate sensory experience without thought – these were qualities to accept, to let in. But never to drown in, as she uniquely could, oh-so-easily.

It was right that the door was open behind her.

It was also right that it remained *behind* her.

Thank the gods she'd not passed through it!

Her watch chimed. *Ding, ding, ding, ding, ding, ding, ding, ding, ding, ding, ding.* Eleven o'clock. Where was she going? She'd not chosen a destination, just set herself to get *away*. But apparently some part of her had chosen, for here she was on the gently curving stairway to the kitchens, nearly at the bottom.

Of course.

She was headed for the third godmother door.

She stopped on the last step before the kitchen anteroom.

This door would require a unique key. Just as had the other two. What shape did its keyhole take?

She closed her eyes, forehead scrunching, trying to bring its image to mind.

If she were in the woods and heard the rustling passage of some hidden beast, she would be able to cast her thoughts back to the tracks she'd barely noticed some moments before and recollect their appearance, identify their creator.

C'mon Fae! You can do this! Aunt Kira again, although *she* would not be coaching Fae on tracking techniques. Nor would she have called Fae by that name. Aunt Kira had always said "Moira" like all Fae's other aunts. *I suppose I've created an Aunt Kira version of myself in my mind.* She snorted a soft puff of breath through her nostrils.

And then she had it. The really peculiarly shaped key hole of the third door swam before her mind's eye: an irregular crescent, sort of like a comma, but with an additional short and narrow slash coming down from the heavier blob at the top left that punctuated the curve of the symbol.

What on earth – ?

And then she knew the answer to that puzzle, too.

Right there on her dressing table – right where she'd left it – the fragment of the wishing bone had exactly that shape where the stub of the one half protruded and the full length of the other connected.

She turned herself around and scampered back up the stairs.

At the top, she stopped again and drained her canteen.

Hah! I remembered! No aqua ribbon, but the essential quality of water had finally drummed itself into her non-thirsting body. *That* was an accomplishment, here in *kairos*.

She detoured to her cooking bay to refill her canteen, and then retrieved the wishing bone from her bedchamber. She glanced around the room. Would she be returning to it ever again? She didn't really care. Sure, it was quirky and fun, with its cheerful blue-stripped walls and its rollicking cornice frieze of grinning suns, but it was no refuge. Aion's malice permeated it as surely as all the other spaces in the castle. All except the godmother doors.

That was interesting. The *godmother* doors. *Milady's* doors. Was Milady as responsible for providing exits from *kairos* as she was for creating Fae's entrance into it?

A renewed sense of urgency surged through Fae.

There was no *time* for this. *No time, no time, no time.*

The Third Godmother Door

SHE RUSHED from the room and dashed for the stairs. Down and down and down. Next, she needed to locate the hidden passageway to the crystal-ceilinged grotto. Could she find it without starting, eyes closed, at the plague door?

Yes, there was the great plaster-covered pier set away from a side wall of the kitchens. And there was the narrow slot behind it, giving access to the dark root-fringed passageway. And there was the passageway itself.

Fae dove into it.

No time, no time, no time.

She walked as quickly as she could manage – not very – through the unseeing blackness, hands outstretched before her.

When a glimmer of light shone ahead of her, dimly illuminating the stone floor and rough walls, she almost sobbed with relief and quickened her stride.

She emerged a moment later in the small hexagonal space with light streaming through its crystal-faceted dome, the bench circling its perimeter, and the third door on one wall.

These doors were almost friends now, so familiar had they become. Small, almost intimate in size. Dull, splintery surface that was common and modest. Point-arched peak: piquant and charming.

Fae homed in on the key hole in the tarnished escutcheon plate, her wishing bone pinched between her thumb and forefinger.

The other end of the bone, with its thicker connecting piece and its broken stub, fit perfectly in the key hole.

Gently, worried the bone might break, Fae turned it.

S-c-r-i-i-i-t-c-h. The springs in this lock were looser. The bone key did not snap as the tumblers turned over. *Clunk.*

Fae bit her lip. What awaited her on the other side of this door? Something beautiful, extravagantly beautiful, but cold and repulsive, like the gate to the cosmos? An echo of her heart's core, irresistible and beckoning, like the portal into mystery? Or something altogether else?

With no other preparation than her questions – bow and arrow had helped her not at all when she stood before the second godmother door – Fae turned the knob on the third.

S-c-r-i-i-i-t-c-h.

Holding her breath, she pushed the door open.

Light, brilliantly gold light, streamed through the first crack between door and jamb, then flooded through the widening gap.

Fae should have been blinded, so fiercely shone the glare, but somehow her eyes were soothed by it, strengthened by it.

A movement of air, too faint to call a breeze, warmed her from crown to toe, and the scent of cinnamon enfolded her.

All her muscles relaxed, but she felt energized, as though she might leap from earth to sky in a single bound, as though she could swim the widest ocean or walk tirelessly from dawn to dusk.

Peace pervaded her.

Life, passion, and engagement – this radiance encompassed all those and more. Love and harmony and joy. The bliss of being.

Everything living craved this.

Fae craved this.

But not uniquely. No special cranny of her nature called for this any more than the rest of her.

I need not step through to receive this. I need only open my heart and let it in.

She widened her stance and lifted her arms, as though welcoming a lover about to enter her embrace, and basked in the life-giving fires.

It was blessed, it was nourishing, it was sustaining.

And she could not stay.

Reluctantly, she turned and walked steadily away, not shrinking from the darkness of the earth passage, carrying a memory of the resplendent light with her.

In the dimness of the castle kitchens, she took a sip from her canteen. The sweet pureness of the water shocked her, in comparison to the heat she'd just experienced – it hadn't felt hot at the time, but in retrospect it blazed.

Then she checked her watch. Half after eleven.

Oh gods, oh gods, oh gods. There was no *time*. She felt sure of it.

But what next?

The Key of Keys

⁂

THERE HAD TO BE another door. A fourth portal from *kairos* to . . . somewhere else.

Three was for change, and four for completion. Milady always said so. There *had* to be a fourth door, a way for Fae to regain *chronos*, the last necessary piece of her wholeness. But where on earth was she to find it?

She'd searched the entire castle for five long days without finding it. And now, on this sixth morning, she *had* to find it with no more delay.

Oh gods, oh gods, oh gods.

She couldn't flail about seeking randomly.

It's the last puzzle, c'mon, Fae. Use your head!

She'd searched the castle, from cellars to tower tops, skipping nothing . . . except for the public reception rooms clustering around the magnificent entrance hall with its polished black marble floors, its great bronze portals, barred, and the hammering presence of demonic power.

She'd skimped there, fled in terror.

I have to go back.

She checked her watch again. Twenty-eight minutes to twelve.

Oh gods, oh gods, oh gods. Her sense of urgency was increasing.

She literally bounded across the kitchens and raced up the stairs, not slowing even at the top when her heaving ribs seemed unable to suck in adequate air. Clutching the cramp that threatened her side, she pounded through the castle hallways – straight, then left, then straight, jog right, then left.

Blown, she arrived at the first hidden door into the public rooms.

Except it wasn't there.

Oh gods, oh gods, oh gods!

She turned away from the blank wall. Turned back to it.

C'mon Fae, no panicking. Think!

Of course that door would do her no good. It led merely to another wing of the castle. She needed . . . a door like the three she had opened this morning. And it had to be . . . somewhere along this wall.

She was going to have to slow down.

A blind rush would get her nowhere.

Or maybe . . . a blind search was exactly the right thing.

Biting her lip, she closed her eyes and stretched out her arm to the marble surface of this wall behind the massive columns of the colonnade.

With her fingertips lightly brushing the cool stone, she walked.

Smoothness, smoothness, and yet more smoothness. How long did this wall extend?

She peeked at her watch. Eighteen minutes to twelve. *Oh gods, oh gods, oh gods.*

Hurriedly she closed her eyes again.

Smooth and smooth and smooth.

And then – sweet Marionya – a bump of something rough and splintery. Then a sudden recess with more rough, splintery wood at its back.

Her eyes flew open.

A door! *The* door! Small and arched with a tarnished knob. But its escutcheon plate lacked a key hole.

Fae grabbed the knob, turned it – s-c-r-i-i-i-t-c-h – and threw the door open.

The cold marble halls of the public spaces stretched away from her, the soulless hammering of the demon slamming through the small doorway.

Oh gods, oh gods, oh gods! This was all wrong. And there was no time, no time, no time.

The gryphons at the head of her bed flashed into her mind's eye, golden and protective by day, ebon and vigilant by night.

She needed a gryphon.

She needed a gryphon *right now*.

But how? And where? And . . . she had *no time*.

This was just like that desperate moment in the study when she *had* to get outside, but the windows were proof against everything, even a weighty glass globe intended to hold paper secure.

The paperweight!

With its colored inclusion that looked like a dragon. Or a phoenix. *Or a gryphon!*

Hoping against hope – praying that she was right – Fae swung around and dashed between the two nearest columns, down two shallow steps, across a rectangular court lit by skylights, and on into a shortcut passage to the southwest wing of the castle.

She thought she'd reached her fastest on the mad rush from the kitchens, but now she discovered she could go faster still. Her bare feet smacked against the white marble floor. Her arms pumped. Her gear rattled.

She skidded into the imprisoning study where she had failed to break a window and snatched the glass paperweight from the floor – not attempting to trace the lines of its colored inclusion. Either she was right or she was wrong. She would get no second chance here.

Lungs heaving and legs burning, she dashed back toward that fourth "godmother" door.

Go! Go! Go!

Sweet Marionya! It was one minute to twelve.

Dear gods, was she already too late?

A moment later she burst out of the shortcut passage and across the interior court.

There was the door. There was the door!

She raised the glass paperweight and *hurled* it.

The heavy globe hit the black marble floor with a dull thud . . . and rolled through the doorway.

Her watch chimed twelve.

Ding, ding, ding, ding, ding, ding, ding, ding, ding, ding, ding, ding.

Fae watched intently as the glass sphere bowled along the demon-oppressed hallway.

Its colorful inclusion flashed bright and brighter.

The globe itself expanded as it grew more distant: large as a melon, large as a boulder, large as the forge in Uncle Leander's smithy.

Fae panted, catching her breath and staring.

The orb rolled to a stop and . . . exploded.

Its colored heart emerged unscathed – vivid and free on the black marble floor – while the enclosing clear glass shards flew through the air, jagged and dangerous. Mid-flight, they melted. And the castle melted with them, its walls vanishing like spun sugar in the rain, the recessed panels of its coffered ceiling fading, blue sky blooming through the misty stone.

As the hallway dissolved and ran like a watercolor painting in a puddle, an unbroken orb coalesced in the air just below the thinning ceiling, drawing the diaphanous gauze of marble into itself. Big as a carriage, but fragile as a soap bubble, its transparent surface gleamed rose and gold and lilac. Within it, a gauzy silhouette issued from the opalescence. The silhouette took on substance and dimension. It passed from transparency to translucency and gained hue. Black boots, black leathers, black vest, black spade beard, black hair neatly combed.

Great gods! It was Uncle Aion!

He pounded furiously on the curving walls of his prison, every line of his body exuding power and wrath. His face was too far distant for Fae to discern his expression, but she could see it in her mind's eye: brow contracted in anger, gaze blazing. Aion's ire was to be feared, not courted.

But the fragile tension of the soap bubble withstood him. Fed by the dissolving castle, its transparency thickened, grew clouded, and then opaque – a gleaming egg that floated high, bobbing as its prisoner struggled.

Opacity complete, the egg shrank.

Smaller, a massive midstream boulder. Smaller, a Turkish ottoman. And smaller yet, a luscious honeydew melon.

The castle hallway was gone, utterly vanished, its interior spaces become gardens in an open air pleasance.

The clear shards of the broken paperweight were equally gone, but its colored heart remained, a vivid nugget on the tan pea gravel of a garden walk.

Fae looked about herself, stunned.

Two thick marble columns from the castle remained behind her. The open godmother door, its threshold, and its jambs, stood in front of her. Around them – door, columns, and Fae – spread a large courtyard paved in the same pea gravel as the path ahead.

As Fae inhaled a trembling breath, the lump of vivid glass – purple and crimson and metallic gold – came to life and grew. The purple darkened to iridescent black feathers covering powerful legs ending in eagle's talons. The crimson became a lion's hindquarters pelted in bronze fur. The metallic gold softened into the gleaming gold feathers of sweeping wings and an eagle's head, its hooked beak imposing, the glare of its yellow eyes fierce.

One of my gryphons! The gryphons who protected my sleep! I was right!

Exultation and anticipation swelled in Fae's breast. Her gryphons were guardians of completion. What would this one complete here?

The beast reared back on its haunches and sprang into the air, wings unfurling for a thunderous downstroke. The first wing clap carried it high, just above Aion's prison. The gryphon's taloned forelegs stretched and closed, snatching the egg prison out of the sky.

The gryphon soared higher, its bronze fur and golden plumage glinting in the sunlight.

Higher and higher it climbed. And then higher still, until Fae could not see it at all. It was gone, Uncle Aion with it.

Now it was safe to step through the godmother door. She hoped.

One step.

Fae stood immediately before the open archway.

Two steps.

Fae stood right under the pointed frame.

Three steps.

She was through!

And the godmother door was gone along with the rest of the castle. She stood in the doorway of a gazebo with honeysuckle twining up its pillars and massing on its roof. The tan pea gravel stretched away to a low hedge at the courtyard's border. Beyond the hedge, hollyhocks reached for the sky, their flower-dotted spires waving gently in the still air.

The plume of a fountain splashed in another direction, and two topiary elephants gamboled in another. These were the gardens of Castle Farnesse. Fae was home.

She could feel it in her bones.

Her breast and belly felt more solid – and more vulnerable – than they ever had in *kairos*. Her arms and legs felt stronger. And tired. And achy. There was a bruise forming on one shin.

She was *hungry*. And thirsty!

A laugh sputtered from her lips.

This was *chronos* alright. With all its disadvantages: fatigue, bumps and bruises, getting overheated. It was hot here, a typical summer afternoon.

It felt good. It felt more than good. It felt marvelous! Fae lifted her arms, taking it in. Taking it *all* in. She breathed the sweet scent of the honeysuckle in, along with the dusty aroma of the pea gravel. It smelled fuller, more complex, than the odors of *kairos*. Mmm.

She tilted her head, listening. There was the play of water in the fountains, rushing and gurgling. There was the drone of bumblebees. And there . . . faint laughter and the calls of her cousins at play.

She wasn't alone any longer!

She skipped out of the gazebo and down a step to the gravel of the courtyard, spinning to absorb her surroundings. Behind the gazebo, and across an expanse of lawns and flower borders, rose Castle

Farnesse in approximately the same spot occupied by the castle in *kairos*.

But the state rooms of the castle in *kairos* would have stood where Farnesse enjoyed gardens. The last two columns of *kairos* were gone. Dissolved like the rest of Fae's *kairos* prison? The configuration of Farnesse's towers was different from the prison castle. And the roofs of Farnesse were gray slate, not red tile. The castle in *kairos* was a version of Farnesse, Fae supposed, but the two were not the same.

As Fae turned back toward the gap in the courtyard hedge, a man in a ruffled white poet's shirt strode through it.

Home at Heart

HE WORE SOFT BROWN moleskin breeches, and dark brown suede boots. His brown beard was neatly trimmed. His brown hair, cut short.

His level gaze met Fae's and he jolted to a stop, startled.

Fae stared at him.

He stared at her.

"Uncle Leander!" Her voice sounded clear, and bell-like.

Then he was running, and she was running.

"Sweetheart!" He swept her up in a strong embrace and spun around with her in his arms. "Thank god, thank god! You're here!" His voice was rough.

He set her down again and tipped her chin up. "You're well? Uninjured by that bastard Aion?"

"I'm hungry!" Fae was laughing. "And thirsty!"

"Of course you are! An hour in *kairos* might feel like an hour, and look like an hour on a clockface, but it isn't. It's half again as long."

"Oh!" That explained . . . a lot.

Uncle Leander flicked her cheek with a gentle tap. "Hunger and thirst I can fix." He drew her arm through his and led her back to the gazebo she'd just exited.

Fae looked around curiously. She'd not actually been *in* the gazebo, even though she'd passed through its doorway. And she didn't know every inch of Castle Farnesse by heart. She'd *lived* in Milady's lodge.

Built-in brown wicker benches circled the space, and a generous wicker table, bearing several pitchers and platters, occupied the center.

"Lemonade?" inquired her uncle. "Or water?"

"Lemonade," answered Fae. "*Definitely* lemonade." She was *so* tired of water!

Uncle Leander looked surprised at her vehemence. She'd always been a water drinker. She was still a water drinker. But . . . not right now, after five and a half days of *only* water.

He poured lemonade into a tall glass and handed it to her, then lifted a small plate from a stack of them and served her two lemon tartlets, three morsels of bacon-wrapped brie cheese, several spears of crispy roasted asparagus, three small meatballs on toothpicks, and a pile of juicy green melon balls.

Gods it looked good after days and days of oatmeal!

Fae chose a bench where she could look at Castle Farnesse. She wanted to see that her prison in *kairos* was not there and not there and *not there*. Gods!

Uncle Leander sat next to her, looking at *her* while she ate and drank, not at the view.

The lemonade was delicious! So tart and citrusy, so sweet. The cheese, creamy and flavorful; the bacon, rich and savory. *Mmm.* Food! Real food! It was beyond good. It was *divine!*

Uncle Leander grinned at her.

"What did *you* eat in *kairos*?" she asked.

He grimaced. "Raw fish."

"Ew!" Fae shuddered and hurriedly bit into a lemon tartlet. The pastry melted on her tongue, blending with the tangy custard.

"It can be quite good." Her uncle frowned. "Prepared properly by a Japanese chef." The corner of his mouth turned up. "*I* am not a chef of any kind. Japanese, French, *or* Italian."

Fae giggled.

Uncle Leander laughed with her. Sweet Marionya, but it felt good to laugh with someone.

"You're sure you're unharmed?" He was serious again, worried.

"I ate oatmeal. And more oatmeal. And yet more oatmeal."

Her uncle touched her other cheek. "What's this?"

Oh! She'd forgotten the cuts on her cheek. The merest thin scratch was all that had remained the last time she looked in the mirror.

"Some hawks dove on me." She raised her chin. "But I shot them with my bow and arrow before they did much damage."

Uncle Leander looked impressed, but his words remained casual: "You always were good with a bow."

"Uncle!" Fae had to know something.

"Hmm?" He was thinking of who-knew-what.

"How did you escape *kairos*? You *were* trapped there, weren't you? Like me?"

His lazy smile straightened. "Yes, I was imprisoned in *kairos*." His voice was curt, hiding anger.

"What happened when you got out? What did you see?" she asked.

He stared at her a moment, then looked away. "Ah. I'd just finished constructing my trebuchet."

"Oh!" Fae interrupted him. "I *saw* you! I saw you in a dream. Building a siege engine."

His mouth curled in a smile again. "Yes. Well. I was loading a cannonball into the sling when the salle de guerre just . . . melted around me." He shook his head. "I was almost disappointed. Almost. I've never built a trebuchet before." He sounded rueful.

Fae laughed. "And you wanted to try it out."

Her uncle shrugged. "Well, yes."

"I bet *you* wanted to be the one who rescued us all from *kairos*." Fae's grin widened.

"No. You did that, and did it well." He nodded. "My solution . . . might have been worse than no solution at all."

"What do you mean?" Had Fae's guess about the results of her relatives' escape attempts been right? Would Uncle Leander's cannonball blasting through the walls of *kairos*, Uncle Nathanos' torrent of water, and Cousin Eulalie's garderobe descent all have resulted in disaster?

"Aion convinced Themis to give up her child." Uncle Leander's voice sounded hard.

"How do you know that?" Fae's heart felt chilled. A mother *consenting* to the loss of her child? How could she? And yet . . . Milady had consented to her foster child's . . . what? Imprisonment? Destruction? What exactly had Milady believed would be the result of that scary ritual in the chapel?

"I dreamed it." Her uncle's words held a distance in their tone. "There in *kairos*, my dreams were . . . sometimes oracular."

"So were mine!" It had been . . . odd. To see the unremembered past, as well as the remembered past.

"Aion intended that Milady should find the daughter of Themis and rear her. And when she was grown, he would then control Fate. But the triune ideals of fate interfered."

"No, Eris interfered!" Fae corrected him.

Uncle Leander smiled. "And who do you think prompted Eris?"

Oh! Of course. That was why the blond-haired baby had ended up with the Spinner, the Alotter, and the Cutter.

"I'm not the daughter of Themis." It was important to have that straight. Would Uncle Leander still love her, if she weren't a Theosian?

"No, sweetheart, you never were." He was smiling tenderly. Then he murmured, "Thank god."

"You don't mind?"

"How could I mind? You're you, Fae, the daughter of my heart. The daughter I never had and didn't even know I wanted."

Oh! He did love her still. Exactly as she was, the mortal daughter of an ordinary weaverwoman.

He bent to kiss her on the forehead. "I love you, sweetheart. Exactly the way you are."

Oh, that felt wonderful. But . . . how did he know her name? The name she'd given herself in *kairos*?

"Uncle, did you dream that I'd named myself Fae?"

He looked puzzled. "But I've always called you Fae. Short for Faine, short for Faline." He paused and winked at her. "Short for Faebio!" He snorted and poked her in the ribs. "You always were 'full of beans,' hah!"

Fae found herself laughing with him at this old, old joke. Faine for "joyful," Faline for "cat-like," and – indeed – Faebio for "bean grower." How had she forgotten?

"Seriously, your godmother was the only one who ever called you Moira. What a stupid name for a child. Bitter? Ridiculous! You were always joyful! And cat agile. And –" he glanced at her sideways at her "– full of beans! Heh heh heh!"

Fae laughed again. Oh, it felt wonderful to laugh. And be laughing *with* someone. The loneliness of *kairos* had been more awful than even the demon spite of Aion that had pervaded it.

"I'd forgotten," she explained. "When I woke up in the castle – trapped there – I'd forgotten who I was. I didn't know anything. Where I came from. Who my family was." Her voice grew small. "Anything at all."

Uncle Leander snugged her in close with a one-armed hug. "Sweetheart, I'm so sorry."

Fae leaned into him for moment. His shoulders felt so solid, so comforting.

She straightened when he released her.

"But I remembered. And I got out!"

"So you did. So you did." Dead serious for a moment, he looked her in the eye. "Good job, Fae. If I had let that cannonball fly, or your Aunt Pallas had cracked *kairos* with her bamboo roots – it would not have been freedom rushing in, but chaos and destruction. You . . . were the only one of us with the right line."

Fae looked down, blushing. Then looked up again.

"You *are* my father? Right? You chose me."

He kissed her forehead again. "You are my daughter. I did choose you. *You.* And – if you'll have me – I am your father."

She nodded, happy in a way too deep and quiet for dance steps or for words.

She was home.

Home in body.

And home at heart.

A flicker of movement tickled the edge of her vision.

She turned her head.

Milady stood in the doorway of the gazebo, garbed in black velvet as always, her pale face very still, her gray eyes very cold.

Fae shifted to face Milady directly. She felt Uncle Leander take her hand in his – it felt heartening – but she didn't look at him. She gazed into Milady's eyes. So cold. So certain. So unloving.

Milady does not love me.

Claiming Herself Fully

IN *KAIROS*, FAE had vowed to learn her godmother's true feelings for her foster daughter.

Now she was learning them, and that learning felt . . . bitter. Awful.

Milady had rescued her, but the love in her face as she held that fosterling baby had been for Milady's sister Themis, not for Fae.

Milady had reared and instructed Fae through all the years of Fae's childhood, but she had not loved her.

And Milady had sacrificed Fae – there in that accursed chapel – when the choice lay between danger and affection.

Fae felt cold, very cold, even though the heat of summer surrounded her, and the warmth of Uncle Leander's hand enveloped hers.

"Fae." Milady's voice was low, almost too soft to be heard.

Fae? Milady called her Moira.

Then Fae noticed Milady's mouth, the lips slightly parted and trembling.

Oh! Milady's truth lay not in her eyes, but on those quivering lips.

Fae bounded to her feet, knocking against the gazebo's table in her eagerness.

The next instant, Milady's arms were closing around her, Milady's cheek was bending to touch her hair, Milady's lips were whispering, "I am so sorry, I am so sorry, dear love, dear Fae, my darling."

Fae felt her own tears start as her arms wrapped around Milady. "Mother?"

Milady's answer was fierce. "Yes! Yes. Darling Fae."

They clung to one another for a time.

Uncle Leander's voice interrupted Fae's crying. "You'll both give yourselves headaches, if you keep that up."

Fae laughed, shakily, and released Milady.

Milady lifted her head, her face uncharacteristically flushed, and fished a handkerchief from the wrist of her sleeve. Composedly, she dried her eyes.

Uncle Leander sauntered up and handed Fae his handkerchief, quite a large one.

She mopped her face, and only then realized that the clothes she'd donned in *kairos* had changed when she re-entered *chronos*. Instead of an acorn-embroidered tunic, she was wearing a cream gown adorned with seed pearls. And her bow and quiver – and water canteen – were gone. She snorted in disgust. Honestly! Apparently, in *chronos*, one's garb was sometimes just as annoying as a bruised shin or a sweaty armpit. She felt the back of her head. At least her hair was still in the practical club-style bun she'd chosen.

Milady had recovered from her spurt of emotion, but Fae was not fooled. Milady might be reserved. Milady might present a collected front, seeming always cool and composed. But it would be a mistake to assume she did not feel deeply.

"Well, it would seem we are having a party," said Milady. "Celebrating our escape, no doubt."

Uncle Leander laughed, easy and deep. "Would you care for lemonade, Dione?"

Milady sniffed. "Water, Leander. You know I avoid sweets!"

Yes, Fae knew, too. She'd acquired her own water-drinking habit from Milady. She felt the corners of her mouth turn up.

Uncle Leander served Milady and ushered her to a seat. He sat near her and beckoned Fae to settle between them.

"You do realize our 'foundling' saved us all, Dione?"

Milady sipped her water, then sniffed condescendingly. How did Milady manage to pack so much looking-down-her-nose in that sniff? "Yes, Leander, I do realize that. Honestly, Fae was not the only Theosian to be attempting a complete escape instead of a limited physical one. Pallas was experimenting with the power of love, and if anyone could have made that work, she would have."

Fae couldn't help chuckling. It just felt great to hear Milady's asperity again.

"*But*," continued Milady, "even my own attempts at vision and prophesy were useless." She took Fae's hand in her own cool fingers, clasping it gently. "My daughter" – oh, wow, could Fae hear the pride in her voice – "was the only one who could succeed. And she *could* have failed. It wasn't an easy puzzle." Milady's fingers tightened on Fae's hand. "Many an old lady goes to her grave without claiming herself fully. *Fae* decided who she wanted to be and how she would go about it."

Leander interrupted her. "What do you think of her choice for us? I imagine you also know about that."

Milady leaned against the slanted back of the gazebo bench and let Fae's hand go.

"It wouldn't have been my choice. I quite liked being the ideal of prophecy. But Aion didn't leave many options. Had Fae walked through the door into cosmos, the very nature of the ideal would have changed. I doubt *you'd* have liked it, Leander."

"I'll admit I'm happy to be released from the necessities of the ideal." He propped one booted ankle on his other knee. "Did I thank you, Fae?"

Fae turned to look at him. He was serious. She shook her head.

"*Thank* you, Fae. Truly. Thank you for choosing humanity instead of godhood. Gods! That would have been dreadful."

Milady overrode him. "If she'd stepped through the door into forest, we'd have all become naiads and dryads."

The meaning of Milady's words suddenly penetrated. Sweet Marionya! Fae'd almost walked through that door! She'd known it wasn't right for her, but – dear gods! She'd not been the only one with a stake in her choice.

"What about the third door?" she wondered aloud. "Where would that have led?"

"The door into sun?" Milady took Fae's hand again. "I don't know. I don't know." Her voice was very soft. "Perhaps the exaltation that comes after death. Or perhaps . . . the oblivion that some call that exaltation. But we would not be here."

Fae shivered.

"Why did you . . . ?" It was hard to ask this question, but Fae had to know. "Why did you help Aion with the rite in the chapel? The one that sent my body into *kairos*?"

Milady sighed. "Aion forced me."

"He *forced* you?"

"And I thought I could make the rite fail. I thought I could make you pass through *kairos* and emerge on the other side. And I did. Just not the way I'd imagined."

"The godmother doors!"

Milady smiled. "Yes, the godmother doors."

"And the gryphons!" added Fae after a moment.

Milady inclined her head. "Naturally I would send protection to accompany you, even though I imagined your passage would be brief."

Fae turned to offer a quick hug. Amazingly, Milady returned it.

Fae still wanted to know more. "How did Aion force you?"

"He'd found out that you were *not* the daughter of Themis, and he threatened to have you exiled from the precincts of our clan."

"Could he –?"

"Oh, yes. The law was on his side." Milady sipped her water.

"Bastard!" rumbled Uncle Leander.

Milady set her empty water glass on the bench beside her. "But Aion was wrong in more ways than one. Because Fae was *not* born a Theosian, she could not be held so completely as the rest of us. Her prison was tighter, but it had exits. Our cells felt looser, but they had no way out."

Milady turned and tipped Fae's chin up to meet her steady gaze. "Thank you, daughter mine." Her lips curved in an ironic smile, but her voice was sincere. "You did a mighty deed."

"So at the end there, when we *all* escaped, what *was* that?" Fae asked.

"There's a balance between *kairos* and *chronos*, and Aion held all the strings. When we emerged from *kairos*, all of us together, the vast power he'd accrued reversed its flow and expelled *him* from *chronos*. May he rot there in *kairos* for eternity, baby killer!" Milady's words held a vicious note quite unusual for her.

"I'm with you on that." Uncle Leander merely sounded definite. "Although, he's clever enough that he'll bear some checking on. Who knows what he might devise, given enough time."

"Oh, he'll be monitored. Never doubt that. I may no longer be the ideal of prophecy with its inherent powers, but I've retained quite a few of my *acquired* skills!"

Leander laughed. "I'll leave you, ladies." He stood and bowed. "I suspect you have quite a bit of talking to do."

Milady nodded and watched him walk to the gazebo doorway, smiling slightly.

Fae wasn't ready to see him go, but felt too turned-inside-out by all Milady's disclosures to protest. So all her relatives were no longer the ideals of their aspects. And Fae had done that. As well as causing Uncle Aion to suffer the same imprisonment he'd dealt out so cavalierly. Huh! It was hard to adjust her world view.

Apparently Uncle Leander sensed her crogglement. "I'll be back in a bit, Fae. I want to go check on your cousins."

Oh, good. She wanted to see her cousins, too. She just didn't want *anyone* departing just yet. She wanted *everyone* around her, in one big crowd. The exact opposite of *kairos*.

But Milady's presence felt good too.

"What did Uncle Aion *want*?" Really, it made no sense.

Milady didn't answer right away.

"Some of your great aunts and great uncles were banished. A long time ago. They were not . . . nice people."

More silence. The afternoon heat hung heavy.

"Aion wanted to bring them back. Themis. Tethys. Iapetus. The eldest generation of Theosians. He is one of the eldest himself. As am I." The corners of Milady's mouth set in censure at the connection. "But bringing them back required deposing the youngest generation of Theosians. Hadrien would never have consented to the reinstatement of Iapetus. Or Rhea." Milady sounded almost pettish.

"Your *sister* was banished?" Evidently Clan Theosis held more family secrets than Fae had ever imagined.

"I'd rather not talk about it, Fae." Milady reached out and stroked Fae's hair. "At least, not right now. I'd rather talk about you."

And Milady proceeded to tell Fae about all the moments when mothering Fae had been thrilling. Fae's first smile. Fae's first steps, exuberant and unsteady. Fae's first word, "M'mm."

"You were so darling." Was that really Milady's voice, so tender and sweet?

Milady gathered Fae against her, holding her close, kissing her cheek. Just like Milady in Fae's dream, holding a baby close, as though it were the most precious creature in all the world.

I'm precious, realized Fae in amazement. Of course. How *could* Milady have devoted herself so thoroughly to Fae for all those years, *unless* she loved Fae. *I'm loved.*

The rattle of running footsteps on gravel sounded in the courtyard, along with a burst of laughter.

The next moment, a throng of young people crowded into the gazebo, exclaiming.

"Fae! Castle Farnesse has a menagerie now. There's a tiger!" That was Lydia. She'd always liked animals.

"That's not the best thing! There's a lake with sailboats!" Zoe loved the water.

"No, no! She'll like the bicycles!" Athletic Theophane.

"Or the new horse trail." Helios, with his breaking boy's voice and his love of riding.

"Let's run a race!" Calanthe. Of course.

They were jostling one another, each eager to secure Fae's participation in her own (or his own) scheme for fun.

Fae started to laugh.

Milady's silvery laughter joined her daughter's.

Fae glanced at her mother, surprised.

Milady gestured, a quick movement of her hand. "Well, go on then! The exercise will do you good. I'll be here."

So she would. They would *all* be here, right *here*. Milady. Uncle Leander. Fae's cousins. All her aunts and uncles. And Fae herself.

The last edge of her uncertainty – a residue from residing in (and withstanding) *kairos* – fled.

Fae felt firmly anchored at last. Herself. Fully human. And powerful in her humanity.

She stood up and allowed her cousins to engulf her, carrying her off to revel in the outdoors.

THE END

J.M. Ney-Grimm lives with her husband and children in Virginia, just east of the Blue Ridge Mountains. She's learning about permaculture gardening and debunking popular myths about food. The rest of the time she reads Robin McKinley, Diana Wynne Jones, and Lois McMaster Bujold, plays boardgames like Settlers of Catan, rears her twins, and writes stories set in the magical realms of myth and fantasy.

Look for her novels and novellas at your favorite bookstore – online or on Main Street.

J.M. Ney-Grimm maintains a blog featuring flash fiction from her North-lands and other tidbits unearthed by her ever-active curiosity.

Visit her at http://JMNey-Grimm.com.

www.ingramcontent.com/pod-product-compliance
Lightning Source LLC
Chambersburg PA
CBHW020558260626
47157CB00003B/758